FATAL FEVER

Also by C. F. Roe

The Lumsden Baby
Death By Fire
Bad Blood
Deadly Partnership

FATAL FEVER

C. F. Roe

HEADLINE

Copyright © 1992 C. F. Roe

The right of C. F. Roe to be identified as the Author of the Work has been asserted by him in accordance with the Copyright, Designs and Patents Act 1988.

First published in 1992
by HEADLINE BOOK PUBLISHING PLC

10 9 8 7 6 5 4 3 2 1

All rights reserved. No part of this publication may be reproduced, stored in a retrieval system, or transmitted, in any form or by any means without the prior written permission of the publisher, nor be otherwise circulated in any form of binding or cover other than that in which it is published and without a similar condition being imposed on the subsequent purchaser.

All characters in this publication are fictitious and any resemblance to real persons, living or dead, is purely coincidental

British Library Cataloguing in Publication Data

Roe, C. F.
Fatal fever.
I. Title
823.914[F]

ISBN 0-7472-0455-1

Printed and bound in Great Britain by
Richard Clay Ltd, Bungay, Suffolk

HEADLINE BOOK PUBLISHING PLC
Headline House
79 Great Titchfield Street
London W1P 7FN

PART ONE

Chapter One

Perth Memorial Hospital stands on high ground overlooking the city, and on a clear day, looking out from the windows on the third floor, where the operating theatres and recovery rooms are, the rounded Sidlaw hills can be seen in the distance to the Northeast, hazy, blue, unthreatening.

Dr Peter MacIntosh, head of gynaecology and obstetrics, stood at the wide window with one hand on the sill, talking to the sister in charge of the operating theatres.

'Thank God it was just a benign cyst,' he said, holding up the specimen bottle containing a floating red blob about the size of a plum. 'I was really concerned.'

'That *was* a relief,' agreed Sister Jan Kelso, a small, pale, determined-looking young woman with a long nose and no makeup. She hesitated. 'Lois is our church secretary, and to be quite honest, she's not exactly the most stable . . .'

They heard the quick sound of running feet along the corridor and Jan turned, annoyed. Nobody was permitted to run in her operating suite. Round the corner appeared a young woman in a student nurse's shapeless grey uniform, her thin blonde hair straggling from under her cap. Sister Kelso was about to greet her with a sharp rebuke when the nurse stopped, out of breath, her gaze fixed on Peter.

'Dr MacIntosh, please . . . your patient, Miss Munday . . . in the recovery room, she's stopped breathing.'

By the time she had the words out, Peter was racing down the corridor as fast as his long athletic legs would take him.

In the recovery room, several nurses and a technician were gathered around a bed, and he hurried over. He took one look at the dead-white face of his patient.

'She has a pulse, sir,' said one of the nurses, but already Peter had put his hand behind Lois Munday's neck and put his face down to hers to start mouth-to-mouth resuscitation. He blew three hard, deep breaths and could feel her lungs expanding with his air.

'Get me a laryngoscope and an endotracheal tube,' he said to the nurse. He held Lois's chin up, watching for signs of spontaneous breathing, but as these did not appear, he started blowing into her lungs again. After three more big breaths, he stood up, went behind the patient's head, put one hand behind her neck, took the laryngoscope in the other, opened her mouth and slid the curved blade of the instrument in until he could see the vocal cords.

'Tube.' He held out his hand, not taking his eyes off the vocal cords. The nurse placed the transparent plastic tube in his hand, and he slipped it deftly between the cords and into the woman's trachea. He blew into the end of the tube, watching Lois's chest expand as he did so, then attached it to the corrugated respirator tubing. The respirator was next to the bed, and Peter secured the tubing and adjusted the controls. In a moment the machine was sighing air into the patient's lungs at 500 mls per breath, 12 breaths per minute, and within a minute, Lois Munday's face became pink again. Peter looked at the monitor above the bed. The heart rate was a little fast, but had not faltered during this life-threatening episode. A few minutes later, she was regaining consciousness and it was clear that the emergency was over.

Peter straightened up with a long sigh of relief and looked at the faces around him. 'Where's Dr Sutherland?' he asked. Dr Sutherland was the anaesthetist who had been on the case.

A quick glance passed between the nurses.

'We called for him first,' said one, plucking up her courage, but her voice was hesitant.

'Well?'

'He didn't answer his pager,' she said. 'I called the operator and she said he'd already left the hospital.' The nurse, knowing the implication of her words, looked at her feet.

Peter's mouth opened in surprise, then his face hardened. 'Thank you,' was all he said, but they could see how angry he was. Anna McKenzie, one of the other anaesthetists, came into the recovery room, and Peter explained what had happened. Anna looked shocked and hurriedly offered to take care of Lois from this point. Having handed the case over to her, Peter strode to the door and ran down the back stairs to the ground floor, heading for the administrative offices. He marched past the secretary and barged straight into the hospital director's room.

Roderick Michie was seated behind his desk, and when Peter started to tell him what had happened in the recovery room, Roderick nervously shook a cigarette out of a packet of Marlboros, lit it and took great, deep puffs, frequently tapping the end of the cigarette on the ashtray. He watched Peter's face and didn't say a word until he had finished.

'I'll talk to him,' he said finally, putting out his cigarette in the ashtray, which already held a dozen fag-ends. Roderick was a pudgy man in his middle fifties, with suspiciously black, thinning hair combed across the top of his head. He rubbed the side of his nose distractedly. 'You know this isn't the first time, Peter . . .'

'I know,' said Peter. 'Apparently he had some major problems in Aberdeen before he came here. Did you know that?'

'It's all in his file,' replied Roderick, avoiding Peter's angry stare. 'There's nothing I can do about it. You know the system. We had a vacancy, and he was the only applicant. Sometimes we have to take who we can get, and that's not always who we want.'

Peter took a deep breath, started to say something, then changed his mind. It wasn't going to help if he lost his temper.

'I hope you can do something, Mr Michie,' he said in a carefully controlled voice. 'Otherwise, sooner or later, there's going to be a serious accident, and someone's going to die as a result of Sutherland's negligence.'

A few moments later, Peter was on his way back to the recovery room to check on his patient. He was still tense with indignation and anger.

Less than fifteen minutes before, Derek Sutherland had just brought Lois Munday back from the theatre when he was called to the phone in the recovery room. Within minutes of hanging up he was dressed and out of the hospital, forgetting in his haste to tell the nurses that he was leaving. He drove out of the car park and headed down the hill, his mind full of what his wife Sheila had just told him. Their son, Bobby, had been sent home from school again, the second time in two weeks. On this occasion, according to Sheila, he'd refused to answer a question from one of his teachers, then had become totally silent and stubborn. Nobody could get a word out of him, not even the astonished headmaster, Dr Robertson, to whom Bobby had finally been sent by his teacher. Dr Robertson personally called Sheila, because Bobby was such an outstanding boy, and he was really concerned about him.

Derek was normally a relaxed, easy-going sort of person, and it took a lot to get his full attention, let alone get him excited. But now he felt really concerned. For several weeks, Sheila had been saying that something was the matter with Bobby, but as usual, Derek had paid little attention to her complaints. Bobby seemed all right to him; about the correct height and weight for a thirteen year-old, active, alert, like all the other kids.

Two days before, Sheila had been ominously silent throughout dinner. After Bobby had gone upstairs, and Derek had picked up the paper, Sheila said grimly 'Derek, there's something the matter with Bobby.' Derek didn't answer, and her voice rose. 'Derek! Listen to what I'm saying! He doesn't talk to me, and he's off his food. Haven't you even noticed? He was always so close to you, and now he avoids even you.'

Resignedly, Derek put the paper down and listened, half his mind still on the football scores. Sheila was still attractive, blonde and big-bosomed, not that he paid much attention to how she looked nowadays. He did notice that the corners of her mouth had turned down in a dissatisfied pout he'd learned to detest.

Derek shrugged, knowing the effect that had on her.

'All that's quite natural for a boy his age,' he replied, picking up the newspaper again. 'Bobby's fine. He's captain of his football team, he's at the top of his class. He has lots of friends. What more do you want? He'll be coming up to puberty soon, and that's going to be a big change . . .'

Sheila's lips tightened. 'Derek Sutherland, I don't think you're listening to me at all.'

He sighed and put down the paper with a martyred expression. 'All right, then,' he said, 'I'm listening.'

'I really think Bobby is ill,' said Sheila, pulling a strand of blonde hair out of her face. She emphasized the word 'ill' and stared at Derek out of her big, pale grey eyes. 'You know that girl Moira who lives on Cairn Street, the red-haired one who came to his last birthday party?'

Derek looked blank, and tried to remember.

'Well, she was diagnosed with leukaemia a few weeks ago, but all the neighbours knew that she'd been looking pale and thin for weeks before that. Only nobody paid any attention, including her parents, just like you're not paying attention to Bobby.' Sheila angrily wiped a tear from her cheek with the back of her hand.

'All right,' Derek said resignedly. 'Tell him to come downstairs and I'll take a look at him.'

Sheila brought Bobby down to the living room, and Derek examined him with some care, but found nothing untoward. Bobby was an extremely good-looking boy, well-developed for his age. Derek looked in his mouth, found it was clean, there was no enlargement of his neck glands. Depressing Bobby's tongue with the back of a spoon, he found that his tonsils and adenoids were not inflamed. Finally, and getting more annoyed by the minute, Derek listened to his son's chest. It sounded perfectly normal. Finally he checked Bobby's muscle tone and reflexes. Again, all was normal. The only unusual finding was that Bobby was a bit pale.

Derek then sent the boy back upstairs, and curtly told Sheila that there was nothing wrong with him, and that it was all in her own imagination. If that kid Moira she'd been going on about hadn't had leukaemia, he told her, it wouldn't have occurred to her that anything was the matter with Bobby.

Not satisfied with Derek's conclusions, Sheila had insisted on a blood test, and they both waited for a week in some trepidation for the results, but to his smug relief, and to Sheila's annoyed surprise, these turned out to be entirely normal.

At the bottom of the hill, Derek turned the car towards South Street and the bridge. He really resented being forced to think about unpleasant or uncomfortable things, and normally Sheila took that and other burdens for him. Sheila paid the bills, argued with tradesmen when necessary, and endured the occasional uncomfortable interviews with the bank manager when the overdraft reached higher than usual levels. And of course Sheila took care of Bobby, his schoolwork, everything except some occasional and infrequent cricket practice on the Inch. Derek had been a good bowler in his day, and occasionally they would go down to the Inch for some practice. Bobby preferred soccer, but was a good enough cricketer and they ran and caught and batted and bowled and generally had a good time.

Derek was, in his careless kind of way, inordinately

proud of Bobby, and would talk about his son's accomplishments to the theatre nurses, to the other doctors, to anyone who would listen. In his wallet, he carried a set of photos of Bobby as a baby, Bobby at the beach, Bobby scoring a goal, Bobby getting the scholar's cup at school. If Sheila and Derek went on a plane trip or a bus ride, just the two of them, she would count the minutes before Derek would start talking to whoever was sitting beside them, and then he'd have the pictures of Bobby out of his wallet in a jiffy.

And now, Bobby had been sent home from school because he wouldn't reply to a question. Derek wrinkled his brow. What a strange thing. He wondered for a moment what question could have elicited such a negative response. Then his mind went back to the hospital, to Lois Munday. Derek realized that his exit from the recovery room had been rather precipitous. Luckily the nurses up there were very capable, and they'd know how to take care of any problems. Lois had been a bit slow coming round, and at the end of the operation Derek had realized that he'd given her a bit more halothane than he'd meant to. Oh well, he thought, luckily there's a big margin of error there, and anyway nobody would ever know.

He waited at the traffic lights, then crossed the old bridge. There wasn't much traffic, and the weather was fine, with some high clouds to his right above Kinnoull hill. The sun shone intermittently on the car, and Derek pulled the sun visor down. To his left the big trees around the North Inch spread their wide, leafy branches over the grass at the side of the playing fields, and a couple of golfers headed towards the golf course, making practice swings as they walked. Under the bridge, the peat-coloured river Tay rolled brown, wide and silent towards the harbour, and the sunlight sparkled up at him from the eddies.

The sight of the golfers made him think that maybe he'd have time for a quick round before going back to check on the patients who'd been operated on that day. Maybe he'd take Bobby with him. He turned right up Kincaid Crescent. His house was half-way up the hill, a semi-detached brown sandstone house with a small garden in front and a bigger one behind, where Sheila grew vegetables and some flowers. Derek didn't know much about gardening, and anyway by tacit agreement all that agricultural stuff was Sheila's affair. She usually took good care of the garden; earlier in the year, she had put in some smaller flowers around the rose bushes; pink, red, and yellow blooms that added a nice touch of colour. But Derek noticed that she seemed to have slackened off recently. The grass was too long, and weeds were springing up around the roses. Derek parked the car outside the low wall bordering the garden.

Inside the house, all was quiet. Sheila appeared from the kitchen, wiping her hands on her apron.

'He's upstairs,' she said, her eyes cold. 'He just went up to his room and wouldn't say anything. He's locked the door.'

Derek sighed, and went slowly upstairs to talk to his son.

A few minutes later, he came down again. 'He doesn't want to talk to me,' he said to Sheila. 'Maybe you should go up. I think he's crying. And I'm off. I'll be at the golf course for the next hour or so.'

It wasn't until some time later that Sheila found out the question Bobby's teacher had asked him at school, the question he had refused to answer. It was a simple enough one, it seemed. In fact, the teacher had asked the same question to all the other children in the class, and until she reached Bobby, they had all answered, one way or the other. The girls had been asked, 'Would you like to grow up to be like your mother?' and the boys were asked the same question about their fathers.

Chapter Two

Three Sundays later, Jean Montrose came into church just as the morning service was about to start, and slipped into her pew past Ann and Joe McIver. Ann was sitting very straight, her strict, pointed features devoid of expression and makeup except for a thin line of mascara around her eyes. She was very carefully turned out in a high-collared dark blue dress with tiny white polka dots. As usual, she looked obsessively neat, making a sharp contrast with her hulking, untidy-looking husband.

The vestry door opened and Duncan Sinclair, the minister, came walking up the central aisle. Tall, in his mid forties, Duncan, with his beaky, patrician nose and big mane of prematurely grey hair, walked past her, his dark eyes fixed in front of him.

It must be a sad life for him, thought Jean sympathetically, watching him climb slowly up the spiral wrought-iron staircase to the pulpit. Duncan lived alone in the big manse, without a wife or even close friends to share his joys or problems.

Jean whispered to her husband Steven, who was standing on her right. Her voice was covered by the rustling of clothes and shuffling of feet as the congregation stood up.

'I couldn't find a place to park,' she said out of the corner of her mouth. Steven said nothing, but passed her a hymn-book, already open at the page for the first hymn. Fiona and Lisbie stood on the other side of Steven; Fiona, slim and immaculately dressed in a dark blue skirt and lacy white blouse, stood next to her father. She grinned past him at Jean, then said something quietly to her sister Lisbie who was on her other side. Lisbie, neat in a pretty blue frock with white collar and cuffs, looked like a younger version of her mother. She stifled a giggle, and both girls smiled complicitly at Jean, who frowned good-naturedly at them. This, she wordlessly reminded them, was a place for respectful contemplation, and where normal family joking around was to be suspended for an hour or so.

Seated at the organ, on the opposite side of the choir from the pulpit, and separated from the choir and the congregation by a faded burgundy-coloured velvet curtain hung on polished brass rails, Ian Farquar glanced into the mirror above his head and watched Duncan arrive in the pulpit. Ian was a small, wiry man with dark, deep-set eyes and black hair swept back from a widow's peak that came far down on his forehead. Lois Munday, the church secretary and Duncan's helper, privately thought Ian looked like a Welsh miner, with his short bow legs and sullen, stubborn disposition. Ian, who had had to have the organ bench lowered by an inch so that his feet could comfortably reach the pedals, had come to Perth a couple of years before to join the music department of the Academy, and soon after was appointed organist and choirmaster at the West Kirk, near the centre of Perth.

Ian came to the end of the piece, a theme with variations by William Boyce, precisely as Duncan opened his Bible, and Ian, still watching in the small mirror positioned above the console, wondered if anybody in the congregation would know or care that the music had been written for the Anglican church, and not for church services north of the border.

Duncan looked down at his congregation from under thick, bushy eyebrows and noted that the church was almost half full, with a fair sprinkling of younger people who sat mostly in the back pews. There was no doubt that the attendance was an improvement on the thin scattering of elderly parishioners he had inherited a year before, but Duncan was unable to derive much pleasure from this. He wondered how his predecessor, a kindly but ineffectual old man who had died at the age of eighty while conducting a wedding, had managed to maintain his faith to the end.

Duncan's gaze swept over the upturned faces and saw that Jean Montrose was there with her family. He felt a muted pleasure that she had managed to find time to come to church.

The congregation sat down.

'Let us pray,' said Duncan trying to sound as if he really still believed in the power of invocation.

After the short prayer, he announced the first hymn, number twenty-eight, 'A gladsome hymn of praise we sing', and the usual coughing and rustling followed as pages were turned and the congregation stood up.

Soon after his arrival at the West Kirk, while he was still full of enthusiasm and faith, Duncan had initiated the custom of the choir singing the first verse of the hymns by themselves, thus avoiding the slow and often out-of-tune start by the congregation. Ian Farquar and he had put together and trained an excellent choir, composed mostly of adult parishioners, but with the addition of half a dozen schoolboys, whose soprano voices added a fine new dimension to the music.

Ian's left hand poked through the curtain occasionally to mark time for the choir, but mainly he led them by subtle emphasis in the way he played. Duncan watched and listened as they sang, and the simple, clear beauty of the music was like a temporary dressing on the hurt of his soul.

The high notes in the last line were taken up by the boys, and two young voices in particular stood out by their purity and strength. The two boys were Bobby Sutherland and Jeremy McIver; Bobby, lithe, slender, with dark hair, a boy with a great personality and liked by just about everybody. Duncan was aware that other mothers secretly envied Sheila Sutherland. Bobby made a strong contrast with Jeremy, his best friend, who was standing next to him. Jeremy was a big, tow-haired, tough-looking boy with hands and feet that seemed too big for him. There was something very physical, very rough-and-tumble about him. That he must have got from his father, Duncan surmised; certainly not from his prim and slightly-built mother, Ann.

The better voice of the two, thought Duncan as he listened, belonged without question to Bobby Sutherland. Although Jeremy McIver's was unusually good, Bobby's voice was spectacular; it had a timbre and intonation that put it in a class apart. The second verse started and the congregation joined in, and Duncan reflected that in only a few months both the boys' voices would be breaking; for a second he thought about the ancient custom of preserving boys' voices by castration. It must have been a blessing for the choirmasters of the time, whereas in this day and age they couldn't expect more than a couple of years of really good singing from their boy sopranos.

And now the whole congregation was singing, and Duncan felt a different, sad, detached pleasure as the music soared and fell. Down in the congregation he picked out Lisbie Montrose, singing with her usual enthusiasm and unaffected joy. Lisbie had a good natural voice, untrained and clear.

After the service, while Ian played the final anthem, Duncan stood outside the door of the church and shook hands with his parishioners as they left. One of the first out was Ann McIver, followed by her lumbering husband, and behind him, the Montrose clan.

'The sermon was wonderful,' said Ann, holding on to Duncan's hand, her dark-ringed eyes staring up into his. 'Thank you, Reverend. It was so . . . uplifting. And the choir . . . I think Jeremy's voice has greatly improved, don't you?' Without pausing, she went on to say that Jeremy was hoping to represent the church in the Scottish Youth Choir. 'Thank you so much for all you've done for him,' she finished, pressing Duncan's hand with her blue-gloved fingers, then went off down the steps looking efficient and self-possessed, followed by Joe, who didn't even look up at Duncan as he passed. Duncan tried to suppress the discomfort that Ann's pushiness made him feel. He knew only too well that if it wasn't for Jeremy, the much-disliked Mrs McIver wouldn't give him the time of day.

When the Montroses came out, Duncan took Jean's hand in both of his. 'I'm so glad to see all of you,' he said, smiling, then turned to Lisbie. 'Why don't you join the choir?' he asked her. 'You have such a sweet voice, and I'm sure you'd enjoy the fellowship. It's a nice group and it wouldn't take up too much of your time.'

Lisbie blushed. 'I'm not nearly good enough,' she said, her eyes lowered.

'Come to a rehearsal, Lisbie,' he urged. 'We meet in the hall on Thursday evenings at seven-thirty. Do come this next week, we'll all be glad to see you.'

Lisbie mumbled something, secretly delighted to have been asked. Her young friend Bobby Sutherland was the star of the choir, and of course Larry French belonged, and the mere thought of him made her heart beat faster.

'Nice sermon, Duncan,' said Steven, feeling he had to say something, but he emphatically did not want to stop for a conversation, and caught Jean's arm lightly and steered her towards the steps. Other people were waiting to speak to Duncan, and Steven was looking forward to his Sunday lunch, and even more to the Bloody Mary that invariably preceded it.

The wind was picking up, and a pink and white straw hat with a red ribbon on it came bowling down the steps and into the street, coming to rest against a parked car. Fiona, who was nearest, ran to retrieve it. Hurrying down the steps after the hat came Sheila Sutherland. Dressed rather extravagantly in a bouffant pink and white organdy dress, and carefully made up, she almost tripped on her high heels when she reached where the Montroses were standing, and only Steven's steadying arm kept her from taking a nasty fall.

'Oh my, I'm sorry,' she said, shaken but less concerned about her near fall than about her hat. She looked over Steven's shoulder, hoping her expensive headgear hadn't finished up in a puddle. When she saw Fiona coming back up the steps with it, she straightened her dress a little self-consciously.

'Fiona, thank you . . .' Sheila took the hat, held it in front of her like a shield, and turned quickly to Jean. She seemed suddenly more anxious than could be accounted for by the errant hat.

'Jean, I'm glad I saw you,' she said breathlessly. 'Do you have a second?' She gave a slightly embarrassed glance at Steven and the girls.

'We'll see you down at the car, Jean,' said Steven, with a note of resignation in his voice. He was used to these after-church medical consultations. He took Fiona and Lisbie gently by the arms and went off towards the gate, but there they encountered Doug Niven and his wife Cathie, and he felt forced to stop and chat briefly with them. Lisbie kept an eye on the people still coming out of the church, hoping that Larry French would appear before she had to leave.

Sheila also looked up towards the church door, where her husband had just finished talking to Duncan and was coming down the steps with his usual cheerful, jaunty air. Duncan still had a friendly hand on Bobby Sutherland's shoulder, but Bobby escaped and followed his father, lagging behind, his gaze fixed on the steps in front of him.

Sheila turned back to Jean, anxious to say her piece before Derek came up. 'Jean, could I bring Bobby in to see you? I'm worried about him . . .' She looked back nervously. 'I'd like you to check him over,' she went on hurriedly. Her big grey eyes had an anxious, hesitant look.

'Of course,' said Jean. 'How about tomorrow, about three in the afternoon?'

Derek joined them at that moment, looking very relaxed, but Sheila tensed even more on his arrival. Bobby stopped on the steps several feet away.

'Bobby, come over and say hello to Dr Montrose,' called Sheila. Bobby hesitated for a second, then advanced and held out his hand, which Jean shook. Jean smiled at the boy, noticing his pallor. He looked as if he hadn't been sleeping well.

'I really enjoyed the choir's singing, Bobby,' she said in her friendly way. 'You're all doing a great job.'

Bobby smiled, grateful that she hadn't singled him out for praise, but he didn't reply. A couple of moments later he walked off to join Fiona and Lisbie, who were still on the street chatting with the Nivens.

'How's business, Jean?' asked Derek. As usual, he sounded cheerful and relaxed, unusual for an anaesthetist, Jean thought, but Derek sounded as if he hadn't a care in the world.

Out of Derek's line of sight, Sheila was making unobtrusive nods and signs at Jean, indicating that yes, she would come down to the surgery the next afternoon. Jean didn't like the way Sheila was doing this; her own direct and open nature resisted involvement in any byplay or secrecy between a husband and wife, especially if it concerned their child.

'We're pretty busy,' Jean replied to Derek's question, although he seemed hardly to expect an answer; his gaze was moving all around, idly checking out the people coming out of church. 'There's a lot of 'flu around, and that keeps us on our toes.'

Derek smiled, but he was obviously distracted, and after a friendly nod, Jean took the opportunity to leave. She saw Steven and the girls, and headed towards the gate, relieved to get away. Jean didn't dislike the

Sutherlands, not by any means, but there was something about the two of them that made her feel uncomfortable, although she could not have said why.

In the car going home, Steven said to Jean 'That was quite an outfit Sheila Sutherland was wearing today, wasn't it? She could have fallen over and killed herself on those heels.'

Jean, who had noticed the same thing, said 'Yes, didn't she look nice? She seems to be taking more interest in how she looks, these days.'

Lisbie, sitting in the back seat with Fiona, said 'That Bobby, isn't he *beautiful*? I just love him. Next week I'm taking him up to Kildrummy Castle if his parents let him.' Lisbie paused, and a concerned look appeared on her face. 'Is Bobby all right, Mum? He was looking sort of . . . quiet, don't you think?'

'He's at a difficult age,' said Fiona wisely, and was mildly annoyed when they all laughed at her.

'What age do you think *you're* at?' asked Lisbie, delighted at the opportunity to tease her sister. 'If anybody's at a difficult age, it's you.'

Quick as a flash, Fiona retorted, 'I heard Duncan ask you to join the choir, Lisbie. Now you'll be able to sing your little heart out right next to Larry French, whether he likes it or not.'

'He'll like it,' said Lisbie, blushing happily. 'As a matter of fact, I think I'm going to marry him.'

Steven swerved and almost went up on the pavement. 'You're going to *what*?' he asked, looking around.

'Daddy, please!' said Fiona, alarmed. 'Are you trying to kill us? You're driving like that time up at Strathalmond Castle.'

'Don't talk to your father in that tone of voice, Fiona,' said Jean mildly, but they all saw her surreptitiously fasten her seat belt as she spoke, and all of them laughed, except Steven.

But Fiona's bad memories of that time wouldn't go away, and she didn't say another word until they were safely home.

Lunch was catch-as-catch can, picnic-style in the dining room, as was the custom on Sundays. Jean had put the cups and plates on the table before leaving for church, and Lisbie went to the kitchen, took the cling film off the plates of sliced ham and cheese, and set them out on the table. Fiona, still subdued, brought in the butter dish and a container of cherry tomatoes. Everyone made his or her own sandwiches according to their preferences. Jean went into the kitchen to make tea for Steven and herself, but both girls preferred Coca-Cola, a recent change in taste that Steven observed with profound suspicion.

'If you're going to drink that stuff, you might at least use glasses,' he said, the remains of his Bloody Mary in a tall tumbler in front of him.

'Come on, Dad, leave us alone, it's Sunday,' protested Lisbie.

'And anyway it tastes better straight out of the bottle, doesn't it, Lisbie?' said Fiona, suddenly coming back to life.

Annoyed, Steven slapped a piece of bread down on his plate. 'Look, you two, I don't intend to get into an argument about this . . .'

'Thank you, Daddy,' said Lisbie demurely. 'I knew you wouldn't really mind.'

Steven went pink, took a deep breath and was about to issue an executive order when Jean, who had heard the discussion, came in from the kitchen, and put an empty glass in front of each of them before sitting down. Jean didn't say anything, but that was the end of the argument. The girls sighed loudly, and Lisbie poured her Coke out too fast so it fizzed up over the edge and spilled onto the tablecloth. Trying to stifle her giggles, she mopped the mess up with her napkin, accompanied by rather ribald comments from Fiona. Steven glowered at Lisbie, but she had long ago learned not to catch his eye at such moments, so the glower withered unrequited. Subsiding into his chair, he started to butter his bread with great vigour, feeling that in some roundabout way he had won that skirmish. At least he'd stopped them from drinking that American stuff straight from the bottles.

As they were finishing lunch, the phone rang, and Fiona went to answer it, then called from the hall. 'Mum, it's for you,' she said. 'It's Mr Farquar. He says his wife is really sick, and could you please go over.'

Chapter Three

After the last of the parishioners had left, Duncan Sinclair walked back to the vestry, slipped out of his gown and hung it on the first of the row of hooks on the wall. The vestry was a big, open room, with dark oak wainscotting and three high diamond-paned windows which faced out on to the small churchyard. A long dark mahogany table stood against the wall opposite, bearing at the far end a large teapot under a red-and-white knitted cosy, a few mugs and a stack of white styrofoam cups next to a plate of biscuits. Half a dozen people, including Ian Farquar, a couple of elders, and a few of the choir members stood in a cluster near the table, waiting for him.

'All right then, who's going to pour?' asked Duncan, smiling and rubbing his long hands together in the way he'd done ever since he was a divinity student.

Lois Munday, the church secretary, a member of the choir and ex-officio pourer, turned towards him. About thirty, Lois was a slender, tense-looking young woman whose pale complexion was marred by a few pitted acne scars on her cheeks. She was dressed in a well-fitting, dark blue business suit; her large horn-rimmed glasses in no way concealed her large, intense grey eyes, and she watched Duncan with a strange, hungry, glittery look. She turned rather clumsily back towards the table; her incision was still giving her some pain.

'No, Lois, let someone else do it today,' said Duncan, firmly. 'You know you shouldn't be lifting anything for a while yet.'

One of the other women choristers poured. Duncan, Ian, and a few of the elders had their own mugs, some with their names on sticky labels; the others got styrofoam cups. The senior elder was busy at the other end of the table with four empty soft dark-red velvet bags in front of him, counting the collection and piling the money carefully before putting it away in an old, grey-painted cash box.

'How did you like the flowers, Reverend?' asked Lois, after insisting that passing the biscuits presented no hazard to her health. She stood as close to Duncan as she dared. 'Most of them came from the manse garden.'

'But the others came from *your* garden, didn't they? The roses and the chrysanthemums? Thank you, Miss Munday, they were lovely.'

Lois blushed, and two spots came alive on her cheeks. The colour spread over her neck and what was visible of the top of her chest, above the high, demure cleavage of her silk blouse.

'Would you care for a biscuit?' she asked, hastily offering the plate. 'They're wholemeal with raisins.'

'Yes, thanks . . .' Duncan picked one up and turned to the group now loosely clustered around him.

'Could they hear all right at the back?' he asked. 'I sometimes feel we should conduct our service like the Baptists, and encourage the congregation to participate more.'

'Reverend Sinclair!' said Lois, her deeply religious mind shocked in spite of her love for Duncan. 'Baptists!' She looked at him uncertainly. 'You're joking, of course . . .'

'Right,' Duncan said easily. He smiled. 'Don't worry about it, Miss Munday. Of course I was just joking.'

Over Lois's shoulder, Duncan saw Ian Farquar staring at him with an unfathomable expression on his face, and went over to talk to him. 'The music went very well,' he said putting a friendly hand on Ian's shoulder. 'I particularly love that piece you started with. William Boyce, wasn't it? He really makes you feel the presence of the Lord through his music, doesn't he?' Hypocrisy had become such a habit with Duncan that he barely noticed.

Ian moved his shoulder slightly, nodded, and muttered something that Duncan didn't hear. Larry French, a young, well-dressed man with a fine moustache and an equally fine baritone voice came up, styrofoam cup in hand. 'Where's Beth?' he demanded of Ian. 'Until now, I thought the two of you were glued together.'

'She wasna' feeling well this morning,' Ian replied, in his rusty-sounding Buchan accent. Larry thought Ian looked sad and preoccupied, and the lines in his face were etched deeper than ever.

Ian put his empty styrofoam cup back on the table. 'It's time I was getting back.' He turned to Duncan again. 'I'll see you all on Thursday evening, then.'

Without further adieu Ian left the room through the door to the church, rather than going directly outside, as he had to pick up some music he'd left on the organ console.

Duncan, feeling faintly uncomfortable as he often did with Ian, watched the organist leave. Duncan knew him to be strong and stubborn, an unlikely sort of person to be a musician, a man whose roots extended deep into the Scottish countryside. He was a typical Buchan Scot, reflected Duncan, strict, fair in a harsh way, burdened with a unswerving code of ethical behaviour, a man who would neither forgive nor forget any injury to himself or to his kin. Ian took his choir very seriously, and had been known to lose his temper with careless singers; he could say dreadful things to them in the heat of the moment. But his teaching was good and the choir members forgave him, usually. Poor Ian, thought Duncan charitably, the tragedy of losing his son must have soured him for life. For a moment, Duncan remembered the sadness in Ian's voice when he told him about it, but since that one time, when he was interviewing Ian for the post of organist, he'd never mentioned his son again.

It took Ian about five minutes driving his old Morris Minor to get to his home up on Graybank Road, a steep, curving street not far from the hospital.

He parked outside, pointing downhill. He carefully turned the wheels towards the kerb, set the handbrake and left the car in reverse. Ian did these routine tasks with a meticulous precision, thinking all the time about Beth, his wife, his companion and best friend. All the anxieties he had been trying to suppress during the service came to the surface again. Beth had woken that morning with a sore throat and a headache. Ian had made breakfast and brought it to her in bed, but all she could take was a few sips of tea. By the time he was ready to leave for church, she was looking flushed and feverish, and although she wanted to go with him, he gave her two aspirins and a glass of water, and insisted that she stay in bed.

The only time he remembered Beth being ill was two years ago, soon after their son Victor died. That was before they moved to Perth from Aberdeen, partly to get away from all the sad memories. They had joined Jean Montrose's practice on the recommendation of one of Ian's new colleagues at the Academy. According to Jean, Beth's illness was more from depression than from any physical cause.

Ian let himself in. There was an immediately noticeable warm, unhealthy odour of illness inside the house; he went into the bedroom, took one look at Beth's feverish, perspiration-covered forehead and the restless movements of her hands. Her breathing made a rasping sound. Barely stopping to touch Beth's hand, he went into the entrance hall and picked up the phone. Jean's phone number was on a piece of paper taped to the wall above the phone, and Ian kept his finger on the number as if it were a good luck charm, while he dialled with the other hand.

Joe had gone on ahead, so Ann McIver, standing stiff and severe, waited alone in the street outside the church for Jeremy. She felt proud and tense at the same time; her son was singing so well that he surely would be selected for the Scottish Youth Choir, especially now that he was taking private singing lessons from Ian Farquar. She'd also repeatedly made quite sure Duncan knew how important joining the SYC was to Jeremy.

Even though Ann knew that Mr Farquar charged her less than his usual fees, the singing lessons were still more than they could really afford. But Ann had made up her mind, ever since she heard the SYC on the radio. Organized by the Church, the choir was composed of about eighty of the best young singers in Scotland. Each year, one young member from each church choir was sent by his choirmaster for an audition. The choir did radio broadcasts and travelled to Europe for a month, giving concerts in various cities, and even did recordings. The Church paid the expenses of those who couldn't otherwise have afforded to go. But the great thing was that many distinguished musicians had got their start in the SYC; for Jeremy, whose chief talent was his music, it would be the entrance to a better, wonderful life. As long as Jeremy got an audition, Ann was sure, the superior quality of his voice would do the rest.

But then there was Bobby Sutherland, who would also be trying for the Choir, Bobby with his rich parents and their high social standing. Ann, always angrily class conscious, knew that in a contest, wealth and social position were usually quite enough to tip the scales in favour of those who had them, regardless of who had the most talent.

Ann watched Jeremy come down the church steps towards her. He was well-built, strong, tall for his age, and *such* a good-looking boy, she thought, with his long blond hair, much longer than his father liked, and his sharp blue eyes. Unfortunately, to many people there was something disturbing about Jeremy's sea-blue eyes; they were shifty, never looked directly into other people's, and often gave more than a hint of duplicity. Ann watched Jeremy approach, and sighed, thinking of the havoc he would wreak in the hearts of so many girls. In fact, unless she was mistaken, that was already beginning to happen. Jeremy was almost exactly the same age as Bobby Sutherland, although much stronger and a couple of inches taller. Ann was well aware of the physiological changes that would be catching up with both of them within a year, and, unconsciously, her fingers tightened into fists. This year would be Jeremy's only chance for the SYC.

'You sounded *wonderful* this morning, Jeremy,' she said as he came up. Most of the churchgoers had left, and only a few stragglers chatted at the foot of the steps and near the gate. 'I could hear you clear over the others.'

'That was Bobby,' grunted Jeremy. He kept walking, and Ann had to hurry to keep up with him. He didn't seem at all concerned about Bobby as a possible rival, and Jeremy's lack of competitive spirit made Ann purse her lips. It seemed out of character, because he was certainly tough enough with the other kids.

'I know the difference between your voice and Bobby's,' she said grimly. They crossed the street, and she tried to hold his hand, but Jeremy pulled away from her.

'I'm not a *child*,' he said.

'Bobby's voice is good, I'll admit that,' conceded Ann as they walked along the almost deserted South Street. 'But he doesn't have . . . I don't know, the same *quality*, let alone the extra training you've had.'

Jeremy shrugged. He had suffered through this discussion so many times that it bored him, although he knew how much his mother wanted him to succeed as a singer.

'What's for lunch?' he asked, looking directly in front of him. He was walking a couple of feet away from her, far enough so that nobody would think they were in any way associated.

'Oh, Jeremy, why can't you ever think about the

important things in life?' Ann cried, exasperated. 'What does it matter what you eat for lunch? Come over here, I don't like having to shout at you.'

Reluctantly, Jeremy came closer, and Ann gripped his arm with both hands in her frustration.

'I wish you'd think a little more about your singing, Jeremy,' she said, 'You know how important it is that you do really well in the auditions.'

Jeremy didn't seem to be paying the slightest attention to her, and was walking nonchalantly along, glancing occasionally into the shop windows. Ann walked a little faster, fighting a rising tide of annoyance.

'You don't appreciate what we do for you, Jeremy,' she said, loudly.

A man passing in the opposite direction gave her a curious stare, and Jeremy shrank with embarrassment. Ann didn't even notice. '*I* never had that kind of opportunity,' she went on. 'When I was your age, my parents wanted me to work in the fish-packing factory because of the money . . .'

Realizing that Jeremy wasn't listening, Ann finally fell silent, but she was still angry. She worked so hard, and had spent so much time and effort to make her son a success. Ann didn't grudge the time or the expense, knowing that success was a *habit*. Once a child really succeeded at something, *anything*, early in life, it became an irreplaceable mental resource that lasted throughout the person's life. That was the treasure she wanted to bequeath to Jeremy, something neither she nor her husband had ever had. That was why she was just a primary school supply teacher, and why Joe worked as a navvy for one of the local contractors, when he wasn't doing other things she didn't want to know about.

* * *

Lois Munday washed and put away the tea things then left with the remaining choir members after shaking Duncan's hand.

'You can go home now,' Duncan said to Mr Archibald, the elderly verger, who had collected the hymn books and was putting them in neat piles on the seat of the rearmost pew. 'I'll lock up.'

Mr Archibald, quite accustomed to Duncan spending time in the church alone, nodded politely, and a few moments later left silently through the vestry door.

Duncan put on his gown, took a deep breath, and walked slowly up the central aisle of his deserted and silent church. The undecorated beige-pink sandstone walls gave the interior a warmth that the more impressive-looking granite churches elsewhere in town couldn't match. Duncan walked slowly past the dark, handcarved old oak pews; the light slanting through the stained glass windows made red and blue splashes on the sisal matting that covered the floor of the aisles.

The gentle serenity of his church made Duncan wish he could again feel a part of all the ancient traditions of Christianity. As he walked towards the altar, he twisted his hands unconsciously, remembering when he was part of an infinitely long, undulating chain, holding hands with all the other children of God in their procession through the ages. But now, he felt alone, utterly and finally alone. The procession was going past without him, and to the marchers he no longer even existed.

Duncan sat down in the front pew, trying to take his mind off his misery. He glanced from the pulpit across to the organ console. The thin red curtain had been drawn back, and the three manuals were visible, terraced one above the other, with the slightly yellowed ivories and old-fashioned, rounded pull-out stops. It was a fine instrument, a Willis, bought for the church almost a hundred years before by Jeremiah Cox, a local adventurer who had made his fortune transporting slaves from the Ivory Coast to Savannah, Georgia. Late in life he had come home to Perth, hoping to save his immortal soul by good works.

Duncan's eyes swept, almost reluctantly, up to the three rows of choir pews set steeply one above the other, then over to the altar, where bright arum, white and tiger lilies sat in a pool of warm sunlight coming into the chancel from the round window in the North wall.

'Dear God,' said Duncan very quietly, looking up at the ceiling with its dark rafters separated by painted coats-of arms, 'If you exist, I sorely need thy help and guidance.' Then, for no reason that training or intellect could explain, Duncan fell abruptly to his knees. With his eyes tightly shut, and both hands clenched in an agony of doubt and remorse, he tried, unsuccessfully, to pray.

Chapter Four

Ten minutes after Ian Farquar phoned, Jean drew up outside the door of his house, still wearing the pretty green and white flowered dress she had worn that morning to church.

She didn't have to ring the doorbell, because Ian appeared in the doorway as soon as she opened the gate. Jean walked quickly up the tidy, rose-lined brick path to the door.

'I'm sorry if I took you away from your lunch, Jean,' said Ian, his gravelly voice genuinely apologetic. He opened the door wider to let her in. 'But I've nivver seen Beth like this.' Ian's lips were pale with concern. He went on talking as he followed Jean down the dark hall towards the bedroom at the back of the house. 'She has a right fever,' he went on, 'and she told me that earlier, while I was in church, she was seeing things that were nae there.'

When Jean came in, Beth looked up with a thin, agitated smile that lasted only a second. Her breathing was fast, and her skin was dry and hot. Jean didn't need a thermometer to tell that Beth had a fever of well over a hundred.

'When did this start, Beth?' asked Jean, putting her

black bag on the floor beside her and sitting down on the edge of the bed.

'I was fine last night, wasn't I, Ian?'

Ian nodded.

'She was really hot this morning,' he said. 'I woke up early, and I could feel the heat coming from her.'

Jean reached down for her stethoscope. 'Pull up your nightie, Beth, please.'

Ian looked away.

Beth's breathing was loud and rasping, but there was no sign of pneumonia.

'You have the 'flu, Beth,' said Jean. 'I'm sure you've heard there's a lot of it around.'

'I didn't know you could get such a fever with it,' said Ian, but he sounded relieved. All kinds of dreadful possibilities had been passing through his mind.

'With 'flu,' said Jean, putting her stethoscope back into her black bag, 'you never know what to expect. Sometimes people get vomiting and diarrhoea, sometimes it's more like this, like a pneumonia. With this particular variety, a lot of people are getting high fevers.'

'Would you like a cup of tea?' asked Ian, and only because she liked the Farquars, Jean accepted. If she drank every cup of tea that was offered her in the course of her working day, she would have been awash in it.

While Ian went off to the kitchen, Jean went into the bathroom to wet a facecloth for Beth's forehead. Everything was tidy and put away, and she felt sure it wasn't because they had been expecting her. Guiltily, Jean remembered the state in which she'd left her own bathroom, but the lived-in untidiness of her home was certainly more comfortable than the severe, stark austerity of the Farquars' house.

One of the things Jean always noticed about a home was the number and style of the mirrors it contained; that single item often told her a great deal about the people who lived in the house. In the Farquars' bathroom, there was only a single small oval shaving mirror set at a height to suit Ian. It was positioned a few inches too high for Jean and therefore also too high for Beth, who was about the same height.

Jean came back into the brown-carpeted bedroom. Apart from the bed and a plain chair, the only piece of furniture was a big chest of drawers. It was solid, well made, with wooden peg handles, no frills. On its shiny, well-polished top was a square, hand-embroidered doily, a small, square mirror in the middle, and on each side, a silver-framed photo; one of their wedding, the other of Beth and Ian camping with their son, a nice-looking boy of about twelve. All three were smiling cheerfully in front of a tent. Next to the photos was a wooden trinket box, and on the opposite end, under a small table lamp with a parchment shade, a large black-bound bible that bore the signs of frequent use.

Jean put the wet facecloth gently on Beth's forehead. The sparse furnishings had given Jean a momentary but weird sense that the Farquars were separate, isolated, and somehow alienated from the world around them.

'Thank you, Jean,' murmured Beth, enjoying the coolness of the wet cloth on her brow. Her eyes showed her gratitude. She coughed, a harsh, dry, cough that shook her thin body. 'How long is this going to last?'

'A week, maybe, if you take care of yourself,' replied Jean. 'A lot longer if you try to keep on doing everything you were doing before. You'll have to stay in bed for a few days, anyway.'

Ian came in quietly with the tea things. He always

seemed to move so unobtrusively, Jean thought. The man would suddenly appear in church, seated at the organ. He had to have walked across the cross-aisle in front of her to get there; she simply hadn't noticed him.

'She's going to have to stay in bed for a few days,' Jean told Ian. 'I'll give you a prescription for her, and she'll need lots to drink, water, orange juice, anything that takes her fancy.'

'Should I cancel my pupils?' asked Ian. Jean knew that he gave private lessons in piano and singing; they had converted the second bedroom into a music room.

'I don't think you need to,' she replied. 'As long as they stay away from Beth.'

'Most of Ian's pupils don't even know I exist,' said Beth with a smile. She was beginning to look better. 'Except that we had a little Christmas party for them last year.'

Ian went to fetch another chair while Jean set out the cups and poured the tea. Normally Beth wouldn't have liked anyone else pouring her tea, but she felt exhausted, and anyway Jean Montrose was different. As far as Beth was concerned, Jean could do anything she wanted, probably even walk on water, not that it would ever occur to her to try.

Jean stayed only a few more minutes, and as she got into her car and headed for home, she thought about the cold, sad bleakness that seemed to pervade both the Farquars' home and their lives, and wondered vaguely if they had been happier before the death of their son.

After seeing Jean out, Ian went back to the bedroom, collected the tea things and put them on the tray. 'She's a fine person, the wee doc,' he said, sitting down on the end of the bed.

'Aye, that she is,' replied Beth. She was now sitting up in bed, feeling much better. Even in the direst circumstances, Jean Montrose often had that effect on her patients.

'I wish there were more like her,' continued Ian. He put his hand out to Beth, and they sat there together, holding hands like two sad children, saying nothing, bonded by their love, their memories, and their life together.

There was never very much conversation at the Sutherlands' home, and this Sunday lunchtime was no exception. Derek sat at the dining-room table, waiting for Sheila to come in with the meal. He had a tumbler of peat-coloured whisky near his left hand, and leafed idly through the latest *Journal of Anaesthesiology*. It didn't take him more than a couple of minutes to flip through, although he did glance at most of the pharmaceutical ads. Then he put the journal down, picked up the *Sunday Post* and turned to the sports pages.

Bobby came in quietly and sat down next to his father. Derek heard him, but didn't look up, or he might have seen the taut, fixed expression on his son's face.

Derek turned to the back page. 'The Dons won yesterday against Partick Thistle,' he said from behind his paper. 'Two penalties against one penalty.' He glanced over the top of the *Post*. 'They all seem to have forgotten how to score real goals any more.'

'Dad . . .' Bobby's voice was high and unsure, and the tension in his face became more pronounced.

Derek was in a good, relaxed mood, and didn't want to be disturbed from it. He could see that Bobby was about to say something that would take him away from the comfortable, peaceful thoughts to which he was entitled. After all, it was Sunday, for God's sake, a day of rest. So he neatly sidestepped his son's overture.

'Bobby, don't just sit there,' he said. 'Go and help your mother prepare lunch, right now.'

'But Dad . . . Please . . . I need to talk to you.'

'When I say now, Bobby, I mean *now*.' Derek's eyes had already moved down to the golf scores; there had been a three-day international match over at St Andrews the day before and he really wanted to see who had come in the top five.

Derek pursed his lips. 'For heaven's sake, Bobby, don't cry like that,' he went on, sharply. It annoyed him to see tears brimming in his son's eyes, and he deliberately chose to misunderstand them. 'You're not a baby any more. It'll just take you a minute, and I'm sure your mother could use some help.'

Bobby got up, his face suddenly expressionless, and went to the door, wiping his eyes with the back of both hands. He returned to the dining-room a few moments later holding a trivet, a big plate and some knives and forks. He was closely followed by Sheila, bearing a tray with a hot meat loaf in one metal pan, and boiled potatoes and leeks in another.

'Bobby!' snapped Sheila, 'you know the trivet doesn't belong there. Put it down in front of your father. How can he possibly reach it there?'

Silently, Bobby repositioned the trivet and sat down. He had been thinking about something else.

'Serving spoons, Bobby. Why do I have to tell you the same thing at every meal?' Sheila seemed upset, and as always, Bobby was certain that it was his fault. He must have done something to annoy her. For months now, he'd been feeling increasingly responsible for his parents' state of mind and for the poor relationship between them. Sometimes it was more than he could stand. His father and mother weren't getting on, and their voices were loud and angry when they talked in their bedroom, and Bobby was sure they were discussing him, blaming him. Whatever was going on, it was his fault.

After lunch, Bobby wheeled his bicycle out of the shed and rode off down the sunlit, leafy street, feeling sad and angry at the same time. He wanted to hit somebody or something. His friend Jeremy met him as arranged, under the statue of Prince Albert at the corner of the North Inch. They rode their bikes slowly, weaving patterns on the path.

'What did you have for lunch?' asked Jeremy riding close behind Bobby.

'Meat loaf.' Bobby was trying to see how slowly he could ride without putting his hands on the handlebars. Doing something difficult like that blanked out the other things he didn't want to think about.

'That's what you had last Sunday.'

'That's what we have *every* Sunday.'

'I bet you can't cycle *this* slow,' said Jeremy, imitating Bobby, but holding on to the handlebars. His front wheel wobbled wildly with his efforts to keep from falling off. 'I bet nobody in the whole *world* can go this slow on a bike.'

'Who cares?' asked Bobby, after trying and almost falling off. 'Who needs to go that slow? I'd rather go *fast*.' And off he went, going like the wind, with Jeremy in hot pursuit.

Later, they tried to ride round the golf course, up and down the steep grassy hillocks, but some man shouted at them and they raced over to the narrow riverside path and back to the Inch.

'What's the matter with you?' asked Jeremy after they'd been riding along in silence for some minutes. 'You hardly talk to me any more.'

Bobby got off his bike, propped it up on the stand, and sat down on a bench. Jeremy cycled slowly in front of him, making tight circles around a large snail cruising majestically across the path.

'You remember a few weeks ago, what Mr Farquar said to me? About my father?'

Jeremy laughed incredulously, wobbled, just missing the snail. 'You're still thinking about that? He's said worse things to me. Once when I wasn't paying attention to him he said *my* father was a good-for-nothing crook.'

'What did you say?'

'I said that if my Dad heard that, he'd probably come and break his neck.'

'You said that to Mr Farquar?' asked Bobby incredulously.

'Sure. We've both forgotten about the whole thing long ago.'

'Well . . .' Bobby obviously wasn't convinced. 'What he said about my father was worse than that.'

'Forget it,' advised Jeremy.

'Why don't you ever come over to my house any more?' asked Bobby after a pause.

'My mother says I'm not to,' replied Jeremy.

'Why not?'

'I don't know,' said Jeremy, sounding uncomfortable. He got off his bicycle and knelt beside it to look more closely at the snail. 'Do you think its shell comes off?'

'Of course. What do you think slugs are? They're just snails that've lost their shells.' Bobby spoke abruptly, suddenly feeling angry with Jeremy, with Jeremy's mother, everybody. He knew the way Mrs McIver looked at him, and knew that she hated him. He hadn't done anything. It wasn't his fault that he could sing better than Jeremy, as if that mattered. But it seemed very important to her, a lot more important than to Jeremy. Bobby scowled. Singing . . . ! How he hated it, hated the choir, hated Mr Farquar, hated everything.

He jumped back on his bike, did a full circle and deliberately ran over the big snail, leaving a wet, crunchy, slimy splash on the tarred surface.

A minute later, as they were going past Albert's statue, Bobby, still feeling angry and wanting to hurt somebody, turned in his saddle to ask Jeremy if he knew how to ride his bike with his hands crossed on the handlebars. Jeremy didn't know, but was quite willing to try, especially after Bobby demonstrated. Jeremy didn't notice that Bobby wasn't actually touching the handlebars. When Jeremy did it, he swerved wildly then fell off his bike with a crash.

Bobby didn't even look back.

Chapter Five

After Bobby left the house and went off to meet Jeremy McIver, Derek picked up his newspaper and returned to his interrupted reading of the sports pages. These were a relief to him, a form of anodyne. Long ago he'd developed an interest in sport, particularly football and golf, and had become extraordinarily knowledgeable about them. As a boy, Derek had already learned to escape anxiety and responsibility by reading, but after finishing medical school, he barely opened a book unless it was about sport. Derek was known everywhere he went for his encyclopaedic knowledge of sporting facts. He could tell you the names, weights and career details of all the men who'd played in all the Cup Finals going back to 1950 and some of the more notable ones before that, and had similar details at his fingertips about Open Championships and all the other major golf tournaments. He possessed all sorts of recondite information about how golf balls were made, how gutta-percha had been used in the old days, and what the little dimples did to the flight characteristics of the ball. He could discuss for hours the detailed rules concerning transfer of ownership of football clubs.

For years now, when something disturbing or unnerving happened, Derek would reach for the record books he kept in his library, or turn to the back pages of his newspaper to dissipate the unpleasant thoughts. It was his own form of self-prescribed anaesthesia.

Sheila's attitude seemed to have changed, he thought, looking for the tennis results. Derek had noticed that apart from her obsession with Bobby's health, Sheila had been nagging him less. If nothing else, Derek was a pragmatist; provided she ran the house with reasonable efficiency, the less she talked to him the happier he was. For years they had really had nothing to say to each other, and when they did speak it was always about some problem; money, Bobby, always something unpleasant.

Sheila, hidden from Derek's eyes by his newspaper, allowed her contempt and disgust for him to show on her face. And her restlessness was fast becoming unbearable.

'I think I'll go out for a walk,' she said a few moments later and started to gather the dishes with a clatter that he couldn't totally ignore. But Derek, engrossed in an account of John McEnroe's most recent spat with the tennis authorities, only grunted something incomprehensible from behind his paper. A few moments later, he heard the front door close softly, then she was gone. Derek barely noticed; he was automatically memorizing the date and the amount of McEnroe's fine, the exact reasons why it had been imposed, which rules had been infracted. One day, Derek knew, in some conversation, he would be able to astound his listeners by recollecting every detail as if he were reading them straight off the newspaper.

* * *

FATAL FEVER

When Jeremy got home, he was trying hard not to cry. His shirt was torn, one of the sleeves was almost off, and his left arm and knee had quite severe abrasions where he had hit the gravel after falling off his bike. Jeremy dropped his bicycle near the front door and came in.

'For heaven's sake, Jeremy, whatever happened?' asked Ann, horrified at his appearance. 'Here, let me see that arm. And your knee . . .' Ann took him into the tiny kitchen, grabbed a towel, wet it and gently started to clean the dirt and blood off his arm.

Joe heard Ann's raised voice, and came and stood in the doorway, both arms raised to the jambs, a beer can in his right hand. Joe was a large, coarse-featured man with heavy, work-hardened muscles. He wore a white sweat shirt over his big belly and ancient leather sandals on his feet. His hands and arms were weathered a deep brown up almost to the shoulders, where his skin became startlingly lard-white.

He looked at Jeremy, who was bearing the torture of cleansing with his eyes all scrunched up and emitting a low wail of pain, then at Ann.

'What the hell happened to him?'

'I don't know,' she said. 'He must have fallen off his bike. He's usually so careful . . .'

'What happened, Jer?'

For a few moments Jeremy said nothing, as he was hurting and couldn't trust his voice.

'Nothing,' he said finally, in an almost inaudible voice. The pain of being betrayed by his best friend was something quite new to him, much worse than the pain from his injuries and his own retaliatory rage was just beginning to take shape.

'Where's the Mercurochrome?' asked Ann, but of

course the only one who had any idea where it might be was herself. She found it, and in a few moments, she had Jeremy's arm and leg all gaudy and luminescent with the brilliant, orange-coloured dressing.

It was only later that day, when Jeremy was about to go to bed, that he finally told his parents what had happened.

'I always told you Bobby wasn't a nice boy,' said Ann, outraged. She put down the shirt she was repairing. 'That'll teach you to stay away from him from now on.'

'That little bastard,' growled Joe. His face flushed and he reached forward to turn down the volume on the television. He was sitting in an easy chair opposite Ann, and had already drunk enough beer to knock out an average man.

'So what are you going to do about him, Jeremy?' he asked.

'I'll get him,' replied Jeremy, his eyes narrowing. He'd got it all worked out already. 'Me and Billy and Sandy. We'll get him after school tomorrow. He'll be sorry.'

Joe nodded portentously, and Ann asked 'What do you need Billy and Sandy for? You're already twice his size.'

Jeremy grinned at his father, who winked back. Ann stared at her son over the half-glasses she used nowadays for close work. There was a lot of his father in Jeremy, she thought, and she knew why Jeremy would recruit his other friends. As a teacher she had seen what even a small gang of boys could do to another boy in a very short space of time. Kids didn't challenge each other then fight it out behind the gym, not these days.

'Just don't get your clothes torn and dirty again,' said Ann, going back to her work, 'I won't have it, do you hear me, Jeremy?' But Ann's voice had no conviction in it. Jeremy understood immediately that she would not be at all troubled if Bobby got his nose bloodied.

Jeremy grunted, and again Joe gave him a fat, complicitous wink before turning the TV up. They understood each other well, man and boy. Although they might not have recognized it by name, they knew that the *lex talionis* remained alive and well in certain circles of Perth. An eye for an eye and a tooth for a tooth; that was how Joe's father and *his* father had managed to survive. Joe was grimly pleased that Jeremy was ready to carry on the family tradition. If the boy let people trample over him, Joe knew, he'd be finished, and the sooner Jeremy realized that, the better. But with his experience of such encounters, Joe also knew that at some point Jeremy might need his help.

Jeremy mumbled goodnight, and limped off to his room. His knee was throbbing a lot, although his arm had stopped hurting. Until he fell asleep, he spent his time working out the details of his revenge on Bobby Sutherland.

After Jean went off to see Beth Farquar, Fiona started to tease Lisbie about Larry French. Steven, who liked to read the paper in peace after Sunday lunch, thought for a moment about leaving the dining room and seeking refuge upstairs, but realized that he would thereby miss a good opportunity to find out what was going on in his daughters' lives. They never told him directly, but all kinds of things came out when the two girls talked together. So Steven kept the paper up in front of his face and listened.

'I don't know about you,' said Fiona in that mocking voice that always infuriated Lisbie. 'Either you're going with boys who are still in short trousers, like that boy . . . What was his name?'

'If you're referring to Neil Mackay,' said Lisbie with dignity, 'he was very grown up for his age, I'll have you know.'

'I'll have you know . . .' mimicked Fiona. 'Well, I'll have *you* know that if you'd been a boy, and he'd been a girl, you could have been had up and sent to jail for carnal knowledge of a minor.'

Steven's hands tightened on his paper, and he drew in a quick breath, but otherwise made no sign that he was listening.

'At least he wasn't an old married man like Douglas,' retorted Lisbie. 'And nor is Larry. You're just jealous that Larry likes me and not you.'

'Well, if you do marry him, is that what you want for the rest of your life, standing behind the counter of a chemist's shop and selling condoms and Tampax all day long?'

The newspaper quivered, and for a second the two girls grinned at each other, Fiona pinching her nose to keep from laughing. But it was only a momentary truce.

'Anyway, everybody always thought Larry was more interested in boys,' went on Fiona relentlessly. 'What did you do to change his mind?'

'That's just a load of rubbish,' said Lisbie indignantly, then laughed, and looked coy. 'All he needed to bring him to life was me . . .'

So that's why Lisbie was so often late home from

work, thought Steven. She was stopping by Larry's shop to have a wee chat with him, to make a pass at him . . . or receive one.

'Well, I don't know,' Fiona was saying more seriously. 'It all seems very strange.'

Lisbie looked at her watch and got up. 'I'm going out,' she said.

The paper came down all the way, quickly.

'Where?' asked Steven.

'Out,' replied Lisbie, grinning self-consciously, and she was gone before Steven had time to ask any more questions.

Larry French left the church soon after Ian went home, but he was in a quite different frame of mind from that of the organist. For the tenth time he looked at his watch, and calculated that if she were on time, he would be seeing her in exactly one hour and twelve minutes. She had warned that she might be late, because she could never be quite certain of getting away from the family. Larry hurried over to his old green Triumph TR6.

Settling in the driver's seat, he pulled down the sunshade on his side; he had glued a large hand-mirror to its top surface when he first got the car. He studied his reflection with interest, patted his thick dark brown hair, found a slightly ragged area in his moustache, right under his left nostril, and carefully repositioned the few errant hairs with a small comb he carried with him for that purpose. More serious, there was a double line of pink on his right cheek where one of the choir women had kissed him. That wouldn't do at all, he thought, and hoped that there wasn't any trace of perfume anywhere on him. He certainly didn't want a scene, or any jealous comments to spoil what should be an afternoon of pure passion and love. He grinned at himself, noting how nicely the left corner of his mouth went up just a little more than the right, giving him a really sexy, slightly crooked smile. It was extraordinary, he thought, how he had a completely different feeling about himself since she had come into his life.

The usually dodgy engine started on the first turn of the key, and he eased out of the car park and waved to a few people still chatting around the church entrance before going home for lunch. It was a glorious morning, warm and clear, and he drove slowly along South Street, looking straight ahead of him, anticipating the afternoon ahead with a warm glow of emotion so powerful that it left him shaken. Larry had always liked girls well enough, but at a distance; he'd always felt shy and tongue-tied with them, to the point where he felt more at ease with his male friends.

There had never been much exposure to females in Larry's life, except to the older women who came into his father's busy chemist's shop. As a child, Larry used to sit perched on a high stool behind the counter, and when a female customer came in, (and most of the customers were female, as in any chemist's shop) they would ask for their bottle of liver salts or tonic or whatever, and while Mr French wrapped their purchase in white paper and sealed it with a dab of red sealing-wax, the women would stand by the till and ooh and aah over little Larry, sigh over his gorgeous curly brown hair, his smooth skin and luminous eyes, to the point where grownup adulation came to him as naturally as his three meals a day.

Larry inherited the business when his father died, and did a good job modernizing the procedures in the shop.

He introduced a computer-based system which not only did the accounts, but held the names of all the patients and the medicines they were taking. The system even alerted the pharmacist to any possible incompatibility or interaction between different medicines. After a couple of profitable years, Larry started a satellite pharmacy across the river in Bridgend, next to the Royal Bank of Scotland branch, and in both locations he was doing very well; he was well liked because he was friendly, respectful and worked hard. Later, because he was so attractive and immaculately turned out, women would apply their makeup with special care and dress up in their best before making a trip to French The Chemist. It was all very good for business, as he treated everyone with the same courtesy and on occasion, a little flattery. For a long time Larry had seemed impervious to female charms, even to the panting young women who gathered around him in droves at various dances and hops and of course at the choir. Larry had made one really congenial friendship which seemed to be going well, but then lightning had struck. He had fallen in love, hopelessly, beyond any reason or caution.

It had happened just over a week ago, on a Friday afternoon, about three o'clock, when there was nobody in the shop except Donna, his assistant, who was in the back unpacking a shipment of medicines.

He'd known her by sight for some time, had seen her in church and heard her sing, and he'd taken notice of the way she walked, straight-backed, with a fine figure, and a certain something about her, a twinkle, a radiance that set her on a different plane from any of the other women he knew. Occasionally, when she was buying something in the shop, she'd smile at him, and he'd feel a warmth and closeness emanating from her, as if he'd been included in her personal aura. Larry felt pretty sure that she liked him, but he didn't think too much about her when she wasn't there. And anyway, he was otherwise occupied.

That afternoon a week ago, she'd come in alone, as she had for the preceding couple of weeks. She'd browsed around for a few minutes, then asked him for something which happened to be up on a high shelf, so Larry came out from behind the counter, brought the wooden ladder over and set it against the wall. He had just climbed to the top when the ladder started to slip, not very fast, but fast enough for him to fall, but luckily she caught hold of him and saved him from what might have been a nasty injury. The feel of her so soft and close against him, the scent of her was like a thunderbolt, and Larry was overwhelmed. Although she let him go almost as soon as he'd recovered his footing, his serenity was gone for ever.

One thing led to another very quickly.

Larry turned left before coming to the pedestrian precinct, and headed for his house in Muirton Bank. It was a large granite-built home with a fine view over the golf course and the river Tay. He had inherited the house with everything else when his father died; at that time his mother already had the early symptoms of Alzheimer's disease, and she was now away in a nursing home, mindless and incontinent. Larry had thought about selling the house and buying a smaller one or a flat, but all his childhood was there within these four solid walls, and he couldn't bring himself to leave it.

He parked the Triumph outside the garage and let himself in. In the huge old-fashioned kitchen, Larry made himself a ham and cheese sandwich, took a bottle of Tennant's lager and a jar of pickles out of the old, round-cornered refrigerator, put it all on a tray with a faded coronation picture of Queen Elizabeth and Prince Philip, and took it into the living room, where he sat on a window seat overlooking the garden with its central lawn and well-tended flowerbeds. Just over an hour later, the garden gate, which led out on to the path that flanked the golf-course, opened, then Larry heard the back doorbell ring.

He got up and ran into the kitchen. He opened the door, pulled her in, and, taking her in his arms, he held her close to him, tenderly, feeling light-headed with the warmth and the perfume of her.

'Oh, Sheila, darling,' he said, not yet comfortable with the language of love, 'I've been waiting for you for an hour, and it felt like ten.'

Chapter Six

The moment he stepped into the classroom on Monday morning, Bobby Sutherland knew something was up. Jeremy was over in the far corner by the window, huddled with two other boys, and they scattered and went to their desks as soon as they saw him come in. Jeremy wouldn't look at him, and there was a bandage on his left hand that seemed to extend up under his sleeve.

During the first period, there was a feeling of tension in the class. Even Mr Allan, the teacher, noticed and his gaze went from boy to boy as he tried to instil some basic principles of mathematics into their heads, but apart from the fact that Jeremy McIver had sustained some kind of injury over the weekend, he wasn't able to work out what was going on.

There was a short break before the second period, and then it was made clear to Bobby what he was in for. Jeremy and Sandy Watt came over and stood by his desk.

'We're going to beat you up after school, pigface,' said Jeremy, looking particularly tough and menacing.

'You and whose army?' retorted Bobby, doing his best to put a brave face on it, but he knew that he was in deep trouble unless he could think of some way of turning the tables on them.

During the next period, which was religious instruction, Bobby thought about what he should do. He wasn't afraid, although Jeremy was bigger and stronger, but Sandy was the strongest and toughest boy in the class, and there was at least one other in Jeremy's gang, Willie Wood – and possibly also Patrick Forbes, both redoubtable opponents.

Bobby knew they would wait for him at the bicycle sheds, out of sight of the main school building, and in any case he had to pick his bike up there to get home. His assigned stall was in the main shed, a long building with a sloping corrugated roof and open at both ends. The two parallel sets of bicycle stalls had a narrow aisle between them, just enough space for the boys to get their bikes out without hitting the bicycle in the opposite stall.

Bobby took care to lag behind after school; if he was lucky, they'd be waiting for him inside the shed. A wave of fear hit him when he saw three of them, Jeremy, Patrick and Sandy, hovering menacingly around the end of the shed nearest the school. Bobby thought quickly, then walked slowly towards them, as if resigned to his fate.

When he was about ten yards away, he suddenly dashed for the opposite entrance to the shed, and heard Sandy Watt shout, 'Come on, we'll get him inside!'

Bobby ran through the back entrance as fast as he could, then charged full tilt down the narrow central aisle. Only a few bicycles remained, and the three boys were clustered near the other end. Without slacking speed, Bobby stuck both elbows out and crashed straight into them, knocking all three of them flying. They tripped and fell in the metal racks, except Jeremy himself, who regained his balance and managed to stagger out of the shed. While the two other boys were struggling to their feet, Bobby grabbed his bicycle, pulled it out of the stall and jumped on. He headed straight for Jeremy, shouting furiously, and tried to run him down, but Jeremy, hobbling because of his still-painful leg, managed to get out of his way.

'You rotten coward, Jeremy McIver!' shouted Bobby over his shoulder as he cycled off. 'Why don't you fight your own battles?'

'I'm going to kill you, Bobby Sutherland!' Jeremy screamed back. 'I'm going to kill you!'

Duncan Sinclair woke suddenly in the big, airy bedroom of the manse, sat up and opened his eyes wide in an effort to dispel the demons that had been pursuing him in his dream. It had been more of a hunt than a pursuit, and it reminded him of a boar chase he'd seen as a divinity student when he did a term at the University of Heidelberg. In his dream, the demons, horned and hairy, with glowing, hateful eyes, first appeared over on his right, so he ran away in the opposite direction, then another group appeared in front of him, equally hideous and frightening, so he ran off in a different direction. The countryside was getting hotter and hotter, the land more parched and bleached, and the trees were shorter, stunted, with scorch-marks on the trunks. It took hours and days for Duncan to realize that all the time, the demons had been patiently driving him closer and closer to the gates of Hell.

Duncan jumped out of bed, and the last demonic howls vanished, leaving him with a strong sense of apprehension and impending doom. Duncan had had that dream before, and knew that if people experienced the same dream again and again, it could reach a point where the dream occupied their every sleeping moment, and ultimately drove them mad.

He went downstairs slowly, still wearing his pyjamas. Every step creaked in the old house. How many ministers had lived here in the hundred years since the manse was built? Not for the first time, Duncan wondered about the dark procession of figures that had preceded him in office. What kind of people had they been? God-fearing, sinful, or the usual mixture of both?

Once, from the pulpit, Duncan had stated the juxtaposition of sin and evil in people in terms of buttered toast – a thin coating of virtue, just enough to cover the far larger slab of sin lurking beneath. He knew that it was true for him, and wondered if any of his predecessors had been as sinful as he.

When Duncan first came to Perth and took over the manse, it had contained several portraits of previous incumbents. Some were hanging in the hall, others in the reception room and even two in the bedroom. Most of them were men of grim countenance, and Duncan, passing them in review with Miss Munday, could easily imagine them standing in the pulpit, shouting about the fire and brimstone to come. On Duncan's orders, all the portraits were taken down and put away in the attic, all but one.

Duncan made himself a mug of coffee in the kitchen, took it back up to his study and switched on the brown parchment-shaded overhead light to look at the portrait he had retained.

Set in a narrow black frame, the fading sepia-toned photograph was of a gentle, thoughtful-looking young man with a big, rather endearing moustache and stiff clerical collar. A faintly apologetic glint in his large brown eyes acknowledged that he should be doing something more useful than sitting there having his picture taken.

Below the portrait, a small rectangle had been cut out of the matting for his name. 'Reverend Jos. McFarland', it read, 'Minister, West Kirk, Perth, 1918–23.' Duncan pulled up a chair and sat down opposite the portrait, aware that his thoughts were jumbled and without apparent sequence, coming into his head rather than out of it, like gunfire aimed at him from all directions. Afraid of his thoughts, Duncan hoped that a few moments of communion with his friend Jos. McFarland would calm his mind. He stared at the photo, noting some minor foxing on the matting around it. Duncan had seen it before, but it hadn't occurred to him that the stains were in the shape of a gallows. Duncan shivered and moved his gaze to Jos.'s features, and concentrated on establishing a communion with his dead predecessor.

What a terrible time that must have been, in 1918, thought Duncan, when the young Jos. first came to Perth, fresh from Divinity School. He would have had to cope with the disruptions that followed the war, the long lines of sad widows and silent, watchful orphans, all the poverty and sadness, all the loneliness. Jos. had been the minister in Perth for only five years, not a very long time. Miss Munday hadn't wanted to tell him the story, but he cajoled it out of her. Jos. McFarland, young and handsome, was covertly eyed by many of the women left single by the war, but had apparently developed a close relationship with a very beautiful sixteen-year old parishioner by the name of Sophie Strachan, and some time later the rumour flashed around the town that she was pregnant. Her father, a wealthy merchant, confronted the minister and threatened dire retribution. The parishioners, up in arms about Jos.'s immoral conduct, requested the presbytery to remove him. The situation had become very tense when McFarland developed typhoid fever and died within a matter of days. Sophie was not allowed to visit him, nor even to go to the funeral, and according to Miss Munday, she died soon after, by her own hand. Examination of her body revealed that not only had she not been pregnant, but was *virgo intacta*, to use the medical terminology of the time.

'Despair,' Miss Munday had said, wiping a sympathetic tear from the corner of her eye, 'that's what killed both of them.'

Duncan continued to stare at the sepia-tinted photograph of Jos. McFarland. Ever since he'd first set eyes on it, the soft highlights in Jos.'s eyes and the slight upturn at the corners of his lips had affected him in a strange way.

Abruptly Duncan got up and pushed his chair back to its place. 'Thou shalt not worship false gods, nor graven images thereof, saith the Scripture,' Duncan spoke out loud to himself in a bitter, accusing tone. But in the last several months, when Duncan was feeling sad or depressed, he derived an unexpected modicum of comfort from the two-dimensional likeness of Jos. McFarland.

An hour later, shaved, washed and dressed, Duncan sat down with Lois Munday, who besides being the part-time parish secretary, also did the book-keeping.

'I don't know what to do about that window,' he said to her, putting a worried hand to his brow. He was referring to the largest stained-glass window in the church, in the centre of the west wall. It was an unusual and fine representation of St Duthac of Ross, standing by a grave with a saltire cross in his left hand, the other raised in blessing over a kite poised over the gravestone with a gold ring clutched in its talons. Duncan had recently noticed that the window was bulging slightly, but seemed otherwise intact.

'Maybe the Reverend Dalgleish over in Forfar could help,' said Miss Munday. She was sitting with her hands demurely folded in her lap but there was nothing demure about her eyes or her thoughts. 'I know that he had some trouble with a stained-glass window in his church last year. It cost them a lot of money to fix, I can tell you that much.'

'That's a good idea, Miss Munday, thank you,' said Duncan, trying hard to concentrate and forge through the gloom of his thoughts. He made a notation on the pad in front of him, looked at the telephone, hesitated, then got up. 'Is there anything else?'

'Reverend Glasgow from the Moderator's office phoned on Friday,' said Miss Munday, staring at Duncan in a way he found slightly unnerving. 'I forgot to tell you. He said that he'll be coming here again next week, probably Wednesday.' Lois put a slight emphasis on the word 'again', and to Duncan's sensitive ear, she sounded vaguely apprehensive.

'Fine,' said Duncan easily. 'It's always a pleasure to see him.'

Miss Munday twirled her pencil, anxiously wondering whether she should tell Duncan that the Reverend Glasgow had also made an appointment to see *her*, but he'd asked her not to mention it to anyone.

'Anything else?' asked Duncan again.

'Here's the list of parishioners in the hospital,' she said, giving him a typed sheet of paper. 'Oh, by the way, did you know that Beth Farquar was ill? The doctor says that she has the 'flu.'

'Oh dear.' Duncan's lips pursed with concern. 'I'm sorry. Actually, Mr Farquar mentioned yesterday that she wasn't feeling well.'

'Well, she has a very high fever, and Dr Montrose had to come out to see her.'

'Do you have their address handy, Miss Munday?' She did, and Duncan wrote it in at the bottom of the hospital visitation list. He didn't particularly like the idea of going to visit the Farquars, but it was certainly his duty to do so.

After a few moments' hesitation, during which she stared at Duncan, seemingly struggling to say something, Miss Munday gathered up her spiral-bound notebook and the two obsidian-sharp yellow pencils she always brought with her.

'Will that be all, Reverend?' she asked, hoping that the yearning in her voice wasn't too obvious, although another part of her was shouting fiercely 'Tell him, go on, tell him you love him and want to care for him and stroke his brow and smooth the sadness away from his mouth, and bring some joy and smiles into his life, and protect him from all the dangers that are gathering around him like a pack of jackals.' Instead, Lois took a deep breath and waited for his response.

'That's it, I think, Miss Munday,' said Duncan, oblivious of the passionate thoughts racing through Lois's mind. 'Oh, and by the way . . .' Duncan raised his eyes and smiled. He actually smiled at her. Lois felt her heart starting to beat at twice the usual speed, and she put a hand on her chest in an instinctive effort to calm it down. 'Miss Munday, I would like to thank you for the devoted care you have been giving the parish. And for the support you have given me personally,' he added.

'It's my pleasure,' replied Lois, her eyes lowered. She felt as if her whole body were blushing; she could feel the warmth on the top of her chest and neck.

In her agitation, one of Lois's pencils rolled off the table, and Duncan quickly went round to pick it up. 'Oh, please, don't bother,' said Lois, bending down too. When they looked up, their faces were only a few inches from each other and Lois thought she was going to explode with emotion.

Duncan straightened up abruptly. 'Here,' he said, glancing at the pencil before returning it to her. 'Luckily it landed on the rubber end.' Once again, he almost smiled. Lois put everything into her old briefcase, and went out, clutching it to her chest. Her heart rate didn't get back to normal until she was almost home.

Lois lived alone in the flat she had shared from childhood with her parents. Both had died there, first her mother, then her father a few months later. Now, in her thirties, Lois had an acute sense of time slipping by; luckily her parents had been able to leave her some money, a modest amount, but enough to live on and have an occasional luxury like the cruise to the Greek Islands she had taken the year before.

Lois took her keys out of her bag and let herself in, closing the door behind her. She then went into the living room, put down her bag, and sat in what had been her father's easy chair by the fireplace. As soon as she was settled, the worries came flying back like bats into her mind. After the morning service that Sunday, one of the women in the choir had whispered a rumour so scurrilous that Lois wanted to slap her face, to scratch and smash her until she was unconscious. But what the woman said had shocked Lois to the core, and although she tried to put it out of her mind, it kept coming back, insidious and horrifying.

She looked up at the leather-framed photo of her parents staring out at her from above the mantelpiece. It was odd how their expressions seemed to change from day to day. What would they think now, she wondered, agonized. What would they tell her to do? Without waiting for a response, Lois got up, picked the poker up from the fireplace and went to the window. From there she could see the spire of the West Church soaring into the grey, cloudy sky. She could feel the acid stirrings of a growing jealousy, and knew that in the heat of her passion, she was quite capable of killing anyone who came between her and Duncan. She looked down at her hands, tightly gripping the poker, and visualized bringing it up, then smashing it down, just the way she'd done with that burglar who'd come through the window a year before. He'd been in hospital for a month, and nobody had believed that she'd had the nerve to bash him like that.

Lois put the poker back in the fireplace. Self-defence was one thing, she mused, but under circumstances where she might face imprisonment she wouldn't dream of using such a crude *modus operandi*.

'Well, Jeremy, I'm glad its no' a piano lesson I'm giving you today.' Ian Farquar eyed the bandage on Jeremy's left arm.

'I can use the hand all right,' replied Jeremy, opening his flat music case and taking out his book of voice exercises. 'It's only the arm that's stiff.'

'All right, then, let's get started.' Jeremy's normal sullenness usually lifted in the Farquars' house, or when he was singing. He liked Mr Farquar, who was a good teacher, and although humourless and undemonstrative, was somehow able to make the recalcitrant Jeremy feel a sense of enthusiasm and respect for the music.

'Which ones were you doing?' asked Ian.

'Numbers eight to twelve,' replied Jeremy, giving Ian a quick, sidelong glance. Mr Farquar usually knew what his pupils were supposed to have practised, but tonight he seemed to have his mind on other things.

'Right, of course, eight to twelve,' repeated Ian. 'Last week you were having a bit of trouble with your approach on the higher notes. I'm wondering if maybe your voice is beginning to break. How was it when you were practising?'

'All right, I think,' replied Jeremy. He shrugged. 'I think maybe I had the breathing wrong.'

'Good. Let's warm up with a few breathing exercises first, then.'

While Jeremy practised breathing with his diaphragm, Ian went out of the room, feeling anxious about Beth. Her temperature had come down earlier in the afternoon, but around supper time she had started feeling feverish, and he felt pretty sure it was going up again.

He tiptoed into the bedroom. 'How are you feeling, Beth?' There was no answer. She was sleeping quietly, and her breathing was regular, so he went back to the music room, feeling slightly reassured.

Jeremy was already doing scales, singing each note crisp and true. Ian sat down quietly on the piano stool, facing the boy.

'All right, now, hold it,' he said after a few moments. 'You're trying to do too much with one breath. If you separate the notes a bit more, just a wee bit, you can breathe without it being over-obvious. Now, take a few good breaths and try it again.'

After the lesson was over, and Jeremy was putting his music away, Ian remained on the piano stool, still watching him. Jeremy wasn't looking very well and hadn't been as attentive as usual during his lesson. Maybe he was getting the 'flu too; Ian knew these epidemics often went through the schools like wildfire.

'Are you feeling all right, Jeremy?' he asked.

Jeremy thought he was talking about his arm. 'I'm okay . . .' He hesitated. 'I fell off my bike.' Then, for no reason other than that he liked Mr Farquar, he told him the whole story, how Bobby and he had gone for a bicycle ride, then Bobby had tricked him into falling off his bike, then gone off without helping him, although he was hurt and bleeding, then how he and his friends tried to get revenge . . . understandably, he missed out the bits where his own part was less than heroic.

'But I thought Bobby was your best friend,' said Ian, getting up.

'He was,' replied Jeremy, 'but not any more.' He tried to look as if it didn't bother him, but inside he was still shaken and upset by Bobby's inexplicable behaviour.

'Jeremy, I'm going to make some tea for Mrs Farquar and me. Would you like a cup?'

Jeremy didn't like tea but knew that it would be accompanied by cake and biscuits, so he said yes, thanks, and went through to the kitchen with Ian.

'What happened?' asked Ian, turning the gas on under the already-filled kettle. 'I mean, did you do something to upset Bobby? I can't imagine he'd have made you fall off your bike for no reason.'

'He's been different for a while now,' said Jeremy,

sullen again. He didn't want to talk about Bobby, he wanted to forget about him. 'He's not jokey any more, and he doesn't talk.' Jeremy grinned. 'He says he's upset because of what you said about his dad.'

Ian shrugged his shoulders.

'Well, as long as it disna' affect his voice,' said Ian, unsmiling. 'Now if you'd like to get the biscuit tin down from that shelf . . .'

'He said he wasn't going to the choir no more,' said Jeremy suddenly. 'That's what he said after the service on Sunday.'

'Oh dear.' Ian sounded alarmed. 'He didn't say anything to me about it.'

'Don't worry, his mother'll make him go,' replied Jeremy.

'Maybe I should talk to him,' said Ian, mostly to himself.

They were drinking tea when the front door buzzer went, and Ian got up, surprised. He had no more pupils scheduled, and wasn't expecting anyone.

It was Duncan. He came in, tall, imposing even in ordinary clothes. 'Well, Jeremy, how's the singing coming along?' he asked, seeing Jeremy in the kitchen. Duncan took his coat off and Ian hung it up on the coatstand in the hall.

Jeremy, suddenly reticent, mumbled something, stuffed a biscuit in his mouth, put his music book in his music case and went off.

'Well,' said Duncan, after the door closed, 'I heard that Beth was not well, so I thought I'd stop in to see if there was anything I could do.' He rubbed his hands together, looking benign and concerned.

'Aye,' said Ian. 'Dr Montrose thinks she has the 'flu.'

'Can I look in and just say hello?' asked Duncan.

'Well, actually, she's asleep,' said Ian. 'I went in to take her a cup of tea just a minute ago, but she was asleep and I didn't want to wake her up.'

Duncan hesitated for a second, and his blue eyes scanned Ian's face. 'Well, just tell her I called, and I'm praying for her swift recovery,' he said.

There was a brief, uncomfortable silence.

'I suppose I'd better be going, then,' said Duncan.

'Nice of you to call,' said Ian.

There was something so totally uncompromising and relentless about this man, thought Duncan, sadly. Once Ian had taken a position, nothing in the world would move him from it, and right now his position was that he didn't want Duncan in the house, however good and sincere Duncan's intentions.

Ian took Duncan's coat off the rack, and held it out while Duncan shrugged it on.

After Duncan had gone, Ian sat by himself in the kitchen, drinking another cup of tea and thinking about Duncan and Bobby and Jeremy. Everything the boy had told made him think that if he was going to do anything at all, he had better do it soon.

Chapter Seven

On Tuesday morning, Jean Montrose woke with the first faint buzz of the alarm, switched it off and got out of bed all in one instinctive movement. The bed creaked, and she glanced over to make sure she hadn't wakened Steven, then went stiffly off to the bathroom, holding up her pyjama bottoms with one hand. It wasn't until several minutes later that she realized she wasn't feeling well: her nose was stuffy, she felt hot and achy, and there was an irritating tickle somewhere in the back of her throat.

Jean stared at herself in the mirror, and brushed her teeth with unusual force to drive away whatever bug had had the impertinence to attack her. By the time she'd dressed and gone quietly downstairs, she was already feeling a little better, and put her symptoms down to the fact she'd had to get up in the middle of the night to see old Mrs Garvie, another patient with the 'flu and a high fever. Mrs Garvie was so ill that Jean had called an ambulance to take her to the hospital.

Jean headed towards the kitchen, and saw Alley, their marmalade cat. He was half-way up the stairs, staring down at her through the banisters. Jean sighed.

Someone had forgotten to let Alley out the evening before. This was part of the household routine; last thing at night, whoever was still up was supposed to let the cat out, lock the doors and turn off all the downstairs lights. Alley had revenged himself for that oversight by leaving what Jean's mother, Mrs Findlay, used to call his 'visiting card' right in the middle of the kitchen floor.

'Oh dear,' said Jean, pulling off a piece of paper towel from the rack over the sink. Alley appeared in the doorway behind her.

'You bad cat,' said Jean severely. 'You know perfectly well you have a box in the pantry . . .' With a little difficulty Jean bent down and started to mop up the offending mound. It was just as well she came down first in the mornings, she reflected; Steven would have had a fit if he'd seen the mess, especially if he didn't notice and trod in it. At the thought, Jean stifled a tiny, guilty giggle.

The door to the basement creaked open, and Fiona appeared, looking thoroughly bedraggled as she always did first thing in the morning. She rubbed her eyes, looked at Alley and then her mother, who was still cleaning up.

'Mum, did I forget to let the cat out?'

'We all did, I suppose, dear. Anyway . . . What time did you get home?'

'About two, I think.' Fiona yawned loudly. 'D'you want some tea?'

'The water'll be hot in a minute,' replied Jean, reaching for the tea caddy on a shelf above her head. 'Where did you go?'

'The Isle of Skye lounge,' replied Fiona. 'Me and Lisbie and Iris Merrick from Accounts.'

Jean took a carton of milk from the refrigerator, was about to pour it into the small red milk jug when a thought occurred to her and she sniffed at it. She made a face, poured the lumpy, sour milk down the sink, and said, 'We're going to have to use that powdered stuff this morning, Fiona. I hope the milk comes before your father gets down.'

'That's all you ever think about, Mum,' said Fiona, smiling, but with a touch of irritation in her voice. 'All you worry about is "Is everything going to be all right for Daddy?" Why don't you think about yourself, just once in a while?'

'I leave that to you and Lisbie,' replied Jean. 'And of course, Daddy. You were telling me about last night. Did you see anybody interesting?'

'Not really. Lisbie's all upset, though.'

'Oh dear. What happened?'

'I don't know. Something to do with Larry French. He hasn't phoned her for a week, and when she went in to buy something he was apparently very cool with her.'

'Well, I've always told both of you not to expect too much from boys,' said Jean. 'They can change their minds for reasons we will never understand.'

'Guess who else was there, Mum.'

'I don't know, dear. Here, can you get the top off the marmalade jar?'

'My boy-friend,' said Fiona, smiling with a faraway look. She took the jar and twisted the top off without any trouble. 'The only bad thing,' she said, her voice changing, 'was that he brought his disgusting pregnant wife with him.'

'Now, Fiona,' said Jean firmly, 'You mustn't talk about Cathie like that. And what's more, it's about time you got Doug Niven out of your mind. He's happily married, and you're just wasting your time. Why don't you forget about him and find a nice boy your own age . . .'

Jean stopped and looked at Fiona. 'What was Cathie doing there? I hope she wasn't drinking anything alcoholic. I told her . . .'

'Relax, Mum,' said Fiona, laughing. 'She was only drinking orange juice. She said she knew you would ask, though.'

Fiona looked up at the clock, and finished her tea with a gulp. 'We'd better get going, Mum, or we'll both be late.'

When she got to the surgery, Jean knew that she was in for a busy morning.

'Fourteen of them in there,' said Eleanor, the secretary, when Jean came in. 'They've all got the 'flu, as far as I can tell. On the radio it said that it was spreading quickly, and there have been several deaths, mostly among older folks.'

Jean shrugged, annoyed with Eleanor. She always exaggerated everything, and what they were dealing with now was no more than the usual seasonal epidemic. 'Let's see the sickest ones first,' she said. 'I hate to keep them hanging around here feeling ill.'

Helen Inkster, Jean's partner, came out of her office. She was a large-boned, athletic, good-natured woman whose brusque manner disguised the kindest of hearts.

'Here's another directive from the Head Office,' she said, waving an official-looking piece of paper. 'According to them, there's a distinct possibility that in the near future we may be faced with a 'flu epidemic. I wanted to be sure you were fully aware of that possibility . . .'

She stopped, and looked hard at Jean. 'Are you all

right? You're not coming down with anything, are you?'

'I'm fine,' said Jean stoutly. 'Why?'

'Well, you're looking a bit peakit,' replied Helen, still looking closely at her partner. 'Anyway, you're not to get sick now, we don't have the time for that kind of luxury, either of us.'

She turned to the secretary. 'Eleanor, put the next patient in my room, please.' Helen waited until she was out of earshot, then said to Jean, 'Have you noticed anything unusual about these 'flu cases we've been seeing, Jean?'

'Well . . .' Jean paused, thinking. 'Do you mean the fever they've been having?'

'Yes. I saw a woman you know, Bella Dornoch, yesterday. Her temperature had gone up past 104°. You could have fried an egg on her forehead.'

'Maybe it's a new strain of the 'flu virus,' suggested Jean.

'Indeed. I'll write a note to these people . . .' she waved the letter in the air, 'and ask them. But you know the kind of reply we'll get.' She slammed the letter angrily down on the desk.

Jean's eyebrows went up. Helen dealt with the finances and most of the administrative aspects of the practice; fortunately she was emotionally suited to dealing with these bureaucratic problems, because Jean found them insufferably frustrating. It was unlike Helen to lose her cool over such matters, but during epidemics everybody tended to get short-tempered.

'It *would* be nice to have some better guidelines,' said Jean. 'Otherwise, we'll be finding that giving aspirin causes meningitis, or something like that.'

'If that Department responds the way they usually

do,' said Helen brusquely, 'we'll get a form letter from them around Christmas. If there *is* a new virus, something we really should know about now, it'll be later.'

Eleanor came back, and Jean went to work. The hot, uncomfortable feeling that she'd had when she got up that morning was coming back, and Jean angrily shrugged aside even the possibility that she might be coming down with something. As Helen said, there simply wasn't time.

'Larry, sweetheart, you know I can't.' Sheila sat up, then swung a long, shapely leg out of bed. Larry watched her hungrily as she picked up her bra from the arm of the chair, slipped it on and started to fasten the three small hooks at the back.

'But we can't just go on like this, Sheila,' he said, 'neither of us. Truly, I really hate all this slinking around.' Larry shook his head with frustration. 'Anyway, somebody's going to find out sooner or later. It's a small town, and you know how quickly the word gets around Perth. Neither of us wants that kind of scandal, do we?'

Larry got up from the bed, still naked, his body beautiful enough to make Sheila feel weak at the knees again. Gently he turned her, undid the bra again and gently cupped both hands around her breasts. To him they felt breathtakingly wonderful: soft, full, mature, bursting with the essence of womanhood.

'I want you to come and live with me here . . .' Larry's hands slipped down to Sheila's waist. 'You're the woman I love, and you love me.' He spoke earnestly and softly, his voice full of tenderness. 'It's time to leave him, Sheila. You don't love Derek, he doesn't love you, and you don't need him. Not any more. I have plenty for both of us, you know that.'

'It's not that, Larry.' Sheila hesitated, then quickly put on the rest of her clothes. 'I'd leave Derek like a shot, believe me. I don't like this any more than you do, but I just don't see how it could work. I'm sorry . . . It's not that I don't want to.' Sheila fastened the buttons on her white silk blouse, then zipped up the skirt with a gesture of finality that alarmed Larry.

'It's Bobby.' she said. '*He* needs me. If it wasn't for him, I'd move in here tonight, I swear.' There were tears in Sheila's eyes, and it was quite apparent to Larry that they were genuine.

'Bring him with you, Sheila,' he urged, as if he were proposing an obvious course of action. But, watching her, he felt a deep sense of desperation start to rise within him. 'There's plenty of room here, and you know that he'd be welcome.'

'He'd never come,' said Sheila with conviction. 'He's a strange boy. If he knew about this, about you and me . . .' Sheila hesitated.

'*What* if he knew about you and me?' asked Larry, smiling. From the tone of Sheila's voice, it almost sounded as if she were afraid of Bobby.

'I think he'd do something bad,' said Sheila, and there was a slight tremor in her voice. 'I mean, he'd do something bad, really bad, to you.'

'Come on, Sheila,' said Larry, laughing. 'Bobby? He's just a boy. He's not about to hurt me or anybody else.' He tried to pull her to him, but she wriggled out of his grasp and went to the door.

'I'm serious,' said Sheila, turning back towards him for a moment. 'I know him a lot better than you do.'

After Sheila left, again slipping out through the garden gate that led onto the path around the Inch, Larry went back to his window seat, feeling a lead weight in the pit of his stomach.

As he sat there, certain things became quite clear to him. There could be no compromise on that one thing; Sheila was going to come and live with him in this house. She was the love of his life, he was quite certain of that. They would get married, and then they would have children of their own. That was going to happen, come what may.

Larry got up, fists clenched. The problem was how to make sure that it did. Sorting out the various possible solutions occupied Larry's mind for the rest of the afternoon.

Chapter Eight

The next day, Wednesday, Jean struggled through her work, did her visits, treated her surgery patients, took aspirins in the morning and the evening, but by the time she went to bed on Wednesday night, she was shivering, aware that she had a fever, and felt terrible. Jean knew that if she wasn't better the next morning, she was in for a major bout of 'flu.

About three in the morning, she woke up after a brief, restless sleep, and found herself soaked in sweat. Getting quietly out of bed, Jean put on an old red woollen dressing gown, and went across the corridor to the spare bedroom. She had the 'flu, she knew it, and there was no point exposing Steven to it any more than he already had been. The sheets in the single bed seemed cold and clammy, and Jean's teeth chattered as she slid between them and tried to get some rest.

Next morning, only moments, it seemed, after Jean had finally managed to fall asleep, Lisbie came quietly into the room. When she saw Jean's flushed cheeks and heard her laboured breathing, she caught her breath with the fear that strikes children when their mother becomes sick.

'Mum?' she whispered.

Jean tried to make a reassuring reply, but at first she could only make a strange, croaking sound. Jean had never been ill, not to the recollection of any of her family, and Lisbie was worried out of her mind.

'Are you all right, Mum? Can I get you anything?'

Jean could feel the fever-heat in her face, and her voice was barely audible. 'Call the surgery,' she said, and couldn't believe how tired just saying three words made her feel. 'Tell them . . .'

'I'll tell them, Mum,' interrupted Lisbie, her eyes fixed on her mother's. 'Don't worry. I'm going to take the day off, they owe me one. I'll take care of you.'

Jean didn't have the strength to tell Lisbie that she would be all right. Lisbie worked in a law office in Perth, and normally Jean would have firmly vetoed Lisbie's notion of taking an unscheduled day off.

Steven looked in a little later to ask how she was feeling. Jean told him to stay out of the room, otherwise he'd catch it too, so he blew her a kiss from the doorway and a few moments later Jean heard his car reversing out of the drive. She looked at the clock, and it was painful to focus; Steven liked to get to the glass works by nine, although as he was part-owner and managing director, it didn't really matter when he came in.

An hour later, the doorbell rang, and Lisbie went down to answer it. Helen Inkster was there, in her thick stockings and sensible black shoes, carrying her black bag.

'All right, then, my dear,' she said to Lisbie, 'where is your mother?'

Lisbie led Helen up the stairs and waited outside while Helen examined Jean. When she came out, Helen's normally jovial expression was grim. 'She's got a real bad dose of it,' she said. 'Unfortunately there isn't an awful lot we can do, except make sure she gets plenty of fluids to drink, and give her two aspirins every four hours until her temperature comes back to normal. If she gets stomach pains with the aspirins, let me know, all right?'

To Lisbie's surprise, Helen then gave her a big hug, and Lisbie saw tears in her eyes. Although it was only because Helen was very fond of Jean and hated to see her ill, the tears scared Lisbie more than anything else could have done.

For the rest of the day Jean hovered in a restless state that was half sleep, half uncomfortable dreamy wakefulness, interrupted from time to time by short but sometimes frightening dreams. Her body and mouth would twitch occasionally, and Lisbie watched and bit her own lip fearfully, wondering if her mother was having a stroke. Lisbie brought water and ice cubes for Jean, and dissolved the aspirin as best she could, put cold washcloths on her mother's forehead, sat by the bed and held her hand, and generally nursed her with all the care that could be expected from a professional nurse, and, in addition, all the love and concern that Lisbie's warm and affectionate heart was capable of.

When Fiona came home from work, she was shocked at how ill her mother seemed, and insisted on taking over from Lisbie.

'And what's more, Lisbie,' said Fiona, using her big-sister voice, 'You're going to that choir practice this evening.'

Lisbie, good-hearted and sentimental, wept, but obediently went off to the church hall after supper, after making sure that Fiona knew how to apply the wet facecloth.

'Get lost,' said Fiona, annoyed with Lisbie's fussing. 'Of course I know how to do that stuff. Off you go. And say hello to Larry French for me. You could put a cold compress on *him* if you like,' she said, with a deliberately crude leer.

'You're just disgusting, Fiona,' replied Lisbie primly, and left, but she felt anxious about her mother, and nervous and unsure at the thought of seeing Larry.

The first to arrive at the church hall, was, as usual, Duncan Sinclair. He let himself in just as the clock struck seven, half an hour before the choir practice was due to start. The place was dark, heavy with the characteristic odour of church halls, a combination of dust, bare floorboards and pine-scented ammonia.

Duncan turned the lights on, went into the vestry and hung his coat on the rack by the door. It was Bobby Sutherland's job to set out the chairs and the sheet music, then put them away again after the rehearsal, but as he didn't usually get there until around a quarter past seven, Duncan went over to the stack of steel and plastic chairs propped up against the wall and started to put them out in four rows. A draught caught the heavy vestry door and it slammed shut with a noise that startled him. Duncan worked quickly, placing the chairs neatly facing the piano. Today they were going to rehearse the cantata 'Jesu, Joy of Man's Desiring', a favourite with everybody, a very rewarding piece and not too difficult for the singers as long as they knew their parts. Duncan hummed the first theme to himself as he put the music out, one xerox copy on each chair, and he felt the tension rising in him as the minutes ticked by.

The outside door opened behind him. He didn't look around, because he knew who it was.

Ian Farquar made some chicken broth for Beth, and held the bowl up to her lips so that she could swallow some of it. Her fever seemed to have diminished a bit, and earlier she had managed to get up to the bathroom to wash and brush her teeth.

'That's the worst part,' she said, trying to minimize her illness because she knew how frightened it made him. 'You feel so sticky and grubby and revolting. I really don't want you to see me like this, dear.'

'Would you like anything else?' he asked. 'A piece of toast, or some tea?' Behind his usual dour expression, Ian was scared and concerned; Beth was the only person he truly cared for in the whole world, and he was mortally afraid that she might fall victim to some complication and die. He knew exactly what he would do if that happened; life without Beth would no longer be worth living.

'You'd better get going,' she said, pushing a strand of damp hair out of her face. 'It's seven o'clock.'

Ian hesitated, but Beth insisted. 'They're all going to be there, and Duncan can't do it by himself,' she went on. 'I'll be fine, dear, don't you worry.'

On the way, Ian forced himself to think about the rehearsal, and decided to hold it in the church itself; the acoustics were better, and the effect of the organ was not only impossible to duplicate with the piano, but there was an added sense of majesty and grandeur from the sound of the organ that always made the singers push in that extra bit of effort.

Ian left his car in the three-car reserved parking space outside the church, and went in through the side door that opened into the verger's storage area. He put on the light, went to the panel to the right of the door and turned on the master switch for the lights, then the separate switch that controlled the power for the organ. Ian loved coming into the church at night; even though he was not a religious man, there was something about the silence, the stillness of the old church that always gave him a sense of mystery, of something akin to awe.

Inside the church he found the switch for the transept lights; they were just bright enough for the choristers to read their music by. Then he headed for the vestry, which was the easiest way to get to the hall. The vestry was dark, and Ian could see a rim of light around the door that led into the hall. Duncan must be there already; Ian knew he always came early. As Ian stepped into the vestry, he heard an indistinct murmur of voices, but something about them made him stop.

He was fairly certain that it was Duncan's voice, followed by the softer murmur of another voice that sounded like Bobby Sutherland's.

There was a noise as the outside door opened, and Ian heard other voices as several of the choir members came into the hall together. Feeling sick, disgusted and angry, Ian went quietly back into the body of the church, swallowing the bile that came up into his throat.

Lisbie found a parking place near the entrance to the church hall, and she was glad of that. The whole area was gloomy and dark, and she had heard that the churchyard contained ghosts, luminous apparitions that had been seen drifting across the old stones, then to disappear through the thick wall into the church. Lisbie repressed a shiver and ran for the door, outlined in friendly light. She heard the noise of car doors closing nearby, and a moment later, a group of choir members came up the short path, talking and laughing together.

With a little shiver of delight, Lisbie recognized Larry French's voice, and waited at the door for them to come up.

'Lisbie!' said somebody. 'So you're finally going to join us!'

Larry saw Lisbie, smiled, and put a friendly hand on her shoulder and held it there for a moment while one of the others pulled the door open against its heavy spring, then they all crowded in.

Lois came up the path a moment later, looking pale and determined, her raincoat collar turned up. She had thought hard about whether she should come to the rehearsal, but finally decided that it would cause unwelcome comment if she didn't. Also, as there were only a few altos, her absence would be doubly remarked upon. A lot of things had happened in the preceding week, and some of her worst fears seemed to have come true.

As Lois came into the hall Ian Farquar came through the other door, and after a brief discussion with Duncan, they all trooped into the church and made their way along the choir pews.

Duncan said a few words of welcome to Lisbie, who blushed and looked at the floor, then Ian climbed up to the organ and played 'Jesu' all the way through, then each part separately, starting with the tenors.

'All right then tenors, take it from the B on the third line,' said Duncan. 'It's a very simple theme, but it's the key to the whole piece. Give each note its full value, and please, no *glissando* at any time.'

Duncan nodded to Ian, who was watching him in his mirror, and the tenors carried the music gently up, then down again, and the organ took up the first theme as a counterpoint to their singing. It was all so beautiful that Lisbie ached to sing with them. Her turn came a few moments later as the sopranos came in with the same theme, this time an octave higher than the tenors. Bobby Sutherland's voice soared above them all, and Lisbie felt such a thrill to be singing with them and making this wonderful, awesome music. She was a part of it now, and realized that she was totally hooked on Bach, hooked on the choir.

Larry was standing right behind her, and as his splendid voice boomed out, Lisbie's heart fluttered. What was going on with him? He'd given her a hug at the door, but he seemed different, preoccupied, remote. She quickly put away her thoughts about him and concentrated on the music. She sang her heart out, feeling Larry's presence behind her, and Lisbie knew that she hadn't felt so happy for a very long time.

After the rehearsal was over, they all had tea and biscuits in the vestry, and then, in ones and twos, went home. Jeremy, who seemed sulky and glum, was one of the first to leave as his mother had come to fetch him. Lisbie noticed that Duncan said something very quietly to Bobby, who didn't look happy, but nodded. Then Larry talked to Bobby for a while, and Duncan came over to Lisbie and thanked her for coming. He was so nice, and so handsome, that Lisbie felt overwhelmed when he spoke sincerely to her and complimented her again on her singing. Ten minutes later when she left, there were only a few people remaining, including Duncan, Ian, and Larry who were all talking together.

Bobby had started to stack the chairs, but he was moving slowly, listlessly, as if he were trying to make the job last as long as possible. Lisbie said goodnight to him, but to her surprise he didn't reply. She was feeling so happy at that moment that she didn't even give the ghosts a thought, but hung around the door, waiting for Larry to come out. A minute or two later he and a couple of others emerged and they all walked down to the gate, laughing and talking excitedly. A few cars down, she recognized Jeremy's parents' car, an old white Honda. The bonnet was up and Joe was looking inside. Larry went over and asked if he could help, but Joe muttered something unpleasant, so Larry laughed and rejoined the little group, and they chatted there for a while until Lisbie got into her car and drove off, in such a haze of pleasure that she didn't notice Joe McIver watching her from under the hood of his car, parked four or five places behind hers.

Throughout the evening, Lois Munday had been intently watching everybody, the body-language, the by-plays, all the meaningful looks and non-verbal communications. Now she felt sure of her facts, and, in the grip of a fury of pathological strength, strode out of the hall alone, lit a cigarette, pulled her raincoat collar up and started to walk the quiet, darkened streets, circling around the quiet church.

Derek had gone to bed early that evening, and Sheila had fallen asleep on the sofa. When she woke up abruptly she was alone; the television was making a soft hissing noise and the screen was a white blank. She shook her head and looked at the clock. It was long after midnight, almost one o'clock. She stood up, feeling groggy and dry-mouthed. Bobby. She hadn't heard him come in, and something, a strange feeling of emptiness and silence in the house, set off alarms inside her head. Suddenly alert and afraid, she ran up the stairs to Bobby's room. He wasn't in the bed, there were no clothes on the chair, and at the sight of that empty bed a feeling of dread rose up and enveloped her until she thought it was going to choke her.

After checking the spare bedroom, Sheila ran down the stairs to the phone on the hall table, and dialled Ann McIver's number. It took nine or ten rings before anyone answered, but Sheila would have let it ring till morning.

'Ann, this is Sheila. Sheila Sutherland. I can't find Bobby, and I was wondering if he was there with Jeremy . . .' Sheila took a deep breath and felt faint, waiting for the answer. It wasn't long in coming.

'Why the hell are you phoning me at this time of night?' Ann screamed into the phone. 'Of course your brat isn't here. I wouldn't have him in this house, not ever again, and that goes for you too.'

Ann slammed down the phone, and Sheila started to tremble. It affected all of her, her hands, legs, and she could even feel her lips and cheeks twitching with the awful fear that was already creeping through every part of her body. She forced herself to go back upstairs, but her legs felt so weak that she had to hang on to the banisters to keep herself from falling. She went into the bedroom, switched on the overhead light and started to shake her husband.

'Derek!'

It took her a while to wake him, but eventually he sat up, rubbing his eyes in the bright overhead light that Sheila had switched on.

'Do you know where Bobby is?' she asked. 'Did he

come home?' Sheila had trouble keeping her voice under control.

'What time is it?' asked Derek, opening his eyes wide.

'It's after one,' said Sheila.

'Then he must have gone home with Jeremy, or somebody,' said Derek, dropping back down on the pillows. 'You worry too much.'

'HE'S NOT AT JEREMY'S!' Sheila screamed at him, at the top of her voice.

Derek jumped up, scared, wide awake. 'Jesus, Sheila, you don't have to shout like that. Where else could he be?' he asked. Then, getting annoyed, he went on, 'for God's sake, woman, why do you always have to panic about every little thing?'

That was the wrong thing to say, because Sheila advanced on him with her long red nails outstretched, and Derek barely had time to get out on the other side of the bed.

They called a couple of Bobby's other friends, with the same result. After making certain that he was nowhere in the house, Derek called the police, while Sheila clung to his arm, prey to an onslaught of fears.

When the phone rang at the manse, Duncan was in his pyjamas, pacing in his study, trying to deal with all the problems that were crowding so inescapably in on him. The shrill sound startled him so much that he let it ring a few times while he got himself reoriented.

Detective Inspector Niven was at the other end, asking if he knew anything of the present whereabouts of Bobby Sutherland, one of the junior members of his choir.

'Well, no,' Duncan replied, sounding mystified. 'I imagine he's home in bed, by now.'

'His parents just phoned, Reverend,' said Douglas. 'Do you know if he left the church with anyone after choir practice?'

'I really don't know.' A primal fear settled like a stone in Duncan's chest, making him feel as if he were suffocating. 'I don't think so. He was one of the last to leave, if I remember correctly.'

'Did you actually see him leave, Reverend?' asked Doug.

'Well, to tell you the truth, Inspector, I'm not certain that I did,' stammered Duncan.

In his office, Doug frowned, puzzled. 'Well, I suppose we'd better start looking for him at the church and we'll go on from there,' he said. 'I'll pick you up at the manse in just a minute, and we can walk over. Please bring the church keys with you.'

Doug was as good as his word, and Duncan had barely time to pull on a pair of shoes and a dressing gown over his pyjamas before he heard the doorbell ringing downstairs. To Duncan, it sounded like the chimes of doom.

Chapter Nine

The bedside phone rang, and Jean woke up instantly and picked it up, hoping that it hadn't wakened Steven in their room next door. She had slept on and off for most of the evening, her fever had gone, and she was feeling quite a bit better. The luminous radio-alarm next to the phone showed that it was almost two o'clock in the morning.

'Dr Montrose?' It was a man's voice, and Jean couldn't immediately place it. 'This is Constable Jamieson,' said the voice, and Jean then recognized his deep, self-important tones.

'Yes?' Jean wondered briefly why he was calling at this hour, and he paused before going on. 'Detective Inspector Niven asked me to phone you,' continued Jamieson. 'He can't come to the phone himself.'

'Well, what is it?' Jean didn't mean to sound so crisp, but Jamieson's ponderous manner usually managed to irritate her.

'He asks if you would kindly come down to the church,' said Jamieson. 'The West Kirk, on Market Street.'

'Why?' Jean sat up in the narrow bed, clutching the phone. She knew without any doubt that she should stay indoors until she'd got over her bout of 'flu. To go out now would be insanity.

'I believe there's been some kind of accident,' replied Jamieson. 'I'm at headquarters now, and I'm on my way down. I'm sorry, Dr Montrose, but I don't know any of the details.'

Jean held the phone and sat there for a moment, thinking. An accident . . . Why did Doug want her to come down there for an accident? Why didn't they just send for an ambulance? And what kind of accident could have happened in the church at that hour?

With a sigh, Jean told Jamieson she'd be down shortly, hung up, and clambered out of bed. She went back into the master bedroom and fumbled about for some clothes, and, now feeling dizzy and weak again, went into the bathroom to dress. As always, when there was talk of an accident, her first thought was of her children; she remembered that Fiona had stayed at home that evening, and Lisbie had come to say goodnight when she came back from her choir practice, so it wasn't anything either of them could be involved in.

Again, Jean sighed. What a relief it was to have two children who so rarely gave her cause for anxiety. There were so many kids their age who were on drugs, out stealing, or unable to hold down a job.

Jean zipped up her skirt and looked in the mirror, wondering if she could get away without putting on makeup. It was such a waste of time. Still . . . Hurriedly she applied a little blush to her cheeks, pursed her lips for the pale pink lipstick, then tucked a protruding corner of her blouse back into her skirtband, and crept quietly out of the bathroom. At the top of the stairs, she stopped and listened, but the only sound she heard was Steven's heavy breathing, interrupted by an occasional muted snort. She was still feeling shaky when she got into the car, and the coldness of the seat made her shiver.

The traffic lights at Bridgend were red, so she waited before turning right to cross the old bridge, although there was no traffic at all. On the town side of the bridge, the streets of Perth were practically deserted; it had been raining, and the cobblestones glistened wetly from the cold orange street lights. Even before turning into Market Street she could see the red flashing reflections in the shop windows. God, how many police cars were there? It seemed as if the whole street were filled with flashing lights, and the vehicles were clustered outside the West Kirk, on both sides of the street.

Jean's anxiety level rose. What kind of accident could this have been? Who did it involve? She geared herself up for whatever she was going to have to face, and parked the car behind a blue Ford that she recognized as belonging to Doug Niven.

Jamieson had arrived a few minutes before her, and was on guard outside. In a rare display of courtesy, he lifted the yellow tape that had already been strung around the church entrance, and Jean passed under it. She smiled her thanks, but got no response beyond a stony glare. Jamieson had a long memory for real and imaginary injuries, and Jean knew that he still remembered the time she'd accidentally almost killed him in a deserted house, long ago when they were investigating the death of that poor little Lumsden baby.

The South door was ajar, and all the church lights were on. When she stepped inside, Jean could see that spotlights had been set up inside, in front of the altar, and there was a brilliant, bluish glow, surely brighter than anything that had ever been seen inside the church before.

It might have been the lights, and the long, grotesque black shadows that moved across the walls and ceiling of the building, that gave Jean the weird impression of a disembodied agony writhing within the fabric of the church itself, as if it were being operated upon without an anaesthetic.

She walked quickly up the aisle, knowing that coming into this church would never be the same; she could never again have that treasured sense of stillness and peace, that feeling of being protected and cherished, cupped in God's careful hands.

Detective Inspector Douglas Niven saw her coming, and detached himself from the group under the lights and walked towards her. Doug Niven was a slim, active-looking man with short, almost crewcut greying hair, a triangular face and round National Health glasses that gave him a curiously innocent and academic look.

'Jean, I'm sorry to call you out at this time, but actually it wasn't my idea.'

'What's happened?' Jean asked. She shivered again, and pulled her coat more tightly around herself. Nothing out of the ordinary could be seen from where she was standing.

'I'll show you,' he said, and led the way up the aisle towards the transept.

The forensic team stepped back to allow them to approach the body. It was a boy of about twelve or thirteen, Jean could see that, but the face and lips were bloated, and the protruding eyes were pink from haemorrhages into the normally white sclera. There was a small amount of blood matting the dark hair on the top of his head.

Jean put a hand up to her mouth and stared at the body.

'Who is it?' she asked, but even as she spoke, she realized that she already knew.

'Bobby Sutherland,' replied Doug.

'Oh my God,' whispered Jean. 'Surely not that lovely Bobby . . .' Then in a louder, anxious voice she said, 'Where are his parents? Do they know?'

'They're here,' said Doug. 'In the vestry. They were the ones who wanted you to come.'

'I'd better go and talk to them . . .' Jean turned to go back to the vestry, but Doug said quietly, 'I wonder if you'd take a look at him first, please, Jean. There's . . . something very weird about this case.'

Reluctantly, Jean came back and got down on her knees. Bobby's body was lying lengthwise, parallel with and a couple of feet in front of the front pew.

She touched his face. 'He's still warm,' she said, looking up at Doug in surprise.

'Did you notice that bag?' asked Doug, pointing to a long bag of paper-thin shiny metallic plastic material lying beside him.

Jean had noticed it, but thought it was probably something the police had brought with them, maybe for removal of the body.

'He was inside that bag,' said Doug. His voice had a peculiar tone. 'It's a lightweight sleeping bag, the kind campers use to protect themselves from really bitter cold. When we got him out he was *hot*, so hot we couldn't believe that he wasn't still alive.'

Jean was puzzled. 'Was he here? In the church? How ever did you find him?'

'He was at a choir practice,' said Doug. 'His parents thought that he'd gone home with a friend, which he does sometimes.' Doug hesitated. 'Do you know his parents, Jean?'

Jean nodded, her gaze wandering back to the body. Bobby looked so sad and small, so pathetic, lying there. For a second she heard his voice, right here in the church, soaring up above all the others, and had difficulty keeping back her tears.

Douglas was speaking to her. 'Well, anyway, Sheila Sutherland says that she fell asleep early in the evening, woke up about one with a feeling that Bobby hadn't come home, so she went to his room, and he wasn't there. She phoned the McIvers, thinking Bobby might be with Jeremy, that's the McIvers' son, but apparently Mrs McIver just shouted at her over the phone.' Doug shook his head. 'Then Mrs Sutherland called us, and as this was the last place he'd been seen, it was the first place we checked.'

Jean frowned thoughtfully, then looked at the shiny bag with a puzzled expression.

'Can I touch it?'

Doug turned to one of his team, a thickset young man who was now sitting on the front pew with the photographer, a pretty girl with long, very straight blonde hair. 'Dave, did you get all the prints you need off the bag?'

Dave, one of the forensic team that Jean had seen on previous occasions, nodded. 'Hello, Dr Montrose. We still have to do the inside,' he said. 'The outside's all done, but we'll have to cut it open to get at the inside.'

Jean noticed that the bag was about six feet long, made of very thin, lightweight plastic, with a draw-string around the top, like a duffel bag. Four or five small holes had been crudely cut out, a few inches below the draw-string.

Jean turned her attention back to the body, and a wave of compassion went out from her, not so much for Bobby himself, but for his parents. For an instant she thought about her own two children, and how she would feel if something like this happened to one of them.

She ran her fingers gently over his head, and felt a slight depression over the back of it, and her fingers came back sticky with blood.

'Can you give me a guesstimate on time?' asked Doug gently.

Jean shook her head decisively. 'Not really. All the normal parameters are changed by his temperature.'

Still, she was able to move Bobby's arm without too much difficulty, although she could feel that rigor mortis had already started to take effect.

'Where's Dr Anderson?' Jean asked, getting rather stiffly to her feet. For a second she felt dizzy, and her vision blurred. With one hand she massaged an aching kneecap. 'Dr Anderson'll be able to tell you more accurately than I can.'

As if on cue, the South door opened again with a crash that reverberated through the high spaces of the church, and Dr Malcolm Anderson, the police surgeon and pathologist, came marching up the aisle with about as much respect for his surroundings as if he were coming into a McDonald's for a hamburger.

As soon as she could, after exchanging a few comments with Dr Anderson, Jean went to the vestry to talk to Bobby's parents and try to console them.

There were three people there, Duncan and Derek sitting silently side by side on chairs and Sheila, walking about in an agony of restlessness, her makeup smudged, her face puffy with tears. Jean's kind heart went out to her, but she couldn't help being appalled by the change that had come over the woman. Sheila had become middle-aged, and looked as if all the liveliness and spirit had been torn out of her heart.

Derek, tieless, was seated with his head down between his hands, his fingers pulling spasmodically at his already thinning black hair. Duncan sat on Derek's right, very still, incongruously garbed in pyjamas and paisley dressing-gown, staring wildly ahead of him, seeing nothing.

Jean looked at him for a moment, astonished, wondering what he was doing there and why he wasn't trying to comfort the Sutherlands. Then she remembered that the manse was right by the church, and Duncan had no doubt been in bed when the police came to get the keys.

Sheila hurried towards Jean, wobbling on her high heels, her arms outstretched. 'Oh God, Jean . . .' Sheila put her arms around Jean, who held her and silently tried to comfort her. Derek didn't even look up.

PART TWO

Chapter Ten

Jean put on the electric kettle and had just made a big pot of tea for everyone when Doug opened the door into the vestry. He looked around briefly, then, in a low voice, asked Jean if she would come back into the church, as both he and Dr Anderson wanted to have a word with her.

The floodlights had been switched off and stacked at an angle against the front pews, looking like a bunch of long-stemmed aluminium flowers waiting to be put in a vase. The photographer had left, and the bloated body of Bobby Sutherland had been taken away. All that remained of him was a chalk outline on the floor. The shiny death-bag had also been removed, and the other members of the forensic team were packing up their equipment, talking among themselves briefly and in low tones; the young age of the victim and the location of the crime had had a subduing effect even on these experienced professionals.

Malcolm Anderson was sitting on the front pew, leaning forward, his elbows on his knees, staring pensively at the chalked outline in front of him.

'There's some really very odd aspects tae this case, Dr Montrose,' he said when Jean and Doug came up.

As usual when he was uncomfortable, his accent was powerful on him. 'I understand from Inspector Niven that you knew the victim pretty well?'

'I saw Bobby Sutherland in my surgery only last week,' replied Jean. She sat down in the pew, next to Malcolm, and a wave of sheer exhaustion came over her. Jean knew very well that she was far from recovered and should have stayed home in bed.

Malcolm sat up at Jean's words, and his bright blue eyes became suddenly interested. 'Oh aye? What was the matter with him?'

'Nothing that I could find. It was his mother who insisted I examine him. She seemed very nervous about something, about Bobby, I suppose.' Jean stopped, puzzled. 'The only thing I could find was that he appeared, well, slightly lethargic, I suppose, for a boy that age.'

All three of them stared at the chalk outline, the last real trace of Bobby Sutherland; everything else about him was now reduced to a few memories fixed insecurely in other people's minds.

'Did you do any tests?' asked Malcolm, still staring at the outline.

'Yes. I did a mono spot check, mainly to satisfy his mother, and that was negative. So he didn't have infectious mononucleosis, if that's what you were thinking. His chest was clear, he didn't have any enlarged lymph nodes, or anything else abnormal on physical examination, not that I could find, anyway. He just seemed quiet.'

Jean broke off for a moment, thinking hard. 'I told Sheila that if he didn't seem better to her in a week or so, to bring him back and we'd do some more tests.'

There was a silence, then Doug said, 'Jean, do you think he could have been depressed? I mean seriously depressed, in a way that might . . .'

'You mean suicidal?' asked Jean. 'Do you think this could have been suicide? How on earth could he tie himself inside a bag like that?'

'The ends of the drawstring were on the inside,' said Doug.

'Couldn't the ends have been pushed in after they were tied?' asked Jean. A dreadful sinking feeling was overtaking her. Could Bobby have been so depressed that he had taken his own life? Had she missed any signs of depression when she examined him? Jean wanted to go home and cry.

'Yes, they might have,' said Douglas carefully. He was watching Jean with a strange expression. 'Suicide's only a possibility here, but we have to explore it just like the others.'

Jean glanced at Malcolm Anderson, but he avoided her look. 'My God,' thought Jean, becoming really alarmed, 'they think I missed the diagnosis. They think Bobby was depressed, came to me for help, didn't get it, and committed suicide as a result.'

She got hold of herself and took a deep breath. 'There was no sign of depression when I examined him. I've been thinking about that since I saw Bobby. He was angry, perhaps, but depressed, no.'

Jean began to feel angry herself, because she could feel an undercurrent of criticism coming from both men. 'In any case, Bobby had a head injury. Do you think he hit himself over the head? If so, how did he do it, and where's the weapon?'

'I don't think it was much of a blow,' said Anderson. 'It didn't feel like a skull fracture to me,' he went on, measuring his words. 'He could easily have done it when he fell.'

'Now come on, both of you,' said Jean, beginning to lose patience. 'You aren't seriously suggesting that he cut air holes in a bag, climbed into it standing up, then fell down, knocking himself out in the process? Get real, you guys, as my girls would say.'

Doug and Malcolm Anderson exchanged a glance, and Malcolm shifted his feet.

'Another possibility is that there may be a psychosexual aspect to this,' said Malcolm, speaking hurriedly and looking at the floor. 'Partial asphyxia is a frequent method for certain persons to get a sexual high, and maybe that was what he was doing.'

'Bobby was just a child,' said Jean. She was trying not to sound annoyed, but this whole thing was beginning to take on ludicrous aspects. 'He was just beginning to enter puberty, and all the cases of that sort I've seen personally were in adolescents or young adults, and I've never heard of anyone getting inside a bag. They usually put it over their heads, with the idea of taking it off as soon as they feel they're reaching orgasm and starting to lose consciousness. Isn't that so?' She looked at each man in turn, sensing their discomfort, but she was not at all inclined to let them off the hook.

'Jean, at this stage, we're just trying to consider all possibilities,' replied Douglas, back-pedalling as fast as he could, and astonished that Jean could discuss sexual aberrations with such sang-froid.

'We'll know a lot more after we've done the full postmortem.' Malcolm's tone was subdued and placatory. 'I'll let you know when we're doing it, Jean, and you're very welcome to come if you like.'

Malcolm could feel Jean's ire, and was also becoming

uncomfortably aware that he and Douglas might have got off on the wrong foot with this case.

'If there's nothing more, then, I'll get back to the Sutherlands.' Jean nodded in the direction of the vestry. 'I'm sure they're too upset to drive, so I'll take them home.'

'We can do that, Jean,' said Douglas quickly. 'I'll have Jamieson take them back. Anyway, I'll be needing to talk to them a bit, first.'

'Douglas, it would be a humane gesture if you didn't interrogate them tonight,' said Jean sharply. 'Let them go home. They're both heartbroken, and they'll be better able to help you tomorrow, after they've had a chance to get some rest.'

Although he felt great sympathy for the Sutherlands, Douglas's instinct was to talk to them now. However, he was acutely aware that for some months he had been on shaky ground with Jean Montrose, and did not want to take the risk of losing her friendship permanently. In any case, Douglas didn't think it would make a big difference if he interrogated the Sutherlands now or later, so it simply wasn't worth arguing about.

'Let's go and see how they're doing,' said Doug reasonably. 'Then we can decide.'

Derek and Sheila looked up when Jean and Doug came back into the vestry. Derek's face was a picture of almost childish bewilderment and despair, as if he simply couldn't understand what had happened. Sheila, red-eyed and puffy-faced, looked wild and disordered, a desperate middle-aged woman whose world was falling apart around her.

'I don't have anything new to report, I'm sorry to say,' said Douglas heavily, standing in front of them. 'Dr Montrose thinks the two of you should be going home now, and that's fine with me. I'll talk to you both in the morning, unless of course there's anything additional you'd like to say to me now.'

He waited, not very hopefully, and Sheila shook her head.

'Would you like one of my men to drive you home?' asked Doug with gruff sympathy. Running a taxi service wasn't part of the C.I.D.'s mission, and his offer was mostly to placate Jean.

'I can drive, thanks all the same, Inspector,' said Sheila. She suddenly raised one hand to her mouth and bit the fleshy part of it. To Jean, who was watching her with the most heartfelt sympathy, it seemed that Sheila was making a painful effort to prevent herself from screaming at the top of her voice.

Sheila stood up, and shakily reached out to Derek with unwilling tenderness.

'Come on, Derek. We have to go home now.' She spoke to him as if to a child, a twelve-year-old. Derek got up, stumbled as he followed her out, looking at neither Jean nor Douglas.

Duncan observed all this silently.

'May I leave now?' he asked when the door had closed behind the Sutherlands. 'I don't think there's anything . . .' His voice faded.

'Of course,' said Douglas, but his voice had changed and his policeman's instincts were surfacing again. He knew that Jean would not come to Duncan's defence the way she had for the Sutherlands.

Duncan stood up, and Doug followed up quietly with '. . . just as soon as I've had a chance to ask you a few questions, Reverend.'

'Would you mind if we did that at the manse?' asked Duncan. He was looking shocked, and his normally carefully arranged hair was ruffled. His benign features and kindly manner seemed to have undergone a sea-change. 'For one thing, it's getting cold, and for another . . .' He glanced at the closed door to the church and shuddered.

'Of course,' said Doug. 'Why don't you go back, Reverend, put some warm clothes on, and the two of us'll come over in about ten minutes.'

'I don't suppose it could wait until the morning?' asked Duncan, a gleam of hope appearing in his eyes, which looked a bit bloodshot to Doug.

'I'd rather we did it now, if you don't mind,' said Doug smoothly, 'while all the events are still fresh in your memory, that sort of thing.' As an apparent afterthought, he went on, 'and of course, as minister of this church, you'll most likely have more insight into this sad business than anybody.'

'I really don't know how much I'll be able to help you,' said Duncan doubtfully, but there was no life in his words, and he didn't argue any further.

'If you don't mind leaving the keys with me, Reverend, I'll lock up and return them to you.'

Duncan pulled a set of half a dozen keys out of his pocket, each with a worn-looking label, and handed them to Douglas.

Jamieson came in at that moment, and stood next to Douglas. The two men watched Duncan as he went over to the door, turned and closed it gently behind him, after giving them a brief but surprisingly sharp glance from under his dishevelled eyebrows.

'Well, Jamieson,' said Doug, jerking a thumb at the door, 'what do you know about him?'

For all Jamieson's slowness of wit, he had been brought up in Perth and had lived there all his life, so he knew a surprising amount about the people of that city.

'Nae much,' replied Jamieson. 'He makes some of the elders a bit nervous because they say he's no a true Christian.' Jamieson paused, then said in his most impressive tones, 'I heard one man even say that the Reverend had no real faith in the Lord.'

'Oh my,' said Douglas, shocked. 'I can certainly understand they widna like that at all. Anything else?'

Jamieson hesitated. 'Well . . . no, not really. But you know how rumours arise around a man that everybody knows is living alone in a big house.'

Chapter Eleven

When Jean got home, she parked her car close behind Steven's Rover; their proximity gave her an inexplicable tiny comfort. She could see the light on in the bedroom; Steven was awake. He had heard her drive in, and met her on the stairs in his bright red Chinese silk dressing gown, a luxury he had permitted himself on a business trip to Hong Kong some years before.

'Would you like a cup of tea, dear?' he asked. 'You look as if you could use one.' He paused on the step. 'Really, Jean, you shouldn't have gone out. You were ill all day yesterday, and you can't be well yet.'

Jean felt worn out and wanted to go to bed more than anything, but she didn't want to appear ungrateful to Steven. 'A cup of tea would be lovely, thanks, Steven,' she said. 'Why are you up?'

'I couldn't sleep,' he replied. 'I have the shareholders' meeting next week, and I'm not looking forward to it. We took quite a loss when Macandon Industries went belly up.'

As often happened when Steven offered tea, Jean ended up making it. She didn't mind; it was part of her job, she felt, not Steven's.

'What was your call?' he asked, holding his mug in both hands. 'Another 'flu?'

Jean told him, and Steven put his mug down on the counter in astonishment.

'Who on earth would want to kill a twelve-year-old boy?' he asked. 'I can understand adults killing each other, I suppose, but that . . . that's really sick.' Steven picked his mug up again and took a thoughtful sip. 'He couldn't have done it himself, could he?'

'Doug and Malcolm Anderson seemed to think so, yes,' Jean replied, her voice carefully non-committal.

'Lisbie's going to be terribly upset.' Steven tightened the silk cord around his waist. 'She really loved that boy.'

Jean was looking silently into her mug. 'Aren't you going to drink your tea?' asked Steven.

'What?' Jean started. 'Oh, yes, of course. I was just thinking.'

'Solving the case?' asked Steven, smiling. He was proud of Jean's talent for finding the secret reasons why people did strange things like kill each other, although the motives usually seemed obvious enough once Jean had explained them.

'No. Maybe they're right, maybe there isn't a case.' Because Doug and Malcolm had made such a big thing of it, Jean couldn't get rid of the idea that Bobby might have committed suicide, although when she tried to put herself in his frame of mind, it simply didn't add up.

Steven yawned. 'Well, I'm going back to bed now.' He put his mug in the sink, then looked at his watch. 'My God,' he said, 'it's almost time to get up again.'

Jean was feeling wide awake now, and pottered around for a while, trying to make sense of what had happened. Those poor parents; they had both been so devastated, and her sympathetic heart went out to both of them. That was the terrible thing about murders; however much the killer must have hated poor Bobby, it was his parents who did the long-term suffering.

Again Jean thought about her own two girls, and before going back to bed, she crept down to Fiona's room in the basement, and stood by her bed for a few moments in the dark, listening to her daughter's quiet breathing. Then she went upstairs to Lisbie's room. Lisbie still liked to sleep with a nightlight on, and in its faint yellow glow, Jean could see her younger daughter lying sprawled on top of her bed, limbs spread out in all directions, her hair making an untidy nimbus on the pillow. Lisbie looked so innocent, so vulnerable, that Jean bent down and kissed her softly on the cheek before tiptoeing out and going back to her own room. She lay in bed quietly but wide awake, shivering occasionally and turning over a whole variety of possibilities in her mind. Every one of them so horrified her that she didn't get to sleep until the grey dawn light began to come in through the window and spread like a sea-mist through the bedroom. Her last conscious thought was that she had promised to be present for Jackie Marshall's caesarean section at the hospital in the morning.

'All right, then,' said Douglas. 'Why don't you sit at the desk, Reverend, and we'll sit here.' Douglas indicated to Jamieson which chair he should take, and it creaked ominously under his weight. The study was large and square, and the plaster of the high ceiling had a brownish tinge around the edges, like the leaves of an old book. A tall, glass-enclosed mahogany bookshelf full of musty-looking bound volumes stretched from floor to ceiling on one side of the room, and dispirited-looking gauze curtains sagged in front of a tall window on the opposite wall. An old sepia-toned portrait, presumably of some long-deceased incumbent, looked out at them from the wall behind the desk. The whole room was draughty and dark, meanly illuminated by a round lamp hanging from a massive brass central fixture, and by an equally weak standard lamp next to the desk. Between them, the two lamps seemed to cast more shadows than light. A small, cheap electric radiator sat under the windowsill.

Douglas always liked to appear slow and stolid when he was interviewing people, particularly when he was dealing with intelligent and able individuals. They often responded in surprising ways; some got irritated, others came to the conclusion that he was just another stupid flatfoot. A few, and Douglas could usually pick them out very quickly, felt the fear of the inevitable descend on them as they watched Douglas lay out his writing pad, place his government issue pencil neatly alongside it, then start asking questions in his careful, meticulous, plodding way. They could sense that he would eventually discover whatever secret they were trying to hide, and as often as not, they gave up the effort right there and then.

'Let's start with your full name and address, then, Reverend, if you please,' said Douglas, carefully licking the end of his pencil.

Duncan gave the information, enunciating his reply in his cultured Edinburgh accent, but with a flat, hopeless tone that made Doug look curiously up at him.

Jamieson watched him and listened, trying to make out where he came from by the sound of his voice. 'Bloody Morningside,' he concluded, although Duncan's voice cracked from time to time and at others became hoarse and unrecognizable.

Douglas was watching Duncan too, but he was looking for different things.

'Wife's name, Reverend?' he asked, knowing perfectly well that Duncan was not married.

'Marriage is one of life's blessings that so far I've had to do without,' replied Duncan. Douglas looked up sharply, and a strange, expansive smile appeared on Duncan's face, then disappeared just as quickly.

'Single,' wrote Douglas laboriously, and Jamieson sneaked a look at his watch. He knew that Douglas could make this kind of thing go on for ever, if it would help the investigation.

Douglas leaned back, and the tension in his body seemed to slacken, as if the difficult part of the interview was now over and they could all relax.

'First tell us about yesterday evening's choir practice, Reverend,' he said. 'Everything you remember. When people came in, whether they came alone or who they came with, when they left, if anything unusual happened, or if anyone said something unusual. That kind of thing.'

'Well . . .' Duncan put a hand up to his jaw, and stroked its unshaven surface. A muscle in his left eye started to twitch repeatedly. 'All right. I came to the church first, about seven, which is half an hour or so before the rest of them usually appear.'

Douglas made a note on his pad.

'Do you mean the church or the church hall?' he asked.

'Yes, the church hall. Of course, I meant the church hall,' said Duncan, sounding flustered. 'You know that the two buildings communicate via the vestry.'

'What did you do while you were waiting for the others?'

'I set the chairs out, pulled the music,' replied Duncan. 'Bobby Sutherland is supposed to do that, but I got there before him.' He paused, before adding 'It saves time if everything's ready when the others get here.'

Douglas wrote something again. Witnesses were usually more careful about what they said when they saw that every word was being taken down.

'Who came in next?'

Duncan's brow wrinkled in an effort to remember. 'Bobby came in around twenty past, I think. Anyway all the others came in soon after.'

'How did Bobby look when he came in?' asked Douglas. 'Did he say anything to you?'

'He seemed all right,' said Duncan, rather vaguely. 'He helped me put out the music.'

'Did Bobby say anything?' asked Douglas. 'Did you get the feeling that he was upset? Scared?'

'I can't say that I did,' said Duncan. 'He's a quiet sort of boy. He doesn't talk that much.'

'Who else was there?'

'Well, Bobby had just come in when a whole crowd of them came, including Lisbie Montrose, who had just that evening joined us.'

'Can you give me a list of the names of the choir members?' asked Douglas.

Duncan went over to a filing cabinet, pulled out a typed list and took it back to his desk. With a thick felt-tipped pen he put a line through three names. 'They weren't here,' he said. 'Cynthia Storer, she's one of our altos, is in Jerusalem on holiday. Frank Dill, he's going to be out on his oil rig for at least another week . . .'

'Just tell me which ones were there,' said Douglas patiently.

Duncan told him, and Douglas ticked their names off the list. Douglas noted that Jeremy McIver and Larry French had been present, as had Lois Munday.

Next Douglas asked him how the rehearsal had gone. 'Ian Farquar wanted us to do the practice in the church rather than the hall,' said Duncan. 'I think it was really because he just loves to play that organ, but he said the choir sings better in the church.'

'What were you practising?' asked Douglas.

'"Jesu Joy of Man's Desiring",' said Duncan shortly. 'It's a chorale from one of the Bach cantatas, and I don't suppose you'd know of it.'

'You're quite right, sir,' replied Douglas, abashed. 'I only know the Myra Hess transcription, and I don't suppose you used that.'

Duncan's eyes opened wide. 'As a matter of fact, we did,' he said, then very quietly added, 'I apologize if I sounded patronizing, Inspector.'

'No problem.' Douglas's grin had something wolfish about it. 'Jesu Joy of Man's Desiring' was one of Cathie's favourite pieces, and it was always on the piano, so he had been able to sound erudite for free, so to speak. 'Now, Reverend, did anyone pay any particular attention to Bobby during or after the practice?'

Duncan bit on a thumbnail and considered the question. 'It's odd that you should mention that,' he said. 'I'd never seen them talk before, but I noticed Larry French had quite a conversation with Bobby in the vestry.' Duncan attempted a smile. 'And to continue in the spirit if not the precise statement of your question,' he went on, 'Jeremy McIver very obviously paid *no attention whatever* to his friend Bobby.'

Jamieson looked up to see if Douglas was going to follow that up, but he didn't. Douglas was watching

Duncan, who had a peculiar, faraway expression on his face.

'Yes?' he prompted.

Duncan started. 'Oh, I was just thinking . . .' He moved uneasily in his chair. 'I suppose I'd better mention this, although I'm sure there's a simple explanation. Lois Munday, one of the altos who is also the church secretary and my assistant, didn't take her eyes off Bobby all evening.'

Douglas shrugged slightly and grinned tiredly. 'Maybe she had a crush on him, like most of the women did,' he said.

Duncan shook his head. 'No . . . I'm pretty sure . . . There was a really strange expression on her face.' Duncan took a deep breath and placed both hands on the desk in front of him. 'At the time, I thought he must have done something very naughty to upset her, because . . . well, Inspector, I don't like to say this, but there was real *hate* in the way she looked at him. I'm sure other people must have noticed.' Again that big, benign smile appeared, and was wiped off in a second.

'Do you know of anything Bobby might have done to upset her?'

If there was any hesitation on Duncan's part, it was virtually imperceptible. 'No,' he said, and shook his head to confirm it.

There was a long pause while Jamieson wrote it all down. As usual, after Doug's early display with his writing materials, Jamieson recorded the bulk of the interview. Without amusement, Doug noted that the tip of Jamieson's tongue was sticking out of one corner of his mouth, apparently from the effort he was putting into his task.

'Who was the last to leave?' asked Douglas.

'Well, Bobby was always last, because it was his job to clear up and put everything away.'

'Would he normally lock up?' asked Doug.

'Yes,' replied Duncan. 'Then he dropped the keys through the letterbox, and the verger picked them up the next day.'

'Last night, Reverend,' said Douglas carefully, 'who was still there when you left?'

'Well, Ian Farquar, the organist, was just leaving. His wife has the 'flu,' he added inconsequentially.

'Anybody else?'

Duncan shook his head.

'Was the outside door open?'

Duncan considered. 'No. It was rather chilly out, but the door wasn't locked, so anybody could have come in when Bobby was alone.'

Another half hour, and they were finished. When Douglas and Jamieson stepped out into the street, the air had the stillness of early morning, with high, thready dawn cirrus clouds making pink streaks above the eastern horizon. Although it was light enough to see, most cars still had their headlights on; Douglas and Jamieson walked over towards Doug's car.

'What do you think of him, sir?' asked Jamieson in a rather disapproving tone, after they had stood in silence for a moment.

'I don't think anything yet,' replied Douglas brusquely. 'I've told you often enough never to have opinions until you have facts to base them on. Actually,' he went on, thinking about Duncan's odd expressions, his twitching face and faraway looks, 'I'm wondering if he's maybe gone batty.'

'That was a nice gold bracelet he was wearing,'

said Jamieson. His voice was as neutral as he could make it.

Doug gave Jamieson a long look and sighed.

'Get up to date, for God's sake, Jamieson. Nowadays wearing a bracelet doesn't mean anything, not any more than if he was wearing an earring. Not for a man of God, anyway,' he added rather vaguely.

'I suppose not, sir.' Jamieson's mouth twisted thoughtfully to one side. Doug recognized the sign, and suppressed a sigh. 'Yes, Jamieson?'

'Whoever it was that killed him must have come back while Bobby was tidying up,' said Jamieson, his eyes screwed up with concentration.

'Or else it was Ian Farquar, or even the Reverend, or maybe both of them together,' said Douglas. 'But you're right, if we can exclude them, it could have been anyone coming in through the door, maybe someone in the choir, maybe not.'

'Right, sir,' said Jamieson, thinking back to Duncan's interrogation. 'Lois Munday, Lisbie Montrose, Jeremy McIver . . .'

'Don't forget Larry French,' said Douglas. He felt suddenly very tired and looked at his watch.

'Do you want a man to stay here on guard till morning?' asked Jamieson.

'No point,' said Douglas. 'We'll go round and lock up. Just make sure you leave the tapes up round the entrance.'

'All the doors were locked,' said Jamieson. 'I checked them while you and Dr Montrose were talking earlier.' He sniffed when he mentioned Jean's name, and Douglas grinned at him. He knew why Jamieson couldn't stand the sight of Jean Montrose.

'Does it still hurt where she got you?' asked Douglas,

grinning again. 'I'll never forget that. You went down like a slaughtered stot.'

'I slipped,' said Jamieson, standing on his dignity. 'Anyway, that was a long time ago, sir, and I prefer nae to think about it.'

'I can well understand that,' said Douglas. He looked at his watch again, turning it so that the dial caught the faint daylight.

'It's just after five o'clock, Jamieson,' he said, then went on in a kindly, paternal voice. 'I want you to get a good night's sleep, now, lad, so I won't expect to see you until nine.'

'This evening, sir?' asked Jamieson, surprised. 'Thank you.'

'No, Jamieson. Nine o'clock this morning, which is in just under four hours. Sleep tight, now.'

Chapter Twelve

After leaving Jamieson at the station, Douglas took his official car home. It was against regulations, but he simply didn't have the energy to change cars. And in any case, he had to be back in less than four hours. On the way home, he felt that strange blend of early morning wakefulness and bone-tiredness. Breakfast . . . It would soon be time for breakfast, but he didn't feel even a bit hungry. That was good, because as Cathie had pointed out, recently he'd been putting on a bit of weight.

'You'd think it was you that was pregnant,' Cathie had said to him. 'Your appetite's gone up more than mine since I started with this baby.' It was true; and sometimes Douglas felt as if he were the one who was having the baby. It was very strange; a couple of times when he was with Cathie, and she said she felt the baby kick, he could have sworn that he'd felt it too, only inside his own belly. When he mentioned it to Cathie, she said a little huffily that she was perfectly able to continue having the baby without his help. 'You did your bit a while ago,' she said. 'Kindly let me do the rest.'

Doug slowed down then stopped behind a baker's van at the traffic lights. That must be a lousy kind of life, he thought, thinking about the baker; getting up in the middle of the night when all good Christians are sound asleep, with never a long lie-in in the mornings.

The lights changed and Doug turned left, following the van past the church, which looked grey, bleak and desecrated in the still-early light. The fluttering yellow police ribbons outside the church separated and excluded it from the outer world of sanity and the comfortable rules of right and wrong. There was a big tree between the road and the manse, and for a second Doug saw a glint of light between the branches and knew that the second floor lights were on.

So the Reverend Sinclair was still up. Anxious to get Sinclair out of his mind, Douglas put his foot down hard on the accelerator and swept past the van. There would be plenty of time later to consider his case in detail, he told himself sternly, but his tired brain refused to get out of gear.

It was evident that Duncan had been crushed, devastated by the tragedy. When Douglas had asked him directly, Duncan couldn't think who possibly might have killed Bobby Sutherland. The lad had no enemies that he knew of, he said, but of course it was normal for boys that age to have occasional rows and fights with their friends. That was part of growing up.

Douglas kept thinking about his interview with Duncan, playing it back like a film he couldn't switch off. The poor chap had been really rather pathetic most of the time the two detectives were there. He kept looking into space with a weird expression and every few minutes a tear would run soundlessly down his cheeks and on to his shirt. Still, they'd managed to get a list from him of all the people who'd been at the church that evening. Not that that list necessarily included or excluded the killer, Doug told himself. It was merely a starting point.

When Doug got home, Cathie was still asleep. She stirred when he came in, although he took his shoes off at the door. He got undressed as fast as he could. Duncan was gone from his mind, and Doug's only concern at that moment was to get next to the now-large softness of Cathie. She had her back turned to him, and wriggled cosily when he put his arms around her. For Douglas, it was completion; he was caught and lifted high on a wave of contentment and tiredness, and was asleep in less than a minute, cocooned in the pleasurable thought that all three members of his little family were sleeping locked tightly together.

After the two detectives left, Duncan closed and bolted the door behind them. He felt shaky and nervous, as if he'd drunk too much coffee. Standing in the dark hall, he held out both hands and looked at them. No, he wasn't shaking, but still, there was no point in going back to bed now; he didn't even feel sleepy, just a strange mixture of fear, sadness, relief that the policemen had gone, and above all, a deep and awe-inspiring sense that the wrath of God had been aroused.

A bright vision assailed Duncan as he stood there, the vision of Bobby Sutherland, with his dark curly hair and lovely smile, singing in the stalls of the choir, with that wonderful voice of his soaring up through the roof of the church, soaring all the way up to heaven. Duncan sat in the high-backed hall chair and put his head down between his hands, weeping for the loss of Bobby, trying to shut out the vision, which had a more fearful clarity than if Bobby had actually been there. And then he saw the two of them again, and that awful, silvery bag coming up around the boy like a shimmering tide, rising, rising, and finally enveloping him in a shroud of blinding light. Who was it? He knew who the person was, because he had been there, seen it, and knew why it had happened, and wondered if it could really have been himself.

Duncan sat there, afraid, his head humming with painful sounds, unable to decide what was real and what was not, and wondered if he could possibly be experiencing a true vision, a revelation. Maybe the whole horror of it was too much for his spirit to bear; maybe he was going mad.

It was past dawn. Duncan stood up, his bones shaking with unreality, went to his bedroom and looked out over the churchyard. The tall yews, dark green during the day, were black with foreboding in the thin light of morning. The sun had not yet appeared; Duncan knew where to look for it, behind the trees, just to the left of the wall. He had watched it come up many times in recent weeks, and only then had he realized that the sun didn't rise in the same place every morning, but started a little farther south every day until the summer solstice, when it reversed direction.

Duncan turned to face the long mirror on the inside door of his wardrobe. Staring at his own tall body, something rose in Duncan, something like a tidal wave that seemed to rush up inside him and out of his mouth with all the strength he could muster.

'Sinner!' he screamed, pointing accusingly at his reflection, 'You God-damned Sinner!' In his fury and despair, Duncan lunged and struck the mirror with his fist, hard enough to crack it up and down and from side to side. Duncan stood back, appalled, not so much by what he'd done as by what he saw. The cracks formed a jagged, fearsome, unholy cross, and as he backed away, Duncan heard it give a mocking, evil, splintery laugh and the cracks slowly extended all the way up and down and across the mirror with a dreadful grinding noise that made him clap his hands over his ears.

Chapter Thirteen

For hours, Derek walked around his house in an agonized turmoil, then phoned the hospital at about seven-thirty. He told the theatre sister what had happened and that he was too distraught to come in.

'My God,' said Jan Kelso, wide-eyed. 'That's just so dreadful. I'm really terribly sorry, Dr Sutherland,' she said with real compassion. It sounded too horrible to be true, and for one cynical second she wondered if Dr Sutherland might have made up the story to get out of coming to work.

'I'll phone Dr MacIntosh,' she said. 'I don't know what he's going to do. He has a pelvic disproportion scheduled for a Caesarean at nine . . .' Jan stopped talking and looked at the phone. Dr Sutherland had hung up.

Derek continued to walk round his house in a fever of restlessness, unable to think about anything except his vast, engulfing hurt. He was like a child in his reactions, as if he'd been struck from a direction he was neither expecting nor watching. Now his mind cowered, too numb even to assess the damage. In some basic area of his brain Derek knew that Sheila was somewhere in the house, but in his condition, even the stimuli of touch and sound and sight were not able to penetrate the mantle of his misery.

When he happened to go past the open door of Bobby's untidy bedroom and saw a pair of socks under the chair, socks Bobby had actually worn and walked around in, Derek realized that it would have been better if he'd gone in to the hospital after all. If he stayed here at home, locked up with his grief, thinking, remembering, hurting, he knew that he would go mad. Derek went back to the entrance hall, picked up the phone, looked at it for a moment, then dialled the hospital's number and was soon speaking to Jan Kelso.

'I hope he's in a fit condition to put her safely to sleep, Sister,' said Peter MacIntosh to Jan. He never felt entirely comfortable when Derek Sutherland was anaesthetizing a patient for him, and now he'd have to be doubly on the alert. For a moment he thought of asking one of the other anaesthetists to take over, but they were all busy in the other theatres with their own cases.

'I'll move Morag from room three,' said Jan. Morag was a very experienced nurse who could keep an eye on what was going on on Sutherland's side of the drapes. 'It'll be all right. Here he comes.'

Peter held out his hand in genuine sympathy when Derek came up. 'Derek, I'm terribly sorry . . .'

Derek nodded, but didn't say anything or even pause on his way to the changing room.

Peter and Jan exchanged a quick glance. 'It'll be all right,' repeated Jan.

She shook her head as Peter went back into the theatre. Being a Theatre Sister was more than knowing how many Kelly clamps were away being repaired, or working out how to keep the operating schedule on time when the water was shut off for a day. It was a very personal job, and she learned all kinds of things about the doctors and her staff. It was like being a mother, negotiator, friend, and general fixer of problems for all of them. It amused Jan to think that only her least important functions appeared on her official job description.

Just as Jan was getting ready to go into theatre herself, Dr Montrose appeared, and Jan got her changed and positioned where she could see the entire operation without getting in the way.

The case did turn out all right, although not without a few scary moments. Anaesthetizing for a caesarean section always took some additional care because if too much anaesthetic were given, some of it could get through the placenta to the baby and could cause cerebral depression and even stop it breathing.

Derek fumbled around, relying on his reflexes, his memory, his training, on Morag. He was a skilful enough anaesthetist, and with Morag making up the dilutions, filling the syringes from the drug vials and handing them to him at the appropriate times, everything went well until several minutes into the case, when the patient's heart slowed, and her blood pressure fell dramatically. Derek, in his rather confused state, didn't even seem to realize that he was facing a major emergency, and bumbled nonchalantly about. Luckily Morag knew exactly what to do, and a few nerve-wracking minutes later all was well again. Jean watched all this, wide-eyed, but silent. There was nothing she could do except keep out of everyone's way.

The next problem arose some fifteen minutes later, when Peter was getting ready to open the uterus. Morag had placed a rectal thermometer in the patient, a standard procedure, and the readout started to rise, indicating that her body temperature was going up. This time, as soon as he noticed what was happening, Derek almost went berserk; sweat poured off his brow and his hand shook. He started to order medication in a loud voice, and Peter, concerned, stopped operating and asked what was the matter. Morag caught Peter's eye, and indicated to him that all was under control. She managed to calm Derek down, showed him that the rise in temperature was only slight, and not anything to be really concerned about. Jean admired the way Morag handled the situation, but she didn't know that Morag was used to covering up for Derek and occasionally for others. There had been one alcoholic anaesthetist whose cases she did almost singlehandedly for over a year. That had been particularly difficult, because at the end of his cases, Morag was faced with the doubly demanding task of waking both the patient and the doctor.

After the incident with the patient's temperature, Derek didn't even try to concentrate on what he was supposed to be doing. His eyes were blank and unfocused, and Morag wondered if he'd taken some drugs to help him through this terrible period. Anaesthetists had access to lots of different kinds of medication, both stimulants and narcotics, and as she well knew, some were not averse to administering their drugs to themselves.

Peter whispered something to his registrar, and they worked fast, afraid that a fresh complication might occur, one that Morag might not be able to deal with. But after the baby was out, and they heard his first wonderful howl of new life, and after the mother's belly had been carefully sewn up, Peter drew what seemed to have been the first breath he'd taken in the entire operation.

Taking no chances, he accompanied the stretcher back to the recovery room and sat there until the patient was fully awake and breathing satisfactorily.

Watching the patient go through the stages of recovery was not entirely a bad experience for Peter, as he saw from closer up than usual the pain and fear and discomfort that his patients went through when they woke up after an operation. In addition, Peter had the real pleasure of telling the young woman that she now had a healthy baby boy, and also of seeing the new mother's tears of joy, a joy that so clearly transcended the pain she was experiencing.

Derek, still in the grip of his pathological restlessness, started to walk down the corridor, intending to leave the hospital, then realized he was still in his scrub suit. Reluctantly he turned and went back to the changing room. The pressure was starting to build in his head again, and he really thought he was going mad, especially as there was nothing he could do to stop the pain or even alleviate it. Worse still, there was no end in sight. Bobby was never coming home, he was never going to ride his bicycle home along the pavement with his hands cockily in his pockets. It never crossed Derek's mind to worry about how Sheila was managing. As always, *his* problems, *his* hurts, and *his* feelings, pushed all other thoughts and concerns out, like fledgling cuckoos in another bird's nest.

Chapter Fourteen

Doug got up late, and after a brief row with Cathie for not waking him, he got to his office a few minutes before ten. He was not in the best of moods, having eaten no breakfast, and the fact that Jamieson was waiting there for him, sitting in the visitors' chair, red-eyed and resentful, didn't help.

'Well, Jamieson, what have you done useful so far?' he snapped. His tone told Jamieson that he was in no mood for either humour or levity.

'I've been waiting for you, sir,' replied Jamieson reproachfully. 'You said to be here at nine, and here I was, sir, on the dot.'

'Is that all? You've just been sitting here?' Doug's tone was a skilful blend of astonishment and sarcasm, but as usual his verbal and inflective artistry was lost on his subordinate.

But for once Doug was surprised by Jamieson's reply.

'I found who has keys to the church,' he said, his voice complacent enough to set Doug's teeth on edge.

'Who?'

'The Reverend himself, of course, the verger, Mr Archibald. The organist, Mr Farquar, Miss Munday . . .'

'Miss Munday has keys?' asked Doug. 'For what reason, I wonder?'

'I asked the very same question, sir,' said Jamieson, his voice deep and important-sounding. 'There is a spare set that's kept for the cleaners, or anybody that was doing work in the church during the week, like electricians. She keeps them when they're not being used.'

Doug thought about that for a moment.

'Who else?'

'That's all, sir. According to the Reverend, anyway.'

'Well, all that's very fine, but of course the killer could have got in while the door was open. I mean, while the rehearsal was on. Anybody could have got into the church hall, right?'

'I don't believe so, sir.' Jamieson had obviously put a lot of thought into the problem. 'There was nowhere for anybody to hide. There's nowhere in the hall itself, there's only one high cupboard in the vestry for hymn books and stuff. If the perpetrator had gone into the church they would have seen him, because the door opens near the choir stalls.'

'For God's sake, Jamieson. Perpetrator? Have you been watching "Miami Vice" again? May I remind you that here we're just the humble Tayside Police, not a SWAT team sinking drug runners off Key Biscayne. We talk about *suspects* here, if you don't mind.'

'Yes sir.' Jamieson's face turned to granite again.

'You're saying that Bobby was killed by someone in the choir, then?' Douglas couldn't help grinning at the thought of these plain, earnest, long-necked choir members. Not a murderer among that lot, he was prepared to bet a month's salary on that.

'It was somebody who was there that evening, somebody everyone saw,' said Jamieson doggedly. The strain of sustaining an argument with Douglas showed in his large, square face; he always felt a lot more comfortable in a mêlée than in a discussion. Jamieson's eyes narrowed with concentration. 'I just canna think of anything Bobby could have done that was so bad it made somebody want to kill him.'

'That's a very good point, lad,' said Douglas approvingly. 'But remember, he must have done something to upset Lois Munday, if we're to believe the Reverend. We need to find out everything we can about the boy. When we know enough about him, we'll know who killed him. And now, Jamieson,' he said, 'I could use a mug of tea, if you please.'

While Jamieson's heavy footsteps retreated down the corridor, Douglas opened his desk drawer, pulled out a pen and a government-issue pad, wrote the date and a heading, *Bobby Sutherland, deceased*. Below that, he made a list of possible suspects, or at least people he needed to interview. He ticked off the top name, Duncan Sinclair. Then there was Ian Farquar, the small, dour organist, followed by Lois Munday, then Jeremy McIver. Douglas tapped his pencil thinking about Jeremy, then put a large question mark next to his name. On the next line he wrote Larry French's name in large, round letters. On the other side of the page, he wrote the names of Bobby's parents, Dr Derek and Mrs Sheila Sutherland. Doug thought about them for a while, then in the middle of the page, in small letters, he wrote Lisbie Montrose's name.

Somewhere in that lot was the killer, and Doug stared at the page, as if he hoped that the guilty name would somehow betray its guilt, made by detaching itself and crawling off the page, or by twisting the letters around and strangling itself.

The door opened quietly, and Jamieson came in holding an overfilled mug, and left a trail of beige splashes from the door to where he deposited the mug on Doug's desk.

Douglas barely noticed. He was thinking about the Sutherlands. He'd met them a few times at the church, the laid-back Derek with his laissez-faire attitude, and Sheila, his flashy, restless-looking wife. Some kind of forensic sixth sense told him that all had not been well with that family, even before Bobby's death.

'Call the Sutherlands and tell them we're on our way over to see them,' he ordered Jamieson, but instead of preparing what he was going to ask them, he found himself thinking about the Lois Munday case that had hit the headlines over a year ago. Lois had hit a burglar over the head with a poker, seriously injuring him, and she herself had narrowly escaped prosecution. For a second Doug had a flashback of Jean feeling Bobby's skull, then looking at her bloodstained fingers.

Jamieson put down the phone and turned to Doug. 'They're waiting for us,' he said.

Jamieson drove, and a few minutes later they pulled up outside the Sutherlands' fine house.

'I wouldn't mind being a doctor,' said Jamieson, looking up at the impressive portal. 'But to tell you the truth, sir, I'd really miss the responsibilities of this job.'

Doug didn't know quite what to answer, so they marched in silence up to the front door. Doug always felt uncomfortable around rich or important people, and although visiting Dr Sutherland in his imposing home wasn't as bad as interviewing the likes of the

Lumsdens or the Strathalmonds, he still felt a knot tightening in his stomach. Then he thought of how the Sutherlands must be hurting at this moment, how dreadful they must both feel, and somehow the thought of their sorrow eased his own tension, and he felt his sympathy go out to them both.

He pushed the door-bell hard, and it was opened quickly.

'Good morning,' said Derek. 'Come in.' He had just come back from the hospital, obviously hadn't shaved that morning, and looked gaunt and ill, more like a tramp squatting in the house than a successful professional man welcoming them into his home.

They followed Derek into the large, black-and-white-tiled hall then turned left after him. Sheila was in the big living room sitting on a couch.

Doug took a quick look around the room. Two long windows, protected by black velvet curtains tied with huge white silk bows, looked out on the garden, and a rosewood grand piano stood against the opposite wall. The white shag carpet was protected from the piano's brass wheels by round wooden pads. A big blue and yellow Nevers vase sat on the piano, exuberantly full of bright pink and red gladioli.

Yesterday's flowers, thought Doug, looking at the display. Today, Sheila would surely have filled the vase with white lilies, or, more likely, put it away empty. On the far side of the room was a stack of stereo equipment, and next to it a big television which could be swivelled around for viewing from the sofa. The fireplace, a large imitation Adam which looked old-fashioned and incongruous in these modern surroundings, was surmounted by a mantel covered with photos of Bobby. Bobby by himself, holding a tennis racquet, Bobby in a chorister's gown, holding music and singing, several of Bobby with his parents standing proudly on either side of him.

The sofa was big, white leather and chrome, and was separated from the fireplace by a low chrome and glass coffee table. Large matching easy chairs were placed on each side of the sofa. It was a strange blend, designer furniture from the 1950s transplanted into a staid Scottish living room. But Doug had never been particularly sensitive to the niceties of interior decoration, and his impression was of a comfortable enough room.

'I'd like to say again how sorry we are,' began Douglas, and he really meant it, but neither of the Sutherlands seemed to hear him. Douglas sat down in one of the easy chairs and swivelled it round to face the sofa, motioning to Jamieson to sit next to Sheila. Jamieson's mere bulk tended to make witnesses nervous, especially guilty ones, but his presence didn't seem to affect Sheila one way or another. She sat there, slumped forward in her dressing gown, immobile, apparently not having even noticed their arrival.

'Herrrumph . . . Mrs Sutherland,' started Douglas, clearing his throat loudly. He'd seen enough people in this condition to know what to do with them. One just had to treat them like foreigners and speak very loudly. That was usually enough.

'I'm not deaf,' said Sheila, staring straight in front of her. For a second Douglas wondered if she was on anything; her expression reminded him of Mac MacFadyen on his way to the drug rehabilitation centre.

Derek sat on the edge of the sofa. He too looked numb and dazed, and Douglas eyed him with some sympathy, and thought about his own feelings a few months back when Cathie almost had a miscarriage. And that was not even a baby, then, just a little blob of human jelly without a face, without anything. Douglas couldn't imagine how it would feel to lose a child one had lived with and loved and cherished for twelve years.

'We're here to try to find out what happened last night,' said Douglas in a quieter tone now that he had gained Sheila's attention. 'Can you tell us if Bobby had any enemies? I know that sounds silly when we're talking about a twelve-year-old boy, but they can have enemies just like us grownups.'

Derek looked up, startled, but Sheila said in a brittle, defensive voice, 'Bobby was a very popular boy at school, and everybody liked him, all the teachers and all the boys.'

'Anyone else?' urged Douglas. 'A neighbour, maybe, or somebody he'd had a row with? Did Bobby ever go over the wall to steal apples, anything like that?'

'Certainly not,' said Sheila, her voice icy. 'He was not that kind of boy at all. He wouldn't have *dreamed* of stealing apples. In any case, there's a wall round the garden.' She stood up and pointed through the window at the high, sheer brick garden wall. 'Look. It's eight feet high, and not climbable.'

'Had Bobby been feeling all right, in the last few weeks?' Doug had a premonition that he was going to have difficulty keeping this interview on track. 'I mean, did he have any worries, with his schoolwork or anything?'

'His teachers were all very pleased with Bobby,' replied Sheila primly, 'and he was going to join the Scottish Youth Choir . . .' A loud, racking sob shook her, and she crumpled back into her seat.

There was a moment's silence, broken by Derek.

'I've been wondering about all that,' he said, standing up. 'A few days ago, Bobby had a . . . well, I suppose you could call it a fight, of some sort.' Derek looked apprehensively over at Sheila as if he were telling tales out of school. 'He had a friend named Jeremy McIver,' he went on. 'He was Bobby's best friend, but they had some kind of a falling out. I don't know the details.' Again he glanced at Sheila. Douglas could see that she knew a great deal more about what had gone on in Bobby's life than did his father.

'Jeremy McIver and a big group of his hooligan friends ganged up on Bobby a few days ago,' said Sheila, tight-lipped and adopting the same defensive tone she'd used earlier. 'They tried to beat him up but Bobby outsmarted them and got away.'

'Why?' asked Douglas. 'I mean, why did they want to gang up on him?'

'Because there were half a dozen of them against just Bobby,' said Sheila, shrugging her shoulders. 'Of course he ran away.'

'I'm sorry, that's not what I meant,' said Doug, wondering if her misunderstanding had been deliberate. 'Why would Jeremy, Bobby's best friend, want to beat him up?' Doug waited for her answer, pencil poised.

'The day before, the two of them had been out on their bicycles. Jeremy was careless and fell off as they were riding along, and of course, being the kind of boy he is, blamed Bobby,' replied Sheila, talking through tightly pressed lips. 'And that was quite ridiculous. Bobby would never do anything like that.'

Sheila took a big breath. 'That Jeremy,' she went on, 'I hate to say this, but he's really not a nice child. What's more, his father works on road gangs, and neither of us ever felt that Jeremy was, well, a suitable friend for our Bobby.'

Douglas felt his ears going red, but he wrote down

what Sheila had said, his pencil digging hard into the paper.

'Do you think Jeremy might have been angry enough to . . .'

'Yes. Either him or his parents,' replied Sheila, interrupting. Her puffy eyes managed to flash; she had obviously come to this conclusion some time ago, and had been incubating it until she could deliver it to Douglas. 'You see, Inspector,' she went on, 'they hated Bobby. Both of them. Bobby was cleverer, and better looking, and they were hoping that Jeremy would get that position with the Scottish Youth Choir. I wouldn't be surprised if they did it together, all three of them.'

'I don't think you should be making such accusations, Sheila,' said Derek, looking very uncomfortable.

'It's not an accusation.' Sheila threw Derek a look which should have shrivelled him up, but, Doug thought, he must be immune by this time. 'I said *I wouldn't be surprised*.'

'Do you know if Jeremy was at the choir practice last night?' asked Douglas, who knew the answer but wondered what Sheila might reply.

'That mother of his would have dragged him there even if he had a temperature of a hundred and five,' replied Sheila shortly.

'How did Bobby usually get home after practice?'

'He rode his bicycle or walked. It's only about ten minutes away.'

'Was there anybody he usually walked home with, or part of the way?'

'No. Most of these people live, well, in another part of town.' Sheila's tone made Doug clench his teeth again.

Douglas sat back and put his pencil in his jacket

pocket. His voice was well-controlled and concerned. 'Is there anything else, anything at all, that either of you can recollect, anything that might help us to find out who did this?'

'We've told you everything we know,' said Sheila, although she knew that it was far from the truth. At least she could point them in the direction of the McIvers, while she came to terms with what had really happened.

Derek glanced at her, then nodded in agreement.

Back in the car, Douglas sighed. 'There's something fishy going on,' he said to Jamieson. 'Something she's not telling us.'

'She was certainly pointing the finger at the McIvers,' replied Jamieson, busy fastening his seat-belt. 'Not just Jeremy, the whole lot of them.'

Doug's hand was on the ignition key, but he didn't turn it for a few moments. 'Could be,' he said. 'Anyway, we'll find out soon enough. That Sheila looks about ready to crack.' Doug looked at his list, and then at his watch. 'I think this would be a good time for us to have a wee chat with Miss Lois Munday.'

Chapter Fifteen

While Doug and Jamieson were on their way across town, Lois was walking like a thin, anxious cat up and down her living room. The air was thick with cigarette smoke, and two ashtrays were already filled with crushed and bent fag-ends, some put out after just one puff. Lois had never felt such turmoil as she was experiencing now; for so many months, her entire life had centred around Duncan Sinclair, and she was dimly aware that her intense interest had become a full-fledged obsession. And then, a couple of days ago, the Reverend Edmund Glasgow from the Church's Central Office had come to see her about 'matters of mutual concern'.

When he appeared at the door, the Reverend Glasgow reminded Lois of the priests she had seen on her last trip to Rome, rounded, bespectacled, each with his worn leather briefcase, and all hurrying on missions of vital ecclesiastical importance.

Seated in Lois's front room, Glasgow came to the point immediately. 'We're concerned about our dear brother Duncan Sinclair,' he said, his pudgy hands pressed tightly together. 'You may know that he had some . . . difficulties at his last parish, and we wondered whether any problems were arising here.'

Lois, astonished, was emphatically denying that any problems existed when she remembered what the woman in the choir had said, and Lois's voice faded away. The Reverend Glasgow observed her discomfort, and for the next half hour, he interrogated her about Duncan, and when she finally asked him what this was all about, his reply had shocked her so much that after he left, Lois hurried to the bathroom and threw up.

And then, today . . . Lois shook with disgust at the recollection. First thing this morning, after spending an almost sleepless night and hearing the news on the radio, she had dressed, made up her face and, driven by an uncontrollable urge, went straight to the manse. All kinds of thoughts flew in disarray through her mind as she hurried along the pavement, her unbuttoned coat flying behind her in the wind. Now that Bobby Sutherland was out of the way, she thought, maybe Duncan would forget about these silly, immature relationships he'd been trapped into, maybe when he saw her he would take her in his arms and they would go forward together in the pure and beautiful life-partnership Lois knew they both craved.

But when Duncan did open the door, unshaven, red-eyed, his pyjamas sagging, and his face bloated and oddly distorted, Lois detected a weird emanation from him, and something horrible clicked in her mind. She stared at him with a sudden stomach-turning revulsion; Duncan really was a faggot, an unredeemable queer, she was certain of it. And that wasn't all . . .

Lois had turned without saying a word and had run back to the gate and into the street, her legs feeling so shaky that she was afraid they might collapse under her.

Lois froze when the doorbell rang, then went over to the window, parted the thin curtains and looked down. She recognized Doug and Jamieson, and although she had been expecting them, her whole body started to shake, and she felt the panic rising in her chest. It took her a few moments to pull herself together. She lit a fresh cigarette, then went down to open the door.

Lois stood aside while the two men stepped in, and a surge of tension tightened every muscle in her body. She led them into the living room, and both men noticed the jerkiness of her movements and the unsteadiness of her hands. Douglas was reminded of comments he'd heard about Lois's emotional instability, and decided to go very gently.

'We're hoping you can help us to find out who killed Bobby Sutherland, Lois,' he said, his tone gentle, confidential.

To Doug's surprise, Lois merely shrugged, and let out two thin trails of smoke from her nostrils. At the sight of the smoke, Doug felt a sharp urge for a cigarette although he hadn't smoked for over five months.

He looked Lois over, and his sympathy faded. After all, if she was tough enough to have smashed a burglar over the head with a poker, she was tough enough to answer a few questions.

Los answered his questions defensively. Yes, she had left the church alone last night; yes, she did have a set of keys to the church; no, she had no idea who might have killed Bobby; no, she hadn't seen anyone suspicious hanging around the church.

Lois had seen the McIvers' car with the bonnet up, but didn't offer assistance. 'I wouldn't know what to do,' she replied when Douglas asked why. She hesitated for a moment, then her voice softened fractionally. 'Anyway, I'm a bit afraid of that family,' she went on, 'like everybody else who knows them, I suppose.'

She had walked around for a few minutes, she told Doug, but hadn't met anyone she knew on the way home, had let herself in, read for a while, then gone to bed.

'What were you reading?' asked Douglas, trying to ease the tension that seemed to be tearing Lois apart.

'Oh, just a murder mystery, nothing very intellectual. It's set here in Perth . . .' Lois picked a paperback off the side table and held it out to him.

'*Bad Blood*, eh,' said Doug. He turned it over to look at the back cover, then gave it back. 'Not my kind of thing, I'm afraid,' he said. He rather ostentatiously put his notebook back in his pocket. 'Now, we're just about done, don't you think, Jamieson?'

Jamieson, who knew his cues, nodded and shifted on his chair as if he were about to get up.

'By the way, Miss Munday,' said Doug carelessly, 'Were you particularly close to Bobby?'

Lois's eyes opened wide. 'Me? No. Not at all. Why?'

Doug watched her as he went on. 'The Reverend told us that yesterday during the practice you couldn't take your eyes off the boy, that's why.'

'That's just rubbish,' said Lois loudly. '*He* was so busy watching Bobby, how would he know?'

'And why would *he* be watching Bobby?' he asked softly.

Lois got up. 'Ask him,' she said in a flat voice. 'I don't know.'

Douglas stood up, slowly, and Jamieson followed his example. 'You used to be very fond of the Reverend, Lois,' he said softly. 'What happened?'

Lois seemed to crumple, and she sat down as if all the wound-up tension had gone out of her, leaving her helpless and vulnerable.

When she raised her head, there were tears running down her cheeks. 'I always thought he was so . . . wonderful,' she said, and a huge sob escaped her, as if all the misery of her life were embodied in it.

'You've changed your mind about him?'

'Well, somebody said that something was going on between him and Bobby – I knew Duncan was fond of him, but I thought . . .'

'What did you think, Lois?' said Douglas after the pause had lasted long enough.

'I thought after Duncan . . . was stopped from doing that, he'd . . . he'd . . .' Lois's voice was high, unsure, and her words were interspersed with uncontrollable sobs. Douglas felt that she was under such stress that she didn't quite know what she was saying. He helped her out.

'You thought that he'd finally see that he belonged with you, that *you* were the person he should be with, isn't that right?' Douglas's voice was loaded with a soft inevitability.

Jamieson's mouth opened slowly as Lois sobbed her agreement, and she blurted out what the Reverend Glasgow had told her about Duncan's previous ministry. She was too distraught to notice the cigarette between her fingers until it burned blisters into them.

'I wouldn't be surprised if she'd done it,' said Jamieson as they drove back to headquarters.

'You think she killed Bobby Sutherland?' Doug's mind had already switched to Larry French, and was wondering about what part he might have played in the case. In any event, he didn't usually pay much attention to the products of Jamieson's cerebral activity.

'Well, she was in love with the Reverend,' said Jamieson through clenched teeth. Doug was negotiating an impossible gap between a tour bus and a truck going in the other direction. Jamieson hated driving with Doug. 'She told us that after the Reverend *was stopped from doing that*, she thought he would take up with her,' he went on doggedly. 'So she stopped him all right, by killing Bobby. There certainly was a motive there.' Jamieson opened his eyes again. 'And of course she already knew how to hit somebody over the head.'

Something else clicked in Doug's mind, and he stared at Jamieson. 'That's an interesting thought, lad,' he said.

Jamieson nodded eagerly, happy that Douglas was for once taking him seriously.

'A very interesting thought,' repeated Douglas in the same tone. 'But now you've had that imaginative trip to Never land, let's get back to reality. Aside from the Reverend and the killer, Ian Farquar was the last person to see Bobby alive, so he's our next stop. Maybe we'll get some *real* help from that wee organist.'

Chapter Sixteen

After her last home visit that morning, Jean hurried back to the surgery, wondering if she'd have time later to visit her mother in the nursing home.

When she came through the door, Eleanor was waiting for her, wearing her usual disapproving look. 'Fourteen of them in there,' she said, first looking at the wall clock, then pointing at the waiting room door. 'Two new ones, both with fevers.'

'Okay, I'll get started right away,' said Jean, then felt annoyed at herself for allowing Eleanor to intimidate her. 'Is Dr Inkster in?'

Helen's door opened and she came out, holding a stack of NHS forms in her hand.

'Get us some tea, please,' said Helen to Eleanor. Helen had a firm, commanding voice, and Eleanor got up hurriedly and went into the little room behind her desk where they did urinalysis and other minor tests, and where the electric kettle and tea things were kept.

Jean shook her head. 'How is it that she jumps when *you* tell her to do something, Helen, but she has me apologizing to her all the time?'

'I'll tell you why,' said Helen, and laughed, a deep,

confident, hearty laugh. 'Did you know we were at school together, Eleanor and I?'

'You may have told me,' replied Jean. 'I didn't actually remember that.'

'Well,' said Helen, not seeming to care if Eleanor heard her, 'she started to work for me about a year before you came. After she'd been here a few months, she was getting more and more bossy so when I'd had enough, I picked her up by her coat lapels, gave her a good shake, and told her that if she didn't shape up and show a little respect, I'd break her in two. I haven't had a moment's trouble from her since.'

'I couldn't do that,' Jean replied. 'I wish I could, but anyway she's bigger than me. I'll have to think of something else or just get used to it, I suppose.'

Jean was about to go into her office when the door of the waiting room burst open and a slender middle-aged woman came out and started to shout at Eleanor, who had just reappeared with the tea.

'How long do we have to wait?' cried the woman. 'I've had my father-in-law in here over an hour, and he's really sick. Does he have to die in there before he gets seen, or what?'

Eleanor banged the tea tray down on her desk with an indignant crash and was starting to shout back at her when Jean came over.

'I'm sorry the two of you had to wait, Ann,' she said quietly to the woman. 'What's been the matter with Andrew?'

Ann McIver turned quickly. 'Oh, Jean,' she said. 'I didn't know you were there.' Ann nodded at her father-in-law. He's been sick for two days. This morning I came over to get him his breakfast, and he was hot, sweating, and looked terrible. So I brought him here.

If I'd known I was going to have to wait so long, I'd have just sent for you.'

Jean turned to Eleanor. 'Let's get Mr McIver into my office,' she said. 'I'll see him first.'

'There's two people in front of him,' said Eleanor, but Jean glared at her, and Eleanor reluctantly went towards the waiting room to fetch him.

In her office, Jean took one look at Mr McIver Senior, and saw immediately that he had been ill for longer than two days. Under his thick jacket, he had no shirt, only a grubby white cotton vest. His trousers, held up by a pair of wide braces, were too big, and above his bony, unshaven, triangular face, Andrew wore a cloth cap in the way usually worn by Scots country people, pulled down against the wind. It looked as if it hadn't come off his head since the day he bought it.

Jean took his temperature. 'A hundred and one,' she said to Ann, who had come in with him.

'I suppose it's the 'flu,' said Ann.

'I'm not so sure,' said Jean, slipping Andrew's braces off his bony shoulders and pulling up his vest.

'His chest sounds pretty clear,' she said after listening for a few moments. 'How much weight have you lost, Andrew?' she asked the old man.

The old man looked at Ann. 'I dinna ken,' he said in a thick countryman's brogue. 'Ask her.'

Ann shrugged. 'He disna eat, that's why he's thin,' she said defensively. 'I bring him food, but he just disna eat it.'

Jean did a complete physical, and felt knots of enlarged, thick, rubbery lymph glands on both sides of his neck.

'No, Ann, it's not the 'flu,' she said when she finished. 'I think he might have Hodgkin's disease.'

While Andrew got himself dressed, Ann seemed agitated and restless, almost excited, and Jean had the feeling that she hadn't taken in what she'd just been told. Ann sat in the chair facing Jean, who was writing her notes on Andrew's chart. A couple of times Ann started to say something; Jean wrote, and waited, feeling that Ann had another reason beside Andrew for coming to the surgery.

'I'm not really surprised about what happened to Bobby Sutherland,' Ann said.

Jean stopped writing and looked up.

'Jeremy says there are things going on . . .' Ann hesitated, but Jean got the impression that the pause was deliberate, and the woman knew exactly what she was going to say. 'At the choir. Maybe other places too.' Ann fixed Jean with a sharp look, as if there was some bond of understanding between the two of them.

'I don't know what you're talking about, Ann,' replied Jean quietly. 'If you feel it's important, shouldn't you discuss it with Inspector Niven?'

Ann shrugged, irritated. 'No, of course not. It's his job to find out, not mine to tell him. But as Lisbie's in the choir, I thought *you* would know.'

'I don't,' said Jean. 'Now, about Andrew . . .'

'He has the 'flu, that's all, and he just needs some medicine.' Ann stood up. 'I'd like a prescription, please.' Her lips were tightly set, and her voice sounded annoyed. Andrew came out from behind the curtain. Ann picked up his jacket and held it out to him. 'Come on, Pa, it's time we went home.'

'We need to get some blood tests,' said Jean. 'What we're talking about is a form of cancer, and he's going to need treatment for it.'

'That's all you doctors do,' said Ann, her voice taut

and stretched with bitterness and anger. 'You just live to find cancer and diseases in people. If you won't give him a prescription, I'll get something at the chemist's.' She got her father to his feet and gave him a push towards the door.

'I'll stop by to see him at home tomorrow, Ann,' Jean called after her. She knew there was no immediate urgency about Andrew's condition, as long as it was taken care of within a reasonable time. 'Meanwhile aspirins should help his fever. Give him two in the evening . . .'

Ann didn't answer, and the door closed behind them.

Jean made a note in her book to visit Andrew the next day; he lived in a council flat not too far from the surgery. Jean was quite sure that with the passage of a little time, and some more sympathetic explanations, she would eventually get him to the hospital for a more complete diagnosis and treatment of his tumour. Putting the chart away, Jean fought back an uncomfortable feeling about Ann. Why had she brought up the topic of Bobby Sutherland? Was that the real reason for her visit? And what did she mean by 'there were things going on in the choir'? Did Ann assume that Jean would immediately report the conversation to Douglas Niven?

Jean shook her head, and pressed the buzzer for her next patient.

Chapter Seventeen

Back at his desk after coming back from Lois Munday, Douglas fiddled with his pen and tried to put some order in his thoughts. Bobby's parents. Douglas had not liked either of the Sutherlands; Derek's hopeless attitude was unmanly, to say the least, and Sheila . . . She certainly seemed to be the one who wore the trousers in the household, but there was something about her bitterness, her mercurial anger that made Douglas think that it had been there before Bobby's murder. Still, they had to be under huge stress at this time, Doug realized, and that would certainly affect the way they behaved.

Why had she been so defensive about her son? Did she realize that her attitude could obscure some hints about who might have been his killer? Was there something strange about Bobby, something she was trying to hide? Had he done something so terrible or so dangerous that he could have been killed for it? Or had Bobby really been the paragon of virtue that his mother had made him out to be, loved by one and all, including all his schoolmates and teachers?

Douglas got up, feeling chilled, and went over to close the window, and at the same time to shut off the noise of traffic going along Caledonian Road. He went back to the notes on his desk to check the name of Bobby's best friend. Jeremy McIver. He would be at school now, unless they'd given the class the day off because of Bobby's death. They were a lot softer about that kind of thing, nowadays. Douglas remembered a boy in his class at school who'd fallen into a piece of agricultural machinery and been cut to pieces, but nobody would have dreamed of cancelling classes for that.

While he was writing his notes on the Sutherlands, Doug thought about Lois Munday. Jamieson's idea that she had killed Bobby so as to clear her own path to the altar with Duncan seemed too preposterous to waste time on. But Lois's near-fatal attack on that burglar a year ago was certainly an interesting coincidence.

Douglas put his notes into the folder and realized that in all probability he would spend a lot of time interviewing innocent people while the killer stayed free. Of course, he might strike again; that would be a pity for the victim, of course, but on the other hand it would improve the chances of catching him. Or her.

Doug sat back, his thoughts passing to the Farquars. Douglas didn't know much about either of them, except that Ian played the organ at the church, conducted the choir with the help of Duncan Sinclair, and gave music lessons. Doug had met Ian a few times, but they never had much to say to each other. Doug's recollection was of a small, dour, unsmiling, humourless man who certainly was a fine organist. He didn't know whether the Farquars had much of a social life; he didn't think so, but Cathie would know more about that. Douglas tried to remember what Beth Farquar looked like. He'd seen her in church a few times, a colourless, mousy, scared-looking woman of maybe forty who wore clothes with wide skirts that looked as if they had been made for a bigger woman. Jean Montrose would probably have something interesting to say about her. That was one of the great things about Jean, thought Douglas; she was shrewd and missed nothing, but somehow she was always able to find and highlight the best attributes of people, features that a casual observer might not even notice.

Douglas put his notes in one of the heavy grey filing cabinets, locked it, then went looking for Jamieson. He found him in the constables' room, in the far corner. He had jammed a chair between the wall and the soft-drinks machine and was dozing.

Doug didn't say anything until he came right up to him. 'All right, Jamieson, let's go!' he barked loudly, almost in his ear. Jamieson leapt to his feet, and the chair went flying.

'Sir,' he mumbled, then shook his head. 'I've been thinking.'

'Jamieson, I've warned you before about that,' said Doug briskly. 'It's not something you can just take up, like macramé. Now let's get going. We have to talk to the Farquars and the McIvers before they all decide to go off on holiday.'

Jamieson followed him to the door. 'Sir,' he said, 'it doesn't make sense, the whole thing.'

'In the car,' said Doug.

A few minutes later, as Doug drove out of the garage area behind headquarters, he said, 'All right, Jamieson, what doesn't make sense?'

'I was wondering if it could maybe have been an accident,' replied Jamieson doggedly, knowing that as a rule Douglas didn't pay much attention to what he said. 'Whoever did it must have brought that funny-looking bag, already with the little holes cut in it. If she . . .'

'Or he,' interrupted Douglas, slowing down for a woman pushing a pram obliquely across the street. These days he noticed prams and babies and pregnant women a lot more than he used to.

'Right, sir,' said Jamieson. 'As I was saying. If she really wanted to kill him, wouldn't she just have hit him a bit harder on the back of the head and not bothered with putting him in the bag and all that?'

'Good point, Jamieson,' said Doug automatically. He was thinking about the shape of Cathie's stomach; now it came out further than her breasts. 'Maybe it was somebody with scruples, or somebody who wasn't too strong, like a woman, like Lois Munday, maybe, is that what you're saying?'

'And the air holes, sir. Do you think it could have been some sort of joke that misfired?'

'Some joke,' retorted Douglas grimly. 'Bashing a kid over the head with a blunt instrument, in church, no less, then stuffing him into a bag to die. Yeah, that makes a really great joke, Jamieson.'

Jamieson subsided glumly into his seat and said no more until they pulled up outside the Farquars' home.

'Do you know anything about them?' asked Doug, indicating the house with his thumb.

'He took over as organist when Mr Falconer retired a couple of years ago,' said Jamieson. 'He came from . . . I don't remember where. Dundee, maybe, or Aberdeen. They're very quiet, don't go out much, no kids, no friends, no nothing.'

'What about her?' asked Doug.

'Beth? They say she's a bit weird.' Jamieson unfastened his seat belt. 'Nice enough, kind and all that, but weird.'

'Okay. Now, listen carefully, Jamieson. Once you get the drift of what I'm talking to them about, you can ask a question from time to time. I like to watch them when they're answering somebody else's questions.'

Douglas didn't mention that many people tended to drop their guard and become careless when answering Jamieson's often inept questions, and on occasion Douglas had been able to use that to his advantage.

Ian opened the door before the bell had stopped ringing; he had watched the car pull up, and had been standing behind the door, waiting for them.

'Aye,' he said in his slow, rasping voice. 'Come in, then.' They followed him into the front room. On the way, Doug looked unobtrusively around. The Farquars' home had none of the panache of the Sutherlands'; it was a mean little place, with small rooms, ancient flowered wallpaper and cheap, hard-worn brown furniture. Not even much of that, thought Doug. Jamieson, walking ahead, seemed to fill the front room all by himself.

'Beth's nae wheel,' said Ian, nodding at the closed door of their bedroom. 'She's got the 'flu and she's staying in her bed. Anyway, she wisna at the church last night, so there's nothing she could tell you.'

Doug sat down on a sturdy ladderback chair, and motioned to Jamieson to sit in the other one just like it. Jamieson's size was an ever-present threat to inferior or delicate furniture.

Douglas put on his impassive, formal expression. 'We're here to get any additional information you might have about the death of Bobby Sutherland last night.'

'I don't know anything about it,' said Ian. 'Except what was on the radio.' His lips tightened. 'I'd have thought that somebody, maybe the Reverend, might have phoned to tell me about it, but naebody did.'

'Bobby Sutherland was found dead in the church, some time after the end of choir practice,' said Douglas. He never gave details to possible witnesses or criminals; a killer could give himself away by inadvertently mentioning something he couldn't have known if he hadn't been there, and conversely ignorance of details would immediately expose someone making a false confession.

'How was he killed?' asked Ian, his small, dark eyes fixed on Douglas, who ignored the question and asked one of his own.

'At what time did you arrive at the church hall for the choir practice, Mr Farquar?'

'About twenty minutes past seven,' he said. 'I usually come a bit early.'

'Why is that?' asked Douglas.

'Och, sometimes to switch on the organ. It's an old instrument that was converted from bellows to electricity, and it takes a wee while for it to warm up.'

'Don't you usually hold the practices in the church hall rather than the church itself?'

'Aye,' replied Ian. 'Not always, though.'

'Was there anybody already there when you came in?'

For the first time, both Jamieson and Doug noted a slight hesitation on Ian's part, and his eyes shifted for a moment.

'Aye, there was,' he said.

'Well?' asked Douglas after it became obvious that

Ian wasn't going to say anything more without prodding. 'So who was there?'

Ian shifted in his seat. He had sat down in one of the two easy chairs on either side of the black, arched cast-iron fireplace. 'I came in through the side door to the church,' he said. 'I had to switch the organ on ahead of time, because I wanted to have the rehearsal in the church. Then I went into the vestry, intending to go through it to the hall. I heard them talking.'

'Who?' asked Jamieson unexpectedly. Both Doug and Ian turned to look at him.

'The Reverend was there,' said Ian in a low, stubborn voice.

'Talking to himself?' asked Doug sharply.

Ian said nothing, and the stubborn expression became more pronounced.

'Mr Farquar,' said Doug after waiting for Ian to respond, 'I want to remind you that withholding important information can be an indictable offence.'

'I'm nae withholding anything,' answered Ian, a touch of defiance creeping into his voice. 'Have I no been answering a' your questions?'

'Who was the Reverend talking to?' Douglas had taken out his pad and was holding his pencil poised over it.

'I'm no sure,' replied Ian.

'Was it one of the choir members?' asked Doug. 'A man? A woman?'

'It was Bobby Sutherland,' said Ian, finally. He was obviously angry to have been put in such a corner. 'And I'm no' going to say ony more about it, except what they were talking about was disgusting and no' the kind of stuff any Christian should be talking about, especially in a church.'

It took a little more persuasion from Douglas, including the threat of arresting him and taking him to the station as a material witness to get anything more out of him.

'You're forcing me tae speak ill o' the dead,' he said angrily.

'That's so, Mr Farquar,' said Douglas smoothly. 'And we don't like that any more than you. But it may help us to find who killed the lad.'

Ian thought about that for a minute, while Jamieson watched him, thinking that if he were unofficially to pick the man up by the scruff of the neck, give him a good shake and hold him against the wall for a little while, it might help him to talk a bit faster.

Ian shrugged. 'Bobby was saying that he'd had enough and that he was going to tell his parents.'

'Enough of what?' asked Douglas, leaning forward in his chair. 'Did he say what?'

'No he did not,' replied Ian, furious that Douglas had so easily overcome his stubbornness. 'But I know perfectly well what he was talking about, and so do you.'

'You're quite sure that's what he said? I mean about telling his parents? You heard that clearly enough?'

'Aye,' said Ian. 'And now, if you'll excuse me I have to get some medicine in to Beth.'

While he was out of the room, neither Jamieson nor Douglas spoke. Douglas looked round the room at the sparse decorations, the few photos on the mantelpiece, and a dark print of a couple of highland cattle knee-deep in a river. He got up and went over to look at them, mostly just to stretch his legs.

When Ian came back, Douglas asked how Beth was.

'She's deein' a' right,' was the curt reply. 'She was wakened by a' the talk in here.'

'I hope we won't need to talk much longer,' said Doug, implying that it was up to Ian; if he answered the questions properly, they'd be out in a few minutes.

According to Ian, he had been one of the last to leave. 'Who was still there in the church when you left, Mr Farquar?' asked Douglas.

'Just the minister and Bobby Sutherland.'

There was a long silence, and Douglas and Jamieson left soon after.

'I hope Mrs Farquar'll be feeling better soon,' said Douglas politely as they went out.

Chapter Eighteen

'Well, that's a right kettle o' fish and no mistake,' said Douglas thoughtfully once they were back in the car.

'Aye, fairly,' replied Jamieson but Douglas could see that his subordinate's mind was not running along the same track as his.

'Did you see the photos on the mantelpiece?' Douglas asked.

Jamieson shook his head.

'There was one of the Farquars with a boy standing between them,' said Douglas, frowning, 'in front of a tent. It can't have been taken that long ago, maybe a couple of years. The thing was,' he went on, 'they were both smiling, and that Ian certainly doesn't do much smiling now.'

'Who knows,' said Jamieson as the car pulled away from the Kerb. 'They could have taken a cousin camping, I suppose.'

'Well, let's go and find out what Bobby's friend Jeremy has to say,' said Doug, abandoning that train of thought. 'If he really was his best friend, maybe he knows something about the Reverend's activities.'

'Aye,' said Jamieson ponderously, 'And maybe from personal experience, at that.'

The McIvers lived in a council flat in one of the poorer sections of Perth, in a development that had been condemned some years previously. Both Douglas and Jamieson knew that although Mrs McIver worked as a temporary schoolteacher and made reasonable money, Joe McIver was a heavy drinker and could never hold on to a job for more than a week or so.

'We're going from the top to the bottom, today, and no mistake,' said Douglas steering around a shattered bottle. Shards of glass, old tins and various pieces of rubbish littered the pavement.

'Aye, fae the palaces o' the rich tae the hovels o' the poor,' said Jamieson sententiously.

Doug stared at him. 'Is that a quote from something?' he asked.

'No, sir, I made it up mysel'.' Jamieson grinned with satisfaction. When they turned the corner into the street where the McIvers lived, he looked at the house numbers, some crudely painted on the side of the doorways. Some of the lower windows of the tenements had been boarded up.

'It's a couple of houses down from here, sir.'

Doug said nothing, but shook his head. This was one of the worst parts of town, and the source of a good number of the crimes committed in the area. When they pulled up outside 18B, a few grubby children appeared from nowhere and gathered round the car. They stared but said nothing when Doug got out and greeted them cheerfully.

All the McIvers were at home.

Joe opened the door of the second-floor flat the moment Jamieson knocked on the door. He glowered at them. 'You couldn't have left your car down the road a bit, could you?' he asked in an unpleasant, aggressive tone. 'Nobody likes to see the police around here.' He pronounced the word 'police' as 'poe-liss'.

Ann appeared behind him, small and wiry, wearing a shapeless slate-coloured dress that came down to her ankles. 'What do you want?' she called out to them in a shrill tone. 'We haven't done anything and we don't need you around here.'

Both Doug and Jamieson felt more comfortable with this kind of greeting than the more formal welcomes they had received at the Sutherlands' and the Farquars' homes. In fact, they found it almost reassuring.

'Aye, that's right,' said Doug tranquilly. 'Nobody said you did. We just need to ask you a few questions about Bobby Sutherland and we'd just as soon do it here than have to take the lot of you down to headquarters.'

Ann visibly wilted. 'We're quiet people,' she said, and opened the graffiti-covered door. 'We just don't want any trouble.'

Doug squeezed past them easily enough, but Jamieson's bulk ran into Joe's. Quite gently, Jamieson pushed him aside; Joe was big, but Jamieson was bigger.

Inside, the place was remarkably clean and tidy; the elaborate Mediterranean-style furniture, though not of particularly good quality, was the kind that appeared in the display windows of furniture chain stores. The cushions and sofa were a brilliant orange, but clean and in good repair. When Douglas and Jamieson came in, Jeremy appeared from another room, took one look at them and was about to turn tail when Doug called out to him. Reluctantly the boy came back and sat down on the orange sofa, where he was joined by his mother on one side and Jamieson on the other. Joe stood with his back to the door after closing it, and stared spitefully at Jamieson out of small, bright blue eyes, and muttered at him under his breath.

'All right, then,' said Doug cheerfully, taking out his notebook and adjusting the elastic band. He looked over at Jeremy. 'Let's start with you,' he said. 'You were Bobby's best friend, weren't you?' He looked encouragingly at the boy.

'No he was not,' snapped Ann. 'He . . .'

'Mrs McIver,' said Douglas gently. 'I was asking Jeremy.'

Douglas watched Jeremy, whose gaze moved suspiciously from Jamieson back to Douglas. Jeremy was a tough-looking, muscular kid. Living in this neighbourhood, Douglas thought, he'd need to know how to take care of himself. It seemed quite weird that he was in a choir, and even weirder that he was a talented musician with a really good singing voice.

'Yes he was my friend,' Jeremy's words came out in a low monotone. 'Right up until the time he pushed me off my bike.'

Ann McIver's breath came out in a hiss, and Jamieson, looking over at her, felt glad that his mother hadn't been like that. This woman sounded like a viper, and Jamieson had noticed a vicious satisfaction on her face when Bobby Sutherland's name was mentioned.

'Why did Bobby do that, Jeremy?' Doug sounded easy and encouraging; he had put on his friendly, I'm-here-to-help-you voice and was watching Jeremy with an expression of relaxed benevolence.

'I don't know,' replied Jeremy, unmoved by Doug's approach. 'I didn't do nothing to him.'

'How long had you been friends?'

'A while.' Jeremy shifted in his chair. It was quite

obvious that he didn't want to talk any more about Bobby Sutherland.

'Did you notice if Bobby had been acting differently, in the last few days, or maybe weeks?'

Jeremy shrugged his shoulders. 'No,' he said. 'But his mother was after him all the time. Bobby said she hated him.'

Douglas waited, silently encouraging Jeremy to go on. 'He also hated going to the choir,' said Jeremy.

'Do you know why?'

'Maybe it had something to do with Mr Sinclair.' Jeremy's voice was flat, uninterested, but Douglas was watching his eyes, and noticed how they shifted. Douglas had an extensive professional experience with liars, and knew one when he saw one.

But Jamieson had difficulty restraining a loud 'Aha!' and threw a profoundly meaningful glance at Douglas, which was neither noticed nor returned.

'What do you think that "something" might have been?'

Jeremy obviously didn't understand the question, and didn't reply.

'I mean, what do you think was the problem between Bobby and Mr Sinclair?'

Again, Jeremy shrugged. 'I don't know. I just don't think Bobby liked him, that's all.'

'Was there anything else, or anybody else that was bothering him, that you know of, Jeremy?'

Jeremy shook his head.

Douglas was almost at the end of his questions. 'Can you think of any reason why somebody might have killed him?'

Jeremy shook his head. 'Me and Sandy Watt and a couple of others would have liked to,' said Jeremy.

'We tried to get him after school for knocking me off my bike.'

'He's just joking,' interrupted his mother loudly. 'It was just a kids' fight, nothing more, wasn't it, Jeremy?' She threw a transfixing glare at Jeremy.

'Did you notice anything unusual during the choir practice last night?' Jamieson asked Jeremy, to Douglas's mild irritation, because he had been going to pursue the boys' disagreement a bit further.

Jeremy shook his head.

'When did you leave?'

'When it was finished,' replied Jeremy. 'I went out just after Lisbie Montrose and Larry French.'

'Did you notice if Bobby was still there when you left?'

'I don't know. He wasn't my friend no more, so I didn't notice.'

'How did you get home?' asked Doug.

'My parents picked me up,' said Jeremy. His voice was very low, and both Douglas and Jamieson noted a sudden tension in the room.

'Both of you?' Doug glanced at Joe and then at Ann. 'Do you both usually go to fetch him?'

There was a silence, broken by Ann. 'Do you object?' she asked shrilly.

'Of course not,' replied Doug easily. 'I just wondered why . . .'

'The car,' said Joe loudly from in front of the door. 'The car was having problems so I went with her.'

Jamieson gave a grunt.

'Did you notice anyone hanging around the church?' went on Douglas, after a glance at Jamieson. There was something going on here that he didn't feel quite comfortable about.

Joe shook his head. Nobody else said anything.

'All right, then. Jeremy,' he asked with an apparent change of tack, 'do you ever go camping?'

Jeremy looked up at Doug in surprise, and shook his head.

Douglas sighed, then snapped the elastic band on his notebook. 'Thank you, Jeremy. That was all very helpful. If you can think of anything else that could be important, you'll let me know, won't you?'

Without a word, Jeremy got up and went back into an inner room, slamming the door after him.

'Now, Mrs McIver,' said Douglas, turning to her and smiling, 'it's your turn.'

'That Bobby Sutherland was nasty and stuck-up, just like his parents,' snapped Ann. 'I know he's dead, and I shouldn't say anything about him, but they all kept filling his head with stuff about being the best singer since that Pavarotti man.'

'He did have a pretty good voice, I thought,' said Douglas, purposely to needle Ann. 'The best in the choir. And just about everybody else said so too.'

Ann's thin frame seemed to swell with rage. 'Let me tell you,' she said, 'my Jeremy's voice is a lot better than Bobby Sutherland's or any of that lot. Even Mr Farquar said so, didn't he, Joe?'

Without waiting for a response from her husband, Ann went on, 'Mr Farquar said he thought Jeremy would get to the Scottish Youth Choir auditions, so that proves Jeremy was better.'

Ann stood, her hands on her hips, a very portrait of a virago.

'Jeremy takes singing lessons from Mr Farquar, doesn't he?' asked Douglas.

'Yes he does. Is *that* all right with you?' Ann's eyes

flashed, and out of the corner of his eye, Douglas could see that Joe was backing up his wife's vituperative attitude, and was waiting for an opportunity to get into the act.

After he had finished with Ann, Douglas turned to Joe, but Jamieson got there first.

'I remember you,' he said suddenly. 'About six months ago.'

'So what of it?' asked Joe, still standing by the door. His voice was as truculent as Ann's.

'Nothing,' said Jamieson. 'You were just lucky to get off.'

'They had no proof,' said Joe, grinning.

'That was only because the main witness died,' said Doug grimly, remembering the case. 'I'm sure you could tell us a fine story about that, too, if you wanted to.'

Doug had not been directly involved, but at the time, the case had received some attention in the media. A Glasgow building contractor had had both his legs broken with a steel bar, allegedly at the behest of a supplier who hadn't been paid, and Joe was suspected of being the hit man. A watchman who had seen the attack had died soon after, and the case was dropped for lack of evidence.

Douglas's interrogation got him nowhere. According to Joe, he knew nothing about Jeremy's friends, and had better things to do than get involved in his son's battles. As for last night, he was watching television all evening with Ann, except for the thirty minutes or so spent picking Jeremy up at the church. Douglas found that Joe's recollection of the programmes he'd watched was fuzzy, to say the least, even when prompted by his wife.

After they finished with the McIvers, Doug drove back carefully, avoiding potholes and broken glass until they were clear of the housing project.

'Do you think his parents were trying to protect Jeremy?' asked Jamieson. 'That mother of his . . .'

When they reached Caledonian Road, Douglas turned the corner and drove into the parking area behind the police headquarters, past a fine display of yellow chrysanthemums at the front of the building.

'That very same thought had crossed my mind, Jamieson,' he said quietly. 'They're a tough family, and I wouldn't want to get on the wrong side of them, in case I met all three of them one night down a dark alley.' Douglas paused. 'It could be,' he went on, pulling up with about an inch to spare before hitting the brick wall at the end of the car park, 'that the stupidest thing Bobby Sutherland ever did was to knock Jeremy McIver off his bike.'

Chapter Nineteen

The Montroses were unusually silent at dinner that evening. They were all shocked by Bobby Sutherland's death, and after exchanging the first horrified news about how his body had been found, none of them wanted to talk any more about him.

Jean wasn't back by the time Fiona got home, so Fiona made the dinner and turned out a surprisingly good meal, considering that nothing was prepared. Jean had carefully trained her girls in the preparation of emergency dinners; she had a couple of sure-fire recipes that only took a few minutes to prepare, and not much longer to cook. On this occasion, Fiona took four haddock fillets from the freezer, put the defrosted fish into a buttered casserole dish, emptied two tins of condensed mushroom soup over them, stirred in some lemon juice, half a teaspoon of marjoram and the same amount of thyme, before covering the whole thing with ready-grated cheddar from a plastic bag. A few minutes in the microwave, a couple more under the grill to brown the cheese, and it was ready.

'And that's all there is to it,' said Fiona, putting the dish in the oven. 'Bob's your uncle.'

'Who was he?' asked Lisbie, red-eyed from crying about Bobby.

'Who was who, for heaven's sake?'

'Bob. You said "Bob's your uncle".'

'I don't know,' replied Fiona, getting the plates ready to warm. 'All I can tell you is he's no relative of ours. Now if you'd like to set the table . . .'

Even after several years of unvarying presentation, the haddock casserole was one of Steven's favourites and he was convinced that the girls had slaved for hours in the kitchen to make it. And for years, they did nothing to disabuse him.

Jean came in just as dinner was about to be served, and she gave Fiona a quick grateful hug for taking care of everything. 'You're just wonderful,' she said. Lisbie came into the kitchen to get glasses. 'Both of you,' added Jean, and they all had a quick 'group hug' in the kitchen.

Lisbie, who knew Bobby best and was heartbroken at the death of her friend, refused to eat anything, and several times during the meal was unable to prevent herself from bursting into tears. Jean, who had had very little sleep in the last few days, and almost none the night before, was exhausted, especially as she hadn't completely recovered from her bout of 'flu. Most unusually, she planned to go to bed directly after supper.

Even Fiona, who was tougher than her sister, was quiet and subdued. The whole idea of anyone being killed in their church horrified her. Steven couldn't think of anything quite like it since Thomas à Becket. He felt rather pleased about remembering that, and twice muttered something about Canterbury and turbulent priests, but neither of the girls paid any attention to him.

Once everybody was served, Steven waited for Jean to say something about the murder, but Lisbie was so visibly upset that Jean kept clear of that topic.

'Fiona,' said her mother, trying to find an innocuous subject of conversation, 'did you remember to take your books back to the library? They already sent you one post card.'

'Oh sh . . .' Fiona started to say, but caught herself just in time. Steven's fork stopped half-way to his mouth and he glowered at her.

'I was going to say "Oh *shhhurely* I can't have forgotten them again,"' said Fiona, grinning cheekily at her father. 'Actually I left the books in my car.'

'Well, I don't imagine they're doing anybody any good there,' said Steven sternly.

Jean sighed. Sometimes it was better just to sit quietly and say nothing, but if she did that she lost any control over what was being discussed. She leaned forward and put a hand on Lisbie's arm. 'Try to eat just a little, dear,' she said, smiling. 'You know how hard Fiona worked to make dinner today, and you don't want to disappoint her, do you?'

In spite of herself, Lisbie smiled, Fiona grinned, and Jean's warm look enveloped them all. Steven felt that some kind of female joke was going on between them that he had completely missed. It wasn't the first time.

'Who's Bob in "Bob's your uncle"?' asked Lisbie, out of the blue. They had all heard the expression, but nobody knew its origin.

The doorbell rang. 'It's my sweetheart, I know his ring,' said Fiona, jumping to her feet. She dropped her napkin on the table and ran to open the front door.

'When are you going to stop your daughter running after Douglas Niven?' Steven asked Jean in a grumpy voice. 'It's really not right, with him being a married man, and about to have a child.'

Douglas came in, looking a bit sheepish as usual when Fiona was around. She hung on to his arm, smiling.

'Sorry if I interrupted your dinner,' he said, standing in the doorway. 'I can watch TV in the living room until you're finished.'

'No, no, Douglas,' said Jean hospitably. 'Sit yourself down. We're having strawberries and cream for dessert, and there's plenty for everybody.'

Douglas sat down, and Fiona fussed around him, getting a plate, a napkin and a spoon for the strawberries and cream. Steven watched her, then addressed Douglas. 'How's Cathie doing?' he asked, pointedly.

'She's wonderful,' replied Doug, smiling. 'I can't wait to see my son and heir, and the truth is that Cathie's already tired of being pregnant. She's just dying to have that baby.'

'I'm really sorry to hear that,' said Fiona with her usual quick wit, and after a moment everybody laughed. Fiona's mostly put-on hostility to Cathie had lasted so long that it was now a family joke.

'Are you working on the Bobby Sutherland case?' Steven asked Douglas, passing his plate to Jean for more mashed potatoes and peas.

Lisbie pushed her plate away at the mention of Bobby's name, got up and left the room in tears.

'Did I say something wrong?' asked Steven, surprised, watching her depart.

'She knew Bobby quite well,' said Jean calmly. 'She's very upset about the whole thing.'

'Daddy!' said Fiona, annoyed. 'You really didn't have

to be so tactless . . . Why do you *always* say things like that when you know she's already upset?'

Douglas got up. 'Excuse me,' he said. 'I'll go and talk to her. I need to ask her a couple of things about Bobby anyway, so I might as well get it over with as soon as possible.'

Doug found Lisbie in the sitting room, and he pulled out his big white handkerchief and dabbed paternally at her eyes. Lisbie was so astonished she didn't resist.

'All right,' he said, 'there, that's better, isn't it?'

'Yes, thank you, Doug.' Lisbie smiled uncertainly up at Doug's serious, concerned face, and for the first time understood why her mother and Fiona liked him so much.

Douglas sat down opposite her and cleared his throat. 'Lisbie, I hate to ask you to talk about it, but I need to know a few things about last night.'

He half-expected Lisbie's tears to start again, but she looked bravely back at him.

'Okay,' she said, her lower lip trembling. 'It's just that Bobby . . . He was just the nicest boy. And it wasn't just me that loved him. We were going to go to Kildrummy this weekend . . .' Lisbie wept softly for a moment, then dried her eyes. 'That's it,' she said. 'I've cried quite enough for one day.'

'Good for you, Lisbie,' said Douglas. 'Maybe you can remember something that'll help us catch whoever did it.'

'Try me. I hope so.'

'Right. Lisbie, who was already there when you got to the Church hall last evening?'

'Well, Reverend Sinclair was putting out the parts; I mean the music for the choir . . . Bobby was there too, he was straightening out the chairs, I think.'

'Lisbie, I want you to think very carefully about my next question. Did you think there was any tension between them?'

'Between Bobby and him? I didn't notice anything, not at the time. Maybe Bobby was a bit quiet, but I don't know what he's like at practices because it was the first time I'd been to one.'

'How about Reverend Sinclair? Did he seem to be different in any way?'

'I don't think so. We arrived in a group, and he came over to say he was happy to see me. No, he seemed fine, to me anyway.'

'Did anything happen during the practice?'

Lisbie thought for a moment. 'I can't think of anything, I'm sorry.' She stared at Douglas. 'Wait a minute. Do you think it could have been somebody who was there who did it?'

'I'm afraid it's more than likely, Lisbie.' Douglas sat back and watched her. Lisbie was round and pretty, a junior version of her mother. Douglas wondered if Jean had been as sensitive, as easily hurt, and as tenderhearted when she was Lisbie's age. He knew that Jean had all these qualities now, more than most people, but modified and made less raw by her life and experience. But unlike Lisbie, Jean had learned to mask her emotions; Doug assumed it was a protective mechanism against all the heartrending situations she came across daily in her practice.

'Well,' said Lisbie in a low voice. 'You know Larry French? I was watching him . . .' Lisbie blushed, and looked at the floor.

Douglas grinned to himself. Jean had once mentioned that Lisbie had a crush on Larry.

'Yes, of course. That's quite a business he's got there

with his pharmacies. He's really changed things around since his father died.'

'When we were having coffee and biscuits after the practice,' said Lisbie, still looking at the floor, 'Mr Sinclair was talking to Bobby, then Larry came and took Bobby into a corner to talk to him. Bobby was looking, well, uncomfortable and . . .' Lisbie's eyes went big. 'Oh, my, Douglas. I shouldn't have said anything about that. I didn't mean that . . . Of course Larry didn't have anything to do with . . . with . . .'

She looked up at Doug, suddenly relieved. 'Anyway, Larry left the church with me and a couple of other people a couple of minutes later.'

Lisbie put her hand up to her mouth, and she went quite pale. Doug waited. Something had obviously occurred to Lisbie; he knew that she didn't have a dishonest bone in her body, and that she would tell him, whatever it was.

'Larry went back,' said Lisbie quietly. 'We'd been chatting at the entrance to the parking area when he found he'd left his car keys behind. He laughed and went back for them.'

'Did anybody go back with him?' asked Doug.

'No. He just looked in his pockets, then turned and went back.'

'Who was still in the church at that time, do you remember? I mean at the time you left.'

'Let's see. Reverend Sinclair was getting ready to go, Bobby was putting chairs away. Mr Farquar was still there, I think . . .' Lisbie wrinkled her brows. 'I don't really remember.'

'Lisbie, that evening, did you see anyone in the church who wasn't a member of the group? A cleaner, a visitor, anybody?'

'No.' Lisbie was decisive. 'There was nobody else there.'

'Let's get back to Larry for a second,' said Douglas, as if he just wanted to tie up a trivial loose end to the conversation. 'How long was it before he went back for his keys? I mean was it just a minute or two?'

'Well, he'd gone to help Joe McIver with his car, then we were all talking and laughing for a while, maybe five minutes or so, then he patted his pockets ... Yes, that's about right, I think, not more than five minutes.'

'Did you notice if the lights in the church were still on?' asked Doug, his voice very quiet.

'You can't really see from where we were, but the door must still have been open, or he wouldn't have got in.'

'Yes,' said Douglas thoughtfully. 'Now how about Joe McIver? Did he get his car going? Did you see them leave?'

Lisbie looked at the ceiling, trying to remember. 'I don't know. The last thing I saw before going home was Lois Munday walking past. I wasn't really paying much attention to the McIvers.' Again she blushed, and Doug smiled at her.

Lisbie stood up, embarrassed. 'I hope you find who did it,' she said, and again the tears came to her eyes. 'I'm quite sure it couldn't have been Larry. He's ... well, Larry's a really nice person, Doug, and he could never do anything so awful.'

Douglas put a comforting arm around her shoulder, and they headed back to the dining room. 'Let's go and try those strawberries and cream,' he said. 'It sounds exactly what the two of us need right now.'

'What's "Bob's your uncle", Doug?' asked Lisbie,

one hand on the knob of the dining room door. 'I mean, who was Bob?'

'Bob was Robert Cecil, Lord Salisbury, a Prime Minister,' replied Doug, smiling. 'His nephew was A. J. Balfour, who kept getting promoted by his uncle. So if Bob was your uncle, it meant you didn't have to worry about getting ahead in life.'

'Oh,' said Lisbie. She thought for a second. 'Do you mind if I tell them?' She pointed through the door. 'And will you pretend you didn't know?'

Chapter Twenty

The next afternoon, after forcing herself to drink a cup of bouillon for lunch, Sheila Sutherland went upstairs to her own bathroom, pulled a comb through her hair, did her best to repair the still-puffy face and eyelids, and got dressed. The phone had rung several times after word of the tragedy had got out, but after the first call, from a concerned and sympathetic Peter MacIntosh phoning from the hospital, she switched on the answering machine in the entrance hall.

In her bedroom, Sheila stood in front of her dressing table and stared at the white phone in her hand as if it were a poisonous snake. Then she forced herself to dial a number. It was answered quickly, and Sheila could hear the sound of talking in the background.

'Larry?'

'Oh, my God, Sheila . . .' There was so much emotion in his voice that Sheila was momentarily taken aback.

'Larry, I need to talk to you.' Sheila gripped the phone tight, and her sense of apprehension soared during the brief silence at the other end.

'I want to tell you how terribly sorry I am,' said Larry in a low voice. Sheila could see him there behind the counter, his head down, trying not to let his assistant Maggie hear what he was saying. 'I'm utterly appalled, Sheila. I would have phoned you at home, but you know that might not be the best . . .'

'I'll meet you at your house,' interrupted Sheila. 'In half an hour, all right?'

Sheila felt his hesitation. Larry never liked to leave the pharmacy during business hours. 'You can leave Maggie in charge,' she told him, and he agreed with a strange, reluctant haste.

When Sheila came downstairs again, Derek was lying on the white leather couch in the living room, curled up in a foetal position. He didn't move or open his eyes when she came into the room.

'Derek,' she said, 'get up.' Her voice was not loud, but there was something about the tone that made Derek sit up instantly.

'Derek, there's a lot of things that have to be done, and it would be better if you got started on them.'

Derek listened, but said nothing. His eyes were fixed on his wife, and Sheila felt a moment's apprehension at the wildness of his gaze.

'We have to find out when . . .' Sheila closed her eyes, but continued, '. . . when they plan to do the post-mortem. You know the people involved, so it would be easier for you to ask.'

Sheila's eyes wandered over her husband's unshaven, sallow face, his flaccid, unresisting, inactive body, and she experienced a sense of revulsion that almost made her want to vomit.

'Then we have to find an undertaker,' she went on. 'The only one I know is Lambert's, over in Bridgend, at the end of Main Street. I've written his phone number on the pad in the kitchen. If you know someone else, that's fine with me. All right, Derek?' Sheila spoke the last three words loudly, as if to make sure he was paying attention.

'Where are you going?' asked Derek, his sunken eyes staring hard at her.

There was a pause, then she looked him straight in the eye, and making no effort to hide her contempt for him, said one word, almost spitting it at him. 'Out.'

Derek said nothing, but watched her go to the door, then a moment later when he heard her car door slam, he got up and went to the window and pulled aside the gauze curtain. Her car was just moving out. He watched it slow at the end of the drive, then turn right before disappearing behind the white rhododendron bushes that separated the end of the front garden from the street.

Sheila drove past the big houses at her end of the street; soon the houses were replaced by neat semi-detached homes with slate roofs and tiny well-kept front gardens, but Sheila saw none of this. Behind her tight lips and fixed gaze, her sense of loss struggled with a growing anger, which she already knew had enough power to consume her.

Sheila found a parking place in Rose Street, in the parking area along the edge of the North Inch. She switched off the engine and sat there in silence for a few minutes, trying to gather her strength and resolve for the confrontation. A noisy soccer game was being played on the grassy pitch in front of her, but she barely noticed the players shouting at each other and running around in their striped jerseys. To Sheila, they were like slow-motion actors in a dream, somebody else's dream . . . Stiffly, moving like an old woman, she got out, locked the car and started to walk along the wide, tree-lined path. She looked up to where the leafy tree-tops met far above her head. She walked past the Sports Arena, past the deserted, velvet-smooth bowling green on her left, partly hidden by an eight-foot hawthorn hedge. There was no one else on the path, and a few yards from her destination, she fished in her purse for the key, and although it felt as if it were burning her hand, she held it tightly until she came to the small wooden door that opened into Larry's back garden.

Out of habit, because she really didn't care now, she looked around to see if anybody was watching her, then she unlocked the gate, closed it behind her, and walked steadily up the cambered path, past the ancient, woody-stemmed rosebushes and their heavy, overblown blooms that today sharply reminded her of herself. The rose-beds were flanked by great patches of big yellow and white daisies, and, feeling as if she were being propelled forward by forces she didn't understand, she passed the pink floribunda roses clustering against the high brick wall next to the house.

Sheila didn't slow down till she came to the back steps, but then her heart seemed to leave her, and she climbed them slowly, painfully, as if they were as steep and exhausting as the final trek up the South escarpment of Everest.

Larry opened the door as she reached out for the doorknob.

'Come in, sweetheart . . .' Larry, his face full of concern and compassion, took her arm and ushered her tenderly inside. Sheila went, unresistingly, feeling nothing, blank, able only to be moved by other forces, like a piece of driftwood. There was no memory left of the other times she'd been here, the flashing excitement, the sense of sparkling adventure, or the deep, almost frightening passions that had so many times threatened to overwhelm her.

After closing the door and turning the key in the lock, Larry turned and took Sheila gently in his arms, pressing her head against his shoulder. She looked at the close-up, out-of-focus pattern of the sports jacket he was wearing, her eyes only an inch from his lapel. It was as if she were aware of everything happening around her, but was unable to respond in any way, as if all the connections from the sensory nerve-endings in her body had been obliterated.

'I'm so sorry,' he was saying, stroking the back of her head, 'Sheila, I'm so sorry . . .'

'Yes,' replied Sheila, suddenly rousing herself from her torpor. 'You should be.'

Her words were followed by a moment of intense, almost frightening silence. Then Larry's hands dropped to his sides, and he took a small step back, and looked at her with what was apparently the same anxious expression. But Sheila, now in the grip of a hyperactive awareness, knew instantly that it was just a pretence.

Larry's brows came together in a puzzled frown.

'I'm not quite sure I know what you mean, sweetheart,' he said.

'On Thursday evening, when we were all having dinner, Bobby mentioned that he'd gone to your shop on his way home from school,' said Sheila.

'Yes . . .'

'He told me that you'd spoken to him . . .' Sheila had trouble speaking through the lump in her throat. 'He said that . . . you wanted to talk to him after choir practice.'

Sheila's voice was a whisper, and her eyes didn't leave Larry's face. Her entire being was in the throes of the worst turmoil she could imagine; on the way to Larry's house, everything had been crystal clear; she was going to confront him, make quite sure, then she had planned to go on to the police station and make a statement to Inspector Niven. But now, so close to Larry, she felt all the hypnotic force of his attraction for her, and to her horror, Sheila heard a ghastly soft voice saying inside her head, 'Bobby's dead, you can't bring him back, so let it go. Let it go . . .'

Larry, who was well aware of the power he could exercise over her, took her hand, and he felt it quiver. She had often told him that his mere touch sent an electric shock through her entire body. He led her, unresisting, to the couch and sat her down beside him.

'Bobby was right,' he said, in the same tone as before. 'He did come in to the shop, and I did talk to him. After the practice, I was going to take him out for an ice-cream or something. I wanted to make friends with him, so that by the time you left Derek it wouldn't be so difficult for him . . .'

Larry left the end of the sentence unfinished. Sitting next to him, enveloped by his aura, feeling the warmth of his body and acutely aware of the touch of his hand, Sheila allowed herself to draw a spurious relief from his words.

'Did you? I mean, did you both go for an ice-cream?'

'No. Bobby liked the idea, but said he had to stay and talk to someone after the choir practice. Next time, he said.'

'Who was he going to talk to, Larry?' Now totally under the influence of Larry's presence, Sheila was fast shedding all the suspicions she'd come with. How could she have even thought that Larry could ever do anything as horrible as kill Bobby? Not sweet, gentle, considerate Larry.

'He didn't actually say . . .' Larry hesitated. 'And I can't tell you exactly why, but for some reason I got the strong impression that it was Duncan Sinclair he was going to talk to.'

'Oh God, Larry . . .' Sheila hardly heard his answer, but felt herself totally caught up again in her passion for him, like a great wave that roared up inside her. She put her arms around his neck and pressed herself hard against him. 'Thank you, Larry, oh, thank you,' she said, her voice muffled in his neck. She didn't know why she was saying it, but she repeated her 'thank you' several times before Larry moved back just enough to allow his hand to slip gently down inside the front of her dress.

Sheila's head was on his shoulder, and she didn't see his expression. He was quietly examining her face, for the first time seeing the puffiness, the wrinkles at the corners of her eyes and the beginning of ridges on her upper lip. Even her large breast felt floppy and lifeless; to Larry, who was about twelve years younger than Sheila, it was the breast of an aging woman.

With a sudden feeling of revulsion, he removed his hand. 'I think you should go home now,' he said.

Sheila looked up, startled, and saw an expression she had never seen before on Larry's face. It was absolutely merciless. A few moments later, she was hurrying back along the path towards her car, heedless of the tears running down her face, and in the grip of a fear so powerful that she thought she'd never make it home.

Chapter Twenty-one

Just a few moments after Sheila ran out, the back doorbell rang again, and Larry took his time going to answer it, thinking that she had come back, probably to beg him not to leave her.

He was startled to see Douglas Niven on the doorstep, with Constable Jamieson close behind him, looking over Douglas's shoulder and grinning broadly.

'Mind if we come in?' asked Doug, but he didn't wait for a reply and pushed his way past Larry into the house.

'Nice place, Larry,' said Doug, looking around. He walked into the living room. 'Nice little love-nest, huh, wouldn't you say, Jamieson?'

'What do you want?' asked Larry. He had gone very pale.

'I think I've just got a new slant on the Bobby Sutherland case,' said Doug slowly, addressing Jamieson and deliberately ignoring Larry.

'Yes, sir,' replied Jamieson, looking at Larry with a hostile, aggressive expression.

'Maybe we should just take him down to the station,' went on Doug.

'Right you are, sir.'

Douglas turned and addressed Larry directly for the first time. 'We're taking you down for questioning,' he said, and when Larry started to protest, he said in the same disgusted tone, 'one more word from you, unless it's an answer to a question, and we'll drag you out of here in handcuffs with the car siren going full blast. Now get a jacket and hurry up.'

Fifteen minutes later, back in his office, Douglas stared at Larry, sitting in the visitors' chair, as if he were some kind of particularly revolting insect. The rest of the available space in the office was taken up by Jamieson leaning against the door. Larry's face was pale, and Doug smelt blood. The look on Larry's face said one thing: guilty.

'Larry, I'm going to give you an opportunity to make a statement,' said Douglas. 'Tell me about your relationship with Mrs Sheila Sutherland, with Bobby, then everything that happened up at the church on Thursday night.'

Larry was sweating, and the whites of his eyes were showing over the irises. There were no arms on his chair, and he gripped his knees until his knuckles went white. He hesitated, and his gaze passed from Doug to Jamieson and back, then went to the floor.

'What do you want to know?' he asked, almost in a whisper, 'I'll tell you whatever you want to know.'

Doug gave a tiny shrug. 'All right, then.' He nodded to Jamieson, who took his notebook out of his pocket but omitted the usual flourish. 'What was your relationship with Sheila Sutherland?'

Larry shifted in his chair. 'We're just friends,' he said, but his voice betrayed him.

'And Mrs Sutherland just dropped by to pass the time

of day, eh?' said Doug, his voice sharp with sarcasm. 'So very soon after her child was killed?'

Larry stared at Douglas as if hypnotized, but didn't say anything.

'Did she stay for lunch?' went on Douglas relentlessly. 'Did you have a little celebration? Champagne maybe?'

'We had some tea,' said Larry in a whisper.

'Is that why she was weeping when she came out of your house?' asked Doug. 'The tea was too hot for her, maybe?'

Jamieson glanced at Doug to see if he should write down the bit about the tea, and Doug shook his head, but his eyes didn't leave Larry's face. All his policeman's instincts were on full alert, and he decided to throw a little petrol on the flames to see what would happen. He banged both fists on the desk with enough force to make the phone ring. 'So you thought Bobby was endangering your relationship with his mother, eh, Larry?'

'Did she tell you that?' Larry licked his lips, and Doug realized that he'd scored a bullseye.

Larry started to rise from his chair, his eyes staring.

'Sit down,' barked Doug, 'until I tell you to get up. Now, if you want to tell us exactly how and why you did this, who helped you, every detail, I can make things a lot easier for you. If you give us a hard time, well . . . you'll certainly have a long time to regret it.'

'I didn't . . . Sheila's wrong. I didn't kill him. Bobby was a nice kid . . .'

'You had a conversation with Bobby after the rehearsal,' said Douglas, quiet again. 'What did you want from him?'

'I asked him if he wanted to go for some ice-cream,' replied Larry, before he realized how his words would sound to two hostile policemen. He hurried to explain himself. 'I mean, I wanted to talk to him, to get to know him because . . .' Larry swallowed, and his adam's apple moved up and down. 'Well, because at the time I was hoping Sheila would come and live with me here. And of course she'd have brought Bobby with her,' he said, but to both Doug and Jamieson his last words sounded too much like an afterthought.

Doug put his hands on his desk and leaned forward. In the small office, it could have been interpreted as a threatening gesture. Then Doug changed his mind and leaned back.

'You invited him for an ice-cream,' he said slowly. 'How often have you had ice-cream with him after choir practice, or any other time?'

'Never,' replied Larry quickly. 'This was the first . . .'

'Well, isn't that a coincidence,' drawled Doug. 'Such a lot of things happening just in that one evening.'

Larry's shoulders drooped. He looked very different from the self-assured young man who'd opened the back door to them half an hour before.

'So you were going to take him out for an ice-cream, were you,' repeated Douglas slowly. 'And what were you going to talk about, over your fudge sundae? Did you have that all worked out?'

Larry sat there, as if in a trance. In order to get him going again, Doug decided to try a new tack. 'After the practice was over, then what did you do?'

'I went home,' replied Larry in a monotone.

'Directly? Did you stop off for a drink somewhere? Was there anybody with you?' Doug's rapid-fire questions were obviously confusing Larry, so he repeated them one by one.

'So you went out with a couple of people, including

Lisbie Montrose, talked for a while, then went to your car and drove straight home? Is that right?'

Larry nodded. He seemed flustered by Doug's intransigent attitude and the loudness of the questions.

'Well then, young man,' said Doug grimly. 'I'm afraid you've got yourself in really deep trouble. We have witnesses who saw you go back into the church hall, allegedly to get your car keys.'

Larry stared at Douglas, and his mouth opened slightly. 'It's true,' he said, stammering, and his eyes opened wide. 'I . . . forgot.'

'You forgot, eh? Well, now that you remember, who was still there when you came back?'

Larry's voice was barely audible. 'I'd left the keys on the top of the hall piano,' he said. 'There was nobody there.'

'*Nobody?*' repeated Douglas, astonished. 'Where was Bobby?'

Larry shook his head. 'He wasn't there. I thought . . . I don't know what I thought. The door wasn't locked, though.'

'You didn't meet him as you went back in? How about Ian Farquar, did you see him? Or the minister?'

'No.'

Douglas sat back and stared at Larry.

'Okay,' he said slowly. 'That'll be all for now. There's just one more thing. We'd like your fingerprints. Jamieson, will you take him downstairs and get that done, please?'

Larry stood up. He looked as if he'd been trampled by every bull in Pamplona. 'Are you going to arrest me?' he asked in an almost childlike voice.

Doug shook his head and grinned his evil grin. 'Not yet, Larry,' he said, 'not quite yet.'

PART THREE

Chapter Twenty-two

Feeling guilty because in the excitement of the last few days she hadn't been able to visit her mother, Jean looked at the surgery clock, calculated that she had almost a whole free hour and decided she had time to pay her a quick visit.

She left her car outside the nursing home in Barossa Place and walked up the ramp. Inside the door, Bess, the matron's old, almost blind golden retriever snuffled at her with his white nose, and the matron, Mrs Kimball, appeared behind her.

'Well, good morning, Dr Montrose,' she said brightly. Mrs Kimball was a cheerful, large, capable woman who ran the nursing home with a nice mixture of gentleness towards the patients and a sergeant-major's strictness with the staff. She always wore an old-fashioned nurse's cap and a blue uniform one or two sizes too small, which made her bulge alarmingly at every seam and buttonhole.

'Aye, Mrs Findlay's doing just fine,' she said, smiling, and pushing a lock of grey hair out of her eyes. 'She had her breakfast a wee bit late today, and she's reading her paper, now that everything's all settled down again.'

'Settled down again?' asked Jean, who knew the circuitous way Mrs Kimball liked to approach difficult topics.

'Aye, well, there was a wee problem earlier this morning.' Mrs Kimball tugged on her uniform, and Jean waited for a button to pop, but they must have been sewn on with wire. 'You know she doesn't like to be wakened up suddenly, and apparently Joannie, our new aide, was a bit brisk with her . . .' Mrs Kimball sighed. 'This morning our board of Governors visited. Once a month they all come, look around, eat cakes and drink tea, then have their meeting and go away.'

'Go on, Mrs Kimball.' Jean's heart was slowly sinking with apprehension.

'Well, just as the Governors were all coming from the kitchens, heading for the dining room, out comes your mother with her zimmer, right into the corridor.'

'Did she fall?' Jean was surprised that the sensible Mrs Kimball would be concerned about such a trivial problem.

'No, Dr Montrose, it wisna that . . .' Mrs Kimball's face turned a shade pinker. 'It was that she had no clothes on, not a stitch.'

Jean sighed. Had it been anyone else, she would have thought the whole thing rather funny, but her mother had caused a fair amount of trouble since coming to the nursing home, and Jean realized that she had lost her sense of humour about the situation. 'I'll talk to her,' she said. 'Did the Governors say anything?'

Mrs Kimball went from pink to red. 'I was so embarrassed . . . Mr Foreman, you know Denis Foreman, the one who married Ilona Strathalmond, well, he's one of our trustees, and he let out such a wolf whistle when your mother came out, the puir thing, and then everybody laughed. Then Mr Foreman kindly got her back into her room. I tell you, Dr Montrose, I've never in my life been so embarrassed.'

Jean got a vivid picture of her naked mother, standing in the corridor, staring truculently at the astonished Governors, and she couldn't help smiling at the thought.

'Well, I don't suppose any real harm was done, Mrs Kimball. At her age, she wasn't going to give any of those men a stroke, seeing her.'

Mrs Kimball, still put out by the incident, went back to her office, and Jean went down the corridor towards her mother's room. People are strange, she thought. When her mother had tried to set fire to the place a few months before by lighting a crumpled newspaper in the middle of her room, Mrs Kimball had taken it all serenely in her stride. But when it was a question of propriety, that was an entirely different kettle of fish, and Mrs Kimball took that very seriously.

When Jean came into the room, Mrs Findlay was indeed reading the paper. Jean kissed her on the forehead and sat down in the comfortable chair facing the bed. It was a pleasant, airy room with white gauze curtains that billowed in front of the big open window. Outside, the carefully tended garden was full of roses and beds of chrysanthemums and irises. Red and pink hollyhocks grew tall against the brick wall at the back. A few old people sat out in their wheelchairs, in the shade of a pagoda-like Victorian gazebo near the end of the garden.

'I hope you didn't catch a cold,' said Jean, trying to

keep her face straight. It occurred to her that she had not seen her mother naked, ever.

'So they told you, did they?' replied Mrs Findlay, putting the paper down. She grinned maliciously. 'My God, you should have seen their faces, out there.'

'Why, Mother? What on earth made you do it? Mrs Kimball was really scandalized.'

'Ach,' said Mrs Findlay contemptuously. 'That Mrs Kimball. She's just a stupid, fat old woman. She'd be more use to humanity if she was rendered for her oil.'

'Mother!' Jean did her best to sound shocked. 'You know you shouldn't talk like that about the Matron. She's a very nice, competent woman and she makes sure you're well taken care of.'

'Don't for one moment think I went out there without any clothes on just to get a few wolf whistles.' Mrs Findlay's eyes flashed with happy reminiscence.

'Why did you, then?'

'Well, this morning I was sound asleep, when into my room comes this young chit of a girl, yelling and screaming into my ear about breakfast, or something equally unimportant.'

'They're supposed to wake you,' said Jean. 'That's part of their job.'

'Well, I have left strict instructions not to be disturbed if I'm asleep,' said Mrs Findlay grandly. 'And I'm tired of this constant interference. So I decided to teach them a lesson.'

'By flashing in the corridor? Oh, Mother, really!'

'These people,' said Mrs Findlay, waving in the general direction of the corridor, 'were the Governors. It's their sworn duty to certify that this place is properly run. How can they possibly do that when they see naked women running around in the corridors?'

Mrs Findlay's eyes sparked disapproval at the very thought. 'If they have the slightest shred of honesty in them, which I doubt, they will be forced to recertify this place as a house of ill-repute.'

'Mother, it's really about time you came home. You've been in here long enough, don't you think?'

'I think I hurt my hip again while I was out there,' replied Mrs Findlay, putting on an expression of extreme suffering. 'The pain is really terrible.'

She moved about in the bed and fixed Jean with an offended look. 'You'd better tell the nurse to bring me my pain medicine. I'm going to have to stay in bed for a few days, I know that, although I'm sure you'd rather have me at home, suffering the tortures of the damned.'

Mrs Findlay's expression changed and she gazed at Jean slyly. 'By the way,' she said, sitting up in bed, 'have you found who killed that boy yet?'

'That's Doug Niven's job, not mine,' replied Jean smiling. 'I'm just a doctor, remember?'

'Well, you've certainly had long enough to work it out,' replied Mrs Findlay in an accusing tone. 'Not that it isn't as plain as the nose on your face, to any *thinking* person.'

'So who did it, Mother?'

'It's perfectly obvious,' replied Mrs Findlay smugly. 'It was that shifty-eyed boy Jeremy, probably with the assistance of his dad.'

Jean's mouth opened and she stared at her mother. 'Why do you say that? Do you know Jeremy?'

'Of course I know him. He delivered my newspaper

most of last year. Nasty little kid, one of those who never looks you in the eye.'

'But why, Mother? Why do you think he'd do something so evil?'

'Jealousy, envy, revenge, and parental pressure,' replied Mrs Findlay airily. 'Not to mention the fact that boys his age tend to be emotionally unstable and prone to commit acts of violence. Is that enough motive for you? You see, Jean,' she went on in a superior tone, picking up the edge of the top sheet, 'I don't just read the paper, I also read between the lines.'

A few minutes later, Jean got back into her car and headed thankfully towards the surgery, but her mother's words kept coming back to her, and in her mind's eye she saw the angry Ann McIver, big Joe with his history of violence, and their shifty-eyed son Jeremy. As Jean waited for the lights to turn green at South Street, the scene changed and she saw the devastated Sheila and Derek, and hovering somewhere in the background, Duncan Sinclair. All these images started to wend their way through her head, coming together like dark, coloured streams in a torrent.

Jean already felt sure that the underlying reasons for the tragedy were twisted and complex beyond her present understanding. She knew that Doug would pursue all the obvious avenues with his usual care, but Jean had an instinctive feeling that the truth would not be found by routine police investigations alone.

The call came from the hospital a few minutes after Jean arrived at the surgery. Permission had been granted by the Dundee authorities to carry out Bobby Sutherland's post-mortem in Perth, and Dr Anderson would be starting it in about an hour.

Jean sighed unhappily. She hated post-mortems anyway, but autopsies on children particularly distressed her. She couldn't help thinking how she would feel if it were one of her own children lying there on the steel and porcelain slab. But this one she had to attend, she knew that. Since Bobby's death, she had been thinking about the weird way that he'd died, the bag, the air-holes.

Already, Jean was convinced that there was much more to the case than a simple murder. For the last twenty-four hours she had been aware of various vibrations, thoughts, recollections and intimations that floated in and out of her head, often not even reaching a level of consciousness where she could classify or consider them in any kind of logical sequence.

Helen was in her office, struggling with a batch of forms that had to be filled up to satisfy the new budget regulations. She looked up and sighed when Jean came in. 'This stuff is really beginning to get out of hand,' she said, pointing to the stack of papers on her desk. 'So what's up, Jean?'

'Helen, Bobby Sutherland's post is starting up at the hospital in about an hour. Can you cover for me while I'm gone? I don't think it should take more than an hour or so.'

To Jean's astonishment, Helen frowned, and after a moment's hesitation, said, 'No, I'm sorry, Jean. Not this time. And what's more,' she went on, pointing to the forms on her desk, 'I'm sick and tired of doing all the paper work for the practice. Jean, I'm sorry, but I have to tell you, you're not pulling your weight around here, and we're going to have to do something about it.'

Jean's eyes opened wide, and her heart sank right

down into her shoes. 'Oh, Helen,' she said, appalled. 'I'm so sorry. Of course I'll try to do my share of that stuff. It's just that I always thought you liked doing it . . .'

Jean's eyes narrowed combatively when she saw that Helen was grinning all over her face as she stood up and pushed back her chair. 'I've been thinking about that Bobby Sutherland business,' she said. 'I happen to know the Sutherlands pretty well, and for a while there's been something really strange going on in that family. Sheila's going around acting like a schoolgirl and dressing in clothes that, well, you've seen her too, so I don't need to tell you what she's been wearing. Anyway . . .' Helen paused. 'I just wondered if any of that might have had something to do with it.'

'I've no idea,' murmured Jean. 'Maybe you should mention it to Douglas Niven. I haven't joined the C.I.D. and don't have any intention of doing so.'

Helen stared at her, then abruptly turned back to her desk and tapped the papers. 'Jean, I'll make a deal with you.'

'I know about your deals,' said Jean, still feeling defensive. 'The answer is *no*.'

'I'll take care of all this paperwork you find so tiresome,' said Helen, ignoring her. 'All you have to do is sign this on the second-from-the-bottom line, just above where they've typed your name.'

'What's the *quid pro quo?*' asked Jean suspiciously.

'Not much. I just want all the details about the post-mortem when you come back, all right? I don't know why, but I have a strange feeling that something important is going to turn up there.'

'If you're so interested,' said Jean, still a bit off-centred by Helen's mock attack, 'why don't you go and see it yourself?'

'Because I would throw up, as you know perfectly well,' replied Helen. 'Honestly, I don't know how you manage to cope with some of the things you deal with.'

Chapter Twenty-three

Jean parked outside the pathology entrance, next to Dr Anderson's new Ford Escort. On the other side was a black undertaker's van, the unobtrusive, unmarked kind used for transporting corpses from hospitals, morgues, and homes. The driver was leaning against it, smoking a cigarette. He was young, hardly over twenty, but already had the lugubrious expression of an old pro. He watched Jean get out of her car, but looked away when she smiled at him.

Jean pushed the swing doors open, squeezed past the line of empty laundry hampers, and headed down the long grey corridor towards the Pathology Department. It was always dark in this part of the hospital, lit only by a few bare light bulbs hanging from the ceiling and long flat windows high on each wall, so dirty and cobweb-covered that Jean was amazed that any light managed to come through them at all.

Jean tried to remember a name as she walked briskly along. Charon, that was it, the one who ferried the dead across the Styx and the Acheron, the two rivers of death, for the price of one *obolus*. Well, nowadays things were different, she thought, trying to keep her mind off what was to come. The corpses were now shuttled along this long, bleak corridor to Hades, under the protection not of Charon but of the smiling, red-gloved and bloody-aproned Dr Malcolm Anderson. And presumably the fee of one *obolus* was paid by the N.H.S. upon completion of the appropriate forms.

At the end of the corridor, Jean got a sudden panicky urge to turn and run, but she pressed the buzzer above the sign that said AUTHORIZED PERSONNEL ONLY. RING BELL FOR ADMITTANCE. There was a click, and she heard the raspy voice of Brian Thomson, the mortuary assistant.

'Push the door, Doc,' he said after Jean announced herself. She did so, and walked in. The smell of formalin tickled her nose as she went past two tiny offices filled with papers and slides and large sealed bottles containing heaven knew what fascinating human remains floating in a turbid brown solution.

Douglas was there already, talking to Dr Anderson outside the double doors of the autopsy room. The red light above the door was out.

'Well, here's the wee doc,' said Malcolm. He grinned. 'Welcome once again to the End of the Road, quine. If you want an apron and a pair of gloves they're on the rack inside.' He jerked a thumb at the double doors.

'No, I think I'll just watch, Malcolm, if you don't mind,' said Jean firmly.

'We were talking about the stuff those mystery writers are putting out nowadays,' said Malcolm, evidently in no hurry to start. 'I was reading this book, I forget its name, by P.D. James.'

'*Devices and Desires*,' said Douglas.

'Right. Anyway, there's this athletic young woman running naked up the beach, and the next thing she's dead with some pubic hair stuffed in her mouth, knifed by another woman, an older, non-athletic one at that.'

'I read it,' said Jean. 'I thought it was a pretty good story.'

'Ach, quine,' said Malcolm with an irritated movement of his head. 'The woman doesn't know what she's talking about. You just canna kill people that easily. The victims dinna just lie down an' let themselves be killed. It's no' so easy to kill somebody, especially if they're young and healthy. They kick, they scream, they bite and fight for their lives. I tell you, I just canna be bothered reading on when I come across rubbish like that.'

'I'd have thought you'd get enough of that kind of thing right here, without reading mysteries in your spare time,' said Douglas, grinning.

'You're right, I suppose,' said Malcolm, still retrospectively annoyed at Baroness James. 'Maybe I should write my own stories; at least they'd be authentic.' He looked at the clock on the wall. 'All right, that's enough chit-chat. Let's get started.'

Malcolm backed into the white-walled, high-windowed autopsy room, followed by Douglas and Jean, who tried to hide her reluctance with a calm and brisk demeanour. She could never overcome the feeling of awe and sadness that invaded her spirit in this place; it was accentuated and brought into focus by Malcolm Anderson's ever-present and often gruesome sense of humour.

There was a body on each of the three tables. One was a fat middle-aged man with the purplish imprint of a steering wheel in the middle of his chest; the other body was that of a thin old woman. Brian Thomson had been working on her; she was totally eviscerated, her chest and abdomen empty, her white hair splayed over the table round her head like a fan. The dead woman made Jean think, unwillingly, of a wrinkled old pea-pod after the peas had been taken out.

On the third table lay the body of Bobby Sutherland, in a different attitude from the other two corpses. The arms were bent at the elbows, the hands were flexed in front of him, almost to the point of making a fist, and the legs were also bent at the knees. The overall impression was that Bobby had been frozen in a defensive posture.

Malcolm started to dictate his preliminary findings into the voice-activated mike that hung over the table. 'The body is that of a young male,' he droned. He had done this so many times that it sounded like a recording. Malcolm checked the pubic area. 'A few small black hairs are noted growing in the pubic area, but the genitalia are pre-pubertal. Post-mortem flexion is noted in all four limbs . . .'

He glanced up at the clock with a look of slight puzzlement, then moved Bobby's left arm to gauge the stiffness. '. . . although rigor should have dissipated by now.' Malcolm passed his gloved hand over the back of Bobby's head. 'A two-inch star-shaped laceration is noted near the vertex, but no fractures can be felt. There is some generalized facial oedema,' he continued, noting the puffiness around the cheeks and eyelids.

Watching Malcolm, and listening to him, Jean suddenly realized that he was going very cautiously, as if there were certain aspects of this case that he couldn't quite understand. She felt Douglas's gaze, and glanced back. Douglas had noticed too.

After finishing with the external appearances, Malcolm called Brian over. 'Right, Brian,' he said. 'You can start on this one now. We'll be right outside, so call us when you're done.'

'Head?' asked the laconic Brian.

'Yes,' replied Malcolm. 'Just take the lid off, don't take the brain out, all right?'

Brian nodded, and went to work. Jean, determined not to look wimpy, took her time following them out.

In the hall, there was a coffee machine with the jug almost full of coffee. Malcolm, who saw himself as host, offered a cup to Jean, but somehow the thought of eating or drinking in this place of bottled organs and disembowelled former people revolted her. Malcolm and Douglas filled their styrofoam cups, adding a teaspoon of powdered milk substitute. Douglas indulged his sweet tooth and stirred in two heaped teaspoonfuls of sugar, and they talked about the Sutherland case. Jean listened to them, and reflected on the Bobby she had known so slightly, a shy, nice-looking boy with the voice of an angel, a voice that soared up to the stars. But here, everything that Bobby really was had been stripped from him, and he was making the penultimate transition from boy to a barely recognizable collection of items of biological evidence.

The high-pitched whine of the portable circular saw put Jean's teeth on edge, because she knew what it was doing. Brian had already made a cut from behind the ear across the back of the head to the other side, then pulled the scalp forward over Bobby's face to expose the skull. Now he was using the saw to cut through the thickness of the skull, carefully, to avoid damage to the meninges and brain beneath. Then when he had sawn all the way round, he would lever the skull cap off with a steel instrument like a jemmy. The noise stopped, and a few moments later Brian appeared in the doorway.

'Ready,' he said.

They all trooped in again, and Malcolm pulled on the thick red rubber gloves he'd removed before coming through for his coffee.

'Good,' he said approvingly as he observed the fruits of Brian's work. 'That didn't take you very long.'

'Skull was easy,' replied Brian. 'Not brittle like the old ones.'

Malcolm already had his hands inside the body cavity, exploring, checking. 'I really like these young ones,' he said reflectively. 'Everything's so clean. Here,' he turned to Jean, 'look at this aorta; nice elastic walls, no arteriosclerosis, no hardening. I hope mine looks like this.' Malcolm laughed his enthusiastic laugh. He took a big syringe with a long needle and tried to aspirate some blood from the heart, but to his surprise it was all clotted.

'Hmm?' he said, and turned his attention to the liver, stomach, spleen and kidneys. 'Liver is firm,' he said, his mouth close to the mike. He took a scalpel with a huge blade and cut into the liver. 'Unusually firm texture,' he said, then looked closely at the cut red-brown surface. 'A few small haemorrhages are noted around the portal vein tributaries. 'Here, take this piece for microscopy,' he said to Brian, handing him a cube of liver. 'We may have to send a piece to the forensic lab, so cut it and put it into two separate containers.'

Malcolm found similar changes in the lungs, and cut pieces out for further examination, but he was obviously not working with his usual assurance now, and he shook his head in a puzzled way. 'Okay,' he said after examining the other organs, 'let's look at the head.' Malcolm went to the end of the table and Jean and Doug stood one on either side. Jean was relieved that Bobby's face was entirely hidden by the flap of scalp.

'The brain is very firm,' he said, and indeed Jean could see that the brain tissue, normally floppy and pink, was stiff and didn't bulge out over the back edge of the cut skull. Malcolm slid his hands around the frontal lobes and cut the cranial nerves that connected the brain to the eyes and nose. After a few minutes of careful dissection, he severed the connection with the spinal cord and stood there holding the brain in his gloved hands. Then he took it over to the cutting board and sliced off one of the temporal lobes. In spite of her repugnance, Jean watched with rising interest, because she could feel the tension growing in the room, although she had no idea what was going through Malcolm's mind.

There were several small red patches on the cut surface of the brain, and after examining them carefully, Malcolm straightened up, pulled off his gloves and motioned Douglas and Jean to come outside with him.

When the double doors had closed and the three of them were alone, Malcolm turned and faced them. He cleared his throat; his voice was strained, and Jean saw with growing apprehension that his expression was sombre and shocked.

'This is all rather weird,' he said in a voice quite different from his usual cheery brogue. 'I honestly don't know what happened here,' he said. 'These are very strange findings, and I don't remember ever seeing anything like it. It's certainly no' what I'd have expected if he'd been killed by the hit on the head, and there were none of the usual signs of suffocation in the lungs. Bobby Sutherland certainly didn't die from that.'

'What did he die of, then?' Douglas was shocked, too. Malcolm Anderson was widely known as a first-class pathologist, and for him to say he didn't know the cause of death was a very unpleasant surprise, because it was something Douglas needed to know to find the killer. If there was a killer. The thought that had occurred in the church when they first saw the victim came back to him. Maybe, somehow, for some reason, Bobby Sutherland had taken his own life. 'Could it have been the 'flu?' he asked in desperation. 'I know that people can die of that sometimes.'

'No way,' replied Malcolm. 'And in any case, putting the patient into a bag is no' an approved method of treatment, would you say, Dr Montrose?'

Jean shook her head. The whole case was getting more and more confusing.

'Poison?' asked Doug, grasping at straws.

Malcolm shook his head. 'We ran a full toxicology profile,' he said. 'Nothing.'

'Was there any sign of sexual abuse, Malcolm?' asked Jean.

'No. We checked for that, of course, with anal and rectal smears,' replied Malcolm, shaking his head. 'And there were no mucosal tears, no sign of any local injury.'

'What are you going to put in your report as the cause of death, then?' asked Douglas anxiously.

'I'm going to have to leave that part blank,' replied Malcolm, looking slightly shamefaced. 'Maybe the lads in Dundee will be able to come up with something. I certainly hope so.'

Chapter Twenty-four

While Bobby's post mortem was still under way, Duncan Sinclair was seated on a hard chair facing the desk in his study. Opposite him, comfortably installed behind Duncan's desk, sat the Reverend Edmund Glasgow, sent to Perth from the Church's central office in Edinburgh. Duncan knew that it was important to pay attention to the Reverend, because his career depended on him, but he couldn't prevent his mind flying off in different directions all the time.

'I read in the paper that there has been a tragedy involving one of your parishioners,' Glasgow was saying. He was short, with pomaded black hair, smooth-faced, his dark clerical garb tight about his middle, rimless glasses flickering with a benign smile that rarely varied, regardless of the topic of conversation. 'I took the liberty of making some further enquiries on behalf of the Church,' he went on.

Glasgow was holding a pencil delicately between thumb and middle finger, then dropping it, rubber end down, on his thigh, just above the knee, repeating the process with maddening regularity. It was beginning to have a hypnotic effect on Duncan.

'A most tragic situation,' continued Glasgow, 'And

with even more serious implications for the Church itself, as I'm sure you'd be the first to agree.'

Duncan could not tell from Glasgow's face, let alone from his prim Edinburgh accent, whether he was being serious or indulging in some kind of macabre ecclesiastical joke. So Duncan said nothing, and that seemed to please the visiting cleric perfectly well. As Duncan knew from past experience, Glasgow was quite capable of keeping up a lengthy monologue apparently without feeling the least boredom.

'As you may remember, Duncan, the first time I came here, you were worried that you might be losing your faith.' Glasgow placed the pencil between his knees and held it there while he placed the palms of his hands together. It was as if he were interposing some kind of quarantine area between them, between Duncan the unbeliever and himself, the dedicated man of God.

Duncan nodded, regretting again that he'd ever mentioned the matter to this inquisitor, but at the time he had been in the deepest despair, and was looking for help in the most obvious place, his own Church. At the time, of course, he didn't know the Reverend Glasgow, M.A., D.D., and was completely taken in by Glasgow's pressing offer of help. He had sounded so genuine, and Duncan had been in such mental pain for so long.

Glasgow picked up the pencil and started to drop it on his thigh again. He was still smiling, and the light glittered on the edges of his rimless glasses. 'I am glad to be able to tell you that the fuss over the sad business you were involved in at your last parish appears to have died away.'

'I wasn't involved in it,' said Duncan quietly. 'It was an invention on the part of an evil child.'

'Of course. What I meant was that there appears to be no more gossip about it now. We spoke to a considerable number of your former parishioners and many of them were quite astonished such an accusation had ever been made.'

Duncan winced.

'Now,' said Glasgow, his smile undiminished, 'would you be so kind as to tell me a little about what's been going on here in Perth?'

Duncan gave him a quick rundown on what had happened, his interview with the police, and the fact that as far as he knew, there were no suspects.

When he had finished, Glasgow reached into an inner pocket and came out with an envelope which he handed to Duncan.

'Please read it,' said Glasgow.

With a vague feeling of dread in the pit of his stomach, Duncan looked at the envelope. It was addressed to the Central Office of the Church at its official address in Edinburgh. The letter was postmarked in Perth, and although Duncan thought he recognized the handwriting, he couldn't think whose it was.

'Go ahead,' said Glasgow. He didn't take his eyes off Duncan, and his pencil kept making a soft tap, tap, tapping sound on his thigh.

Duncan pulled the letter from the envelope.

'"Dear Sir,"' he read. '"I think you should be aware of some of the facts surrounding the death of a twelve-year-old boy, Bobby Sutherland, who was murdered early this morning."' Duncan felt as if the world was caving in around him, and Glasgow's smiling face rotated at the centre of his field of vision. Duncan had glanced at the bottom of the letter and seen the signature.

'Go on,' said Glasgow. His eyes were glittering now. Duncan started to read again, more slowly. '"I regret to have to tell you that an illegal, immoral and indecent relationship existed between Bobby Sutherland and . . ."' Duncan stopped reading, and his hand started to shake to the point where he had to put the letter down on the table in front of them.

'Please continue,' said Glasgow, still watching Duncan with satisfaction. His palms were now together again, separating him, the child of God, from Duncan Sinclair, that unspeakably foul infidel. But Glasgow was here to help Duncan in his time of misery, so his smile didn't fade for a second.

Duncan sat up very straight, and some strength came to him from nowhere. His voice was clear, as if he were reading out his own death sentence from his pulpit. He even re-read part of the letter. '"An illegal, immoral and indecent relationship existed between Bobby Sutherland and the Reverend Duncan Sinclair, minister of the West Kirk where the murder was committed.

'"I am prepared to back up these accusations, and will be happy to meet you or your representative to discuss this matter at your convenience. Signed, Ian Farquar."'

'Yes,' said Glasgow, putting the pencil down flat on the table. 'Indeed. An interesting document, don't you think?'

'It's a damnable lie,' said Duncan hotly. 'And as nothing of the sort ever happened, I'll be most interested to hear what proof Mr Farquar has.'

'Nothing of what sort?' asked Glasgow, silkily.

'That Bobby and I . . .' Duncan stopped, like a stag at bay, exhausted but still defiant. 'I have nothing more to say,' he said finally, and put his head down between his hands.

'As you might expect, Reverend Sinclair,' said Glasgow in his silkiest voice, 'the Church is extremely distressed by this matter,' said Glasgow. 'Especially as it redounds to the discredit of the entire Church.'

'Can you help me?' asked Duncan, his eyes staring. 'Can I talk to the Church's lawyer?'

'Of course we'll help you,' said Glasgow encouragingly. 'In every way we possibly can. But you must understand that this is a criminal matter, and the assistance we so willingly give has to be limited to religious and doctrinal issues.' He smiled at Duncan's face, which was now twitching uncontrollably with a growing panic. 'I think the best thing we can do now, is for the two of us to pray together to the Lord for his forgiveness and help.'

Duncan closed his eyes and tried to pray, but even in his fear and panic, he felt like the ancient mariner who was unable to pray after killing the albatross, *because a wicked whisper came, and made his heart as dry as dust.*

When he opened his eyes, Glasgow was staring at him. 'I hope that God almighty will show his mercy to you,' he said. He got up, and his plump hands straightened his waistcoat in an oddly final gesture. Without another word, he walked to the door, and Duncan heard his footsteps get fainter as he went down the stairs.

With a feeling of total despair, not knowing where to turn for help, Duncan looked up at the wall, where from his narrow wooden frame, his old confidant Jos. McArthur looked back at him today with a slightly awkward, reproachful expression. Unable to take his eyes off the old sepia portrait, after several minutes Duncan fancied that Jos.'s lip curled ever so slightly in a smile so full of contempt that Duncan got up and stumbled out of the study and back up to his bedroom where he fell face down on the bed, feeling that he had nowhere to hide.

Chapter Twenty-five

Douglas was opening his post when the phone rang, and the clipped, precise voice at the other end announced himself as the Reverend Edmund Glasgow, speaking from the Central Office of the Church. After ascertaining that Douglas was indeed in charge of the Sutherland case, Glasgow took a big breath.

'Inspector, in this morning's post, you should have found a copy of a letter we received yesterday,' he said. Feeling pretty sure that the man was overestimating the efficiency of the Post Office, Douglas spread out the remaining unopened envelopes on his desk. Sure enough, there was a long envelope with the embossed stamp of the Church in the upper left hand corner.

'Yes. I have it,' he said. 'Hold on.' He opened it with one hand and read the Xerox copy while Glasgow talked.

'The Reverend Duncan Sinclair has been with our Church for seven years,' said Glasgow in his clipped, unctuous voice. 'As we are dealing with a criminal situation, we have felt obliged to inform you about some additional problems Sinclair encountered in his previous ministry . . .'

While he spoke, Douglas pulled a pad across the desk

and started to scribble on it. Then, after Glasgow hung up, Douglas took a deep breath, sat back and reread the letter. This was a serious accusation, and fitted with what Ian Farquar had hinted at when he'd been interviewed at home, but Douglas was curious about why he'd written to the Church authorities rather than tell him and Jamieson when he had the opportunity to do so. He didn't wonder very long, because that kind of thing happened all the time; most people simply did not like to give information to the police.

An hour later, he and Jamieson were back at the Farquars' home, and this time Beth opened the door. Beth was a slender woman, insubstantial, as if a breath of wind would blow her away. Douglas knew her by sight, from church and occasionally seeing her around town. She always had a scared, bewildered look as she flitted around the shops. Nobody knew much about her, not even Cathie. Now, her eyes were big with fear as she faced Douglas and the figure of Constable Jamieson, who loomed even larger next to her.

Ian appeared behind her, and Beth disappeared into a back room.

'You said in your letter that you were prepared to back up your statement, Mr Farquar,' said Douglas after they were settled in the front room and he'd explained the reason for his visit.

'Well, this is a church matter,' said Ian in his cold, dour way. He stared dispassionately at the two men from under his stubborn, contracted eyebrows. 'I wanted to prevent any further risks to the morals of the parish.'

'Actually, this is a *police* matter, as I'm sure you're well aware,' said Douglas sternly. 'I must remind you that a murder has been committed.'

Ian hesitated, and his small, dark eyes seemed to harden.

'I've already told you everything I know,' said Ian. 'And from what I know about you people and your methods, nothing'll ever come of it, and you or your bosses will hush up the whole matter. That's why I told the Church authorities. Those people, over at the Church headquarters, they understand.' There was disgust in his voice. 'I suppose it's because they have to deal with that kind of thing all the time.'

'Well, I'm sure you understand why we have to follow your letter up.' Doug's voice was curt. 'To go back to that evening, do you remember exactly what the Reverend replied when Bobby told him he was going to tell his parents?'

'I dinna know. I went back into the church. I'm no a listener at doors.'

Douglas sighed. 'Do you have anything more concrete than that, Mr Farquar? You said that you could back up your statement, but in a court of law, what you said would just be hearsay evidence.'

Ian stood up. 'I know that, Inspector, but what I said is right all the same. That man . . .' Ian seemed to swell up with an internal fury. 'That man's been *buggering* boys . . .' Ian spat the word out as if he'd had a piece of excrement in his mouth. 'There's no place for him in this church, in this town, or anywhere else.'

Doug snapped the elastic on his notebook, and he and Jamieson stood up. 'Oh, by the bye, Mr Farquar,' said Doug, as if he'd just thought of it, 'I understand you give singing lessons to Jeremy McIver?'

Ian glowered at Doug. 'So, what of it?'

'I suppose that *now* he has a very good chance at the Scottish Youth Choir, wouldn't you say? He'd be your star pupil, and it would all be pretty good for business, wouldn't it?'

Ian's face went an ugly, dark red colour and a vein stood out on his neck. 'If you have no more questions,' he said between his teeth, 'I'd be obliged if you'd both get yourselves out of my house.'

'We're on our way,' said Doug calmly. 'But that and the fact that you were the last person with Bobby Sutherland begins to add up, doesn't it?'

The door slammed hard behind them as Doug and Jamieson walked back to the car.

'What a nasty wee man,' said Jamieson, fastening his seat belt.

'People were no' put on this earth to meet your standards, Jamieson,' replied Douglas sternly. 'And we canna let our personal feelings interfere with the way we deal with a case.'

Jamieson didn't let the rebuke interrupt his train of thought.

'Do you really think he could have done it?' he asked.

'For God's sake, Jamieson, I don't know,' replied Douglas, irritated. 'Right now there are far too many people who *could* have done it, and too many who also had some kind of reason to.'

Douglas pulled away from the kerb and Jamieson said nothing until they stopped at the lights before the old bridge. 'Did you ever read that story, *Murder on the Orient Express*?' he asked Doug, who shook his head. 'It's an Agatha Christie,' went on Jamieson, pleased. 'There's a man with lots of enemies who gets stabbed to death on this train, and it turns out that all his enemies are on the train too, and each of them sticks a knife in him once so nobody knows who actually killed him.'

The lights changed, and Doug eased the car forward. 'So?' he asked.

'It was just a thought,' replied Jamieson. 'Are we going back to see the Reverend now?'

Doug considered that for a minute. 'No, I don't think so,' he said. 'We need a bit more background on that gentleman.'

Back in his office, Douglas took a piece of typed paper from his desk drawer and handed it to Jamieson. 'This is a list of phone numbers, kindly supplied by the Reverend Edmund Glasgow,' he told him. 'They're mostly people who knew Sinclair at his last ministry. Talk to them, find out if there's any truth to that story.'

Jamieson hesitated, his eyes searching Doug's for clues.

'The story about Sinclair and some young boy in his last parish,' said Douglas patiently. 'What I'm saying is, find out if there was any truth to it.'

Duncan jumped when the phone rang. He was getting worse, he knew it. All the warning signs were there, the insomnia, the shakiness, the feeling that everybody was talking in a derogatory way about him behind his back, and, worst of all, he now knew for sure that there was no God to help and succour him. Even his only real friend, Jos. McFarland, had his limitations as a confidant; as an adviser, he was no help at all.

It was Denise Harmon on the phone. Denise was Lois Munday's next-door neighbour and a regular churchgoer. Lois was sick, probably with the 'flu, she told him, and wouldn't be in, probably until next week. Duncan, in his hypersensitive state, thought he detected a censorious tone in Denise's voice, but as the conversation was brief he couldn't be sure.

'Tell her I'll be over to see her,' said Duncan. It was the least he could do for his most devoted helper, and he was curious to find out why she'd come over to the manse on Monday only to hurry away when he appeared. 'It probably won't be until later this afternoon, but I'll try to come sooner. Has she called the doctor?'

'Yes, she has,' replied Denise. Her voice was definitely curt, Duncan was certain of it now, and his brows furrowed, wondering what was the matter. 'And,' Denise went on, 'I don't think she wants to have any visitors for a while.'

'Well, I'm hardly a visitor, am I?' said Duncan, smiling at the telephone. There was a brief silence, then Denise said, 'She just wanted me to tell you she was sick, Reverend, that's all.' There was a click, and the phone was dead.

Every day that passed added to the ever-increasing weight of sadness and guilt that Duncan carried around with him; everybody he spoke to, everything that happened was inevitably transmuted into the burden of leaden misery that was already heavy enough to make him totter. Duncan was dimly aware that this could not go on, that he was getting close to breaking point, but at this point, there didn't seem to be anything he could do to break the cycle.

Lois Munday didn't live far away, and in his agitation Duncan decided to walk over now. First he went into his small garden and picked a little bunch of pansies, added some green leaves to make the bouquet more substantial, then wrapped it in some cellophane before setting off up the road, holding it in his hand.

He waited for a long time after ringing the doorbell, then Duncan heard the shuffle of slippers, and the door opened.

Lois was looking bleary-eyed, her usually neat hair sticking up all over, and her pale face went blotchy red when she saw him.

'Oh, Reverend,' she said, embarrassed. She hesitated in the doorway. 'Really, there was no need.' She crossed her arms in front of her. 'You'd better come in, I suppose.'

Duncan stared at her in astonishment. It was the most ungracious invitation, and totally unlike Lois's usual adoring manner.

He came in and held out the bouquet to her. 'Here are a few flowers to help your recovery,' he said, smiling, trying to regain whatever it was that he seemed to have lost with Lois.

'Oh, thanks, but . . .' Lois eyed the little bouquet. 'I'm actually allergic to . . . to pansies,' she said, stammering, and looking at the floor. 'I'm sorry, Reverend.'

'Oh, *I'm* sorry,' said Duncan, nonplussed. Lois had never mentioned allergies to him before. 'In that case, I'd better take them back with me.' He looked at her questioningly, and Lois pulled her nightgown more closely around her. 'How are you feeling?' he asked, truly concerned about her. 'Lois, is there anything I can bring you?'

'I'm fine,' replied Lois, trying to speak firmly through her stuffed-up nose. 'Dr Montrose said I was to get lots of rest and sleep.' She moved her feet uncomfortably but didn't invite Duncan beyond the front hall.

'Well, in that case . . .' Duncan still wore his smile, but it was frayed around the edges, and, if Lois had been looking, she might have seen signs of the desperation spreading like a malignant growth behind it.

'Thank you for coming,' said Lois, her hand on the doorknob. Now she was looking at Duncan again, but with a strange expression, as if she were really afraid of him.

'My pleasure,' replied Duncan mechanically. The lead in his heart was absorbing another incremental load, and he could hardly stand it.

After Duncan had stepped outside, Lois said, without looking directly at him, 'I won't be coming back, Reverend Sinclair. I'm sure you understand why.'

The door closed firmly in his face, and Duncan, staring at the door, had to force himself to walk out and down the street, and not crumple right there on the steps and break down completely. He held on to the small now-poisoned bouquet for a few yards, then with a jerky, hopeless movement, threw it into a rubbish bin at the corner of the street.

Chapter Twenty-six

Malcolm Anderson looked through the reports that had come in with the mail, then picked up the phone to call Jean. 'Well, quine,' he said, all the old joviality back in his voice, 'I got the blood chemistries and the histology back on Bobby Sutherland. They sent the duplicate slides back with the report. Do you want to come over and take a look at them under the microscope?'

Jean thought quickly. She had to go up to the hospital anyway to see Jackie Marshall, who had developed a post-operative partial collapse of one lung and was feeling very unhappy.

'Yes I would,' she answered. 'Can I stop by this afternoon, maybe about four?'

'That's fine, Jean,' he replied, 'but don't come any later than four, if you don't mind. I have a golf game at five.'

Jean put the phone down and went through to the office. Eleanor was just putting her phone down; Jean quickly checked to see which button was lit. Eleanor had not been eavesdropping, which she occasionally did, but had been on the other line. Before Jean had time to feel guilty about her unfounded suspicions, she glanced at Eleanor's face, and could see that she hadn't been talking business. There was an expression of suppressed excitement, a mixture of elation and disgust that showed only too clearly in her eyes.

'It's terrible about the Reverend, isn't it?' she said. Eleanor had never been able to keep her information to herself.

Jean stopped with her hand reaching for the phone directory. 'What's terrible?' she asked, a sudden fear coming over her. 'What's happened to him?'

'Well,' said Eleanor, 'listen to this.' She leaned forward and spoke in a tone of smug confidentiality which nauseated Jean. 'Apparently he's been doing filthy things with some of the boys in the church choir, and that Bobby . . .'

'Just stop right there, Eleanor,' said Jean sternly. 'Unless you have proof of such a thing, that's just vile gossip. And please, don't repeat any of it outside the surgery, all right?'

Eleanor went red and started to mumble something when Helen opened the door of her office and put her head out. She was looking very serious.

'Jean, do you have a second?' she asked, and Jean went in and Helen closed the door.

'I've been hearing the rumours,' said Helen, sitting down at her huge desk and pointing at the telephone. 'Do you think there's anything to them?'

'You mean about Duncan Sinclair?'

Helen nodded.

'I don't know anything at all,' said Jean, feeling very uncomfortable. 'The first I heard was just this minute from Eleanor. I must say I'm surprised you heard them before she did.'

'Apparently one of the boys in the choir told his parents that Duncan had . . . I don't know what the technical term is, propositioned him, I suppose. Anyway the parents told the police, and according to my sources they've been interviewing the boy.'

Jean was shaking her head. 'Oh dear,' she said. 'Do you know which boy it is?'

'Jeremy McIver, I believe. It's such a sordid business, but if you believe what you read, there's an awful lot of that kind of thing happening these days, although I must say I would never have suspected him.'

Jean frowned, upset by being thrust again into the evils that civilized life covered with such a thin veneer. And this was not a development she had expected, although she had no evidence either way, and not even enough information to make an educated guess. But it was a question she had given some thought to, and it did fit in to the larger picture, perhaps, when she thought about it.

Derek Sutherland sat by his anaesthesia machine. Somewhere in his mind, in a distant region of his auditory cortex, he heard the regular soft sighing of the ventilator. The other parameters of the case, the amount of succinylcholine he'd given to relax the patient's muscles at the beginning of the case, the concentrations of halothane and oxygen in the gases being pumped into her lungs, the blood pressure, heart rate, and body temperature all were being monitored, more or less, in some other, equally remote place in his brain.

His mind was mainly concentrating on the conversation he'd overheard in the changing room. He'd been in the adjoining dictating area, and when he came through, they'd stopped talking abruptly, but he'd heard enough. Duncan Sinclair, the Reverend Duncan Sinclair, that holy man of God, had been having homosexual relations with certain members of the church choir, and all of a sudden everything fell into place in Derek's overwrought mind.

'She's bucking a bit.' Derek heard Peter MacIntosh's voice through the fog generated by his own thoughts.

'All right, Peter. I'll take care of it.'

Derek injected a little more relaxant, so that even if the patient was awake enough to feel the pain, the muscles would be paralysed and the surgeon could go on operating without interruption.

'Give her about a minute,' said Derek, looking at the clock, then he went back to his thoughts. For some reason that possibility had never occurred to him, although now it seemed such an obvious risk, having a middle-aged single man working with a choir where there were both adults and boys. A vision of Duncan in his ecclesiastical gown welled up in front of him, and Derek gritted his teeth. An involuntary exclamation escaped him.

Peter MacIntosh and Mary Kelso, the theatre sister who happened to be working with him, exchanged a worried glance.

'Everything all right, Derek?' asked Peter after a pause. Derek glanced back at him and nodded, but the expression in his bloodshot eyes was frightening, and it startled Peter.

But from that moment on, the case went smoothly, and afterwards in the recovery room when Peter went to see the patient, he noticed that Derek was staring fixedly at a small bowl of roses on the nurses' table. What Peter didn't see was that to Derek, the flowers seemed to come to life in front of him, to glow, to become bright, almost incandescent. The roses were all clustered together, some crimson, others so dark they were almost black, with startling yellow centres and lighter streaks in the line of the soft, wide, God-loved petals. Derek stared, hypnotized, at the waxy, shiny green leaves as they insinuated themselves so intimately between the flowers. Caught in a waking trance, Derek dimly understood that there had to be a cosmic significance to these multicoloured roses, and that somewhere, like him, they had their place in the ultimate fabric of time.

It was during this weird and otherworldly time that Derek came to a conclusion. In his misery, Derek knew that he had to do something, otherwise he would go mad. Now he had a goal, or rather a target, and had spent the latter part of the operation deciding what he would do, and how he would do it. He didn't care a jot for risk or retribution; he was beyond caring about such things.

The pathology lab was on the first floor of the hospital, directly above the mortuary and connected to it by steps and a kind of dumb waiter that was mainly used for sending specimens upstairs for X-ray or microscopic examination. It was clean and airy, with big windows, and had none of the dungeonesque qualities that pervaded the floor below.

Jean walked in, greeting the white-coated laboratory assistants, and went over to the long laboratory table where Malcolm Anderson and Douglas Niven were sitting. Douglas looked up from the beige folder he was reading from and nodded pleasantly to her. Malcolm was adjusting the stage on a powerful binocular Zeiss microscope.

'Aye, quine,' he said, without looking up. 'One of the things I like about you is that you're always on time.'

Jean sat down on the chair on the opposite side of the table so that she could look through the second eyepiece.

'The first one's a slice of brain,' said Malcolm, waving the slide in the air and speaking as if he were discussing a particularly fine item on a menu. 'It's from the hypothalamus. Did you know that area has a very dense blood supply?'

Jean said nothing. She knew that Malcolm wasn't expecting an answer.

'A' right . . .' Malcolm put the slide on the stage and focussed the low-power eyepiece. 'Here we are . . . Now . . .' he turned the knob that controlled a small illuminated arrow. 'Here, you see the blood vessels? The ones with the thicker walls are the arteries. Well, look at the veins right next to them, here . . . and here . . . you can see the blood's clotted inside them – see the strands of fibrin, and the clumping of red cells?'

Jean could see what he was showing her, but she could not independently have interpreted what she saw.

Then he showed her the swollen brain tissue cells, and the damage they had undergone. 'All that happened before death,' he said. 'Not long, mind you, but long enough to get some early tissue reaction, infiltration of macrophages outside the blood vessels, that sort of thing.'

After showing Jean slides of the liver, where similar changes had occurred, Malcolm rolled his chair back from the microscope table and picked up the beige folder that Douglas had put down in front of him. It had Bobby Sutherland's name on it.

'The blood chemistries were very interesting too,' he said, flipping through the loose pages. 'He had well above the normal amount of lactic acid in his blood, and a blood pH of 6.1, which is so acid that he could have died from that alone.'

Jean could see that Malcolm was quite prepared to discuss the laboratory values until he was due to leave for his golf game without having told her what it all added up to.

'Malcolm,' she said, 'what does all this mean? Does it tell us what Bobby died of?'

'Aye, fairly,' said Malcolm, leaning back and looking very solemn. 'All the tests support the same diagnosis.' He turned over a few sheets of paper and stopped when he got to the official report from the pathologist in the central laboratories in Dundee. He pulled the sheet then passed it over to Jean.

'. . . Changes are consistent with acute heat stroke,' she read. Jean's head reeled, and she put the paper down on the desk.

'Oh, my goodness, Malcolm,' she said. 'Surely that's not right. How could he possibly have developed heat stroke?'

'Aye,' said Malcolm, 'that's right enough. I talked to the head of the department in Dundee, and the two of us worked it out.'

Malcolm stood up and walked over to the window. Douglas looked at Jean and shrugged. It was all getting a bit beyond him. Outside, the wind was blowing hard across the car park, and the leaves of the young trees that lined it were fluttering bravely. To Malcolm's golf-oriented imagination, the leaves looked like tiny green flags on top of the pins, all pointing in the same direction. He turned back to face Jean and Doug.

'This is how we pieced it all together,' he said. 'First, the boy was knocked out by a blow to his head. It was a light blow, certainly not severe enough to have killed him, not by any means. Then he was put into that bag of shiny reflective plastic material; the Dundee people did some checking, and found that it was a sleeping bag, the kind they use in survival kits to preserve body temperature and prevent people from freezing to death. It's made of mylar, strong enough so that he couldn't kick his way out even if he did wake up. The surface is specially designed to reflect heat back into the body.'

With a growing horror, Jean was beginning to understand the implications of what he was saying.

'Being unconscious, the boy's temperature-regulating reflexes were gone,' Malcolm went on. 'He was still alive, and could breathe through the air holes, but there was no way he could lose heat, so his body temperature went up and up, and of course that increased his rate of metabolism, and so his body produced more heat.'

'Oh my God,' said Jean.

'So Bobby Sutherland died of a heat stroke,' finished Malcolm, picking up a pencil and tapping it on the folder. 'The poor kid was cooked to death inside that bag by his own body heat.'

Jean felt her stomach contracting. 'Doug, do you know yet who did this?'

Douglas shook his head. 'There are still a lot of possibilities,' he said cautiously. 'But now they do seem to be pointing in one direction.'

Jean recognized the signs; the closer Doug got to making an arrest, the more reticent he became.

Chapter Twenty-seven

Duncan hurried back to his manse, neither seeing nor hearing the traffic noises, the horns, even the sound of a road drill crackling in the middle of the street. He couldn't get Lois's expression out of his mind, and a scream was starting somewhere inside him, an eerie, outlandish, silent sound that he could feel spreading through him until it had invaded every part of him.

Duncan didn't notice the car outside the manse, but when he came in, he found the ever-smiling Reverend Edmund Glasgow installed upstairs behind the desk, with Jos. McFarland looking down at him from the wall with an expression of gentle surprise.

'Come in, come in,' said Glasgow, apparently not at all abashed by having pre-empted Duncan's place. He closed the magazine he had been reading and waved a pudgy hand at Duncan. 'Pull up a seat, do. The church authorities have asked me to come and talk to you again.'

Feeling numb and ill, but grateful to both the Church and Glasgow because they were paying attention to him, Duncan obediently pulled a chair up to the desk.

'Thank you,' he said simply.

Glasgow, watching Duncan through his rimless glasses, pressed the palms of his hands together, more as if he were stretching the muscles than as if in prayer. He didn't waste any time with preliminaries.

'We are all most concerned about your ministry here,' he said, 'and also on the larger effect it is having on the *corpus* of the Church.'

Duncan smiled and nodded. He was walking through a wide field of flowers, and the air was warm.

'You have previously approached me about your loss of faith, and for these last several months, it has been my privilege, as a fellow worker in the vineyards of the Lord, to help achieve your spiritual recovery.'

Glasgow went on talking, but although Duncan could clearly hear his smooth, glossy, unctuous voice, and recognized it instinctively as the voice of a preacher to rich men, the words seemed to be in some foreign language and Duncan could make no sense out of them.

The sun was high, and Duncan's bare skin felt to him like warm velvet. The smell of crushed grass followed his footsteps, and the bees sang high in the lambent sky.

Glasgow's eyes narrowed, and the smile vanished momentarily as he watched Duncan's eyes travel heavenwards, then turn back to him with the most gentle of expressions. There was no anger, no resentment, Glasgow noted, and for some reason that caused him a brief flash of annoyance. He would have expected at least a little fear to have followed his words, but Duncan's look held only a beatific, childlike wonder.

Glasgow's voice hardened fractionally. 'But these prayerful and dedicated attempts by me have not, I fear, met with success. In fact . . .' Glasgow thumped his hand on the blotter, 'they have *failed*, and failed miserably.' He stood up, a picture of sorrowful anger, a man who had given of his best, who had struggled valiantly against the powers of evil, but who had finally been forced to acknowledge defeat, although nothing would ever crush his spirit.

Duncan smiled, a far-seeing, open smile. The poppy-scattered landscape was opening up ahead of him. The air was sweet and pure, and the breezes curled and fluttered around his body. He ran, in this glorious place, and his feet made no sound.

Glasgow sat down, frowning, but his gaze remained on Duncan, whose reaction to what he surely knew was coming seemed woefully inappropriate. The last minister he had had to deal with in this way had actually attacked him, and strangely, Glasgow had experienced a fierce joy in that.

'Do you have anything to say, any comments at this stage?' he asked. In a way, this was the part he liked the best; at this moment, Glasgow was the Lord's executioner, and was raising his axe. After a long pause, Duncan shook his head, but Glasgow was not convinced that his victim had understood, and repeated his question.

'No,' replied Duncan, smiling gratefully. Already, he knew that his burden was gone. 'But I would like to thank you for all the help you have given me.'

'Yes, of course.' Glasgow's palms were pressed back together, and he sat up very straight in Duncan's chair. 'Within a few days, you will be receiving an official, registered letter from the Central Office which will formalize and confirm the action I, as duly accredited and confirmed representative of the Church of Christ Almighty, am about to undertake. Now . . .'

The Reverend Edmund Glasgow gathered himself

and stood up. At this point, he allowed a long pause, as befitted the dignity of the occasion, and mentally placed the black cap on his head. 'Duncan Sinclair,' he intoned, 'by order and authority of the Holy Church, your ministry here is hereby terminated. Henceforth you will no longer be a part of the living Church, nor be permitted to officiate or participate in its sacrament.' Glasgow raised his right hand in solemn benediction. 'And now may the grace and forgiveness of the Father, the Son, and the Holy Ghost be upon you.'

Glasgow surveyed Duncan in silence for a moment, then in a different, more business-like voice, said, 'Your stipend will be paid until the end of the month, but I'm afraid you'll have to leave the manse by the end of next week as we shall need to get it ready for your successor.'

A thought struck the Reverend Glasgow, and he took his glasses off and polished them with a spotless white handkerchief. 'The last incumbent left the place in an untidy, not to say unhygienic condition,' he said, 'and it cost the church a substantial sum to clean it up. We trust that there will be no such problem with your departure.' Glasgow's smile was frank; he knew from long experience that it was always better to be open about such matters, and before rather than after the fact.

'I should like permission to conduct one last service this coming Sunday,' asked Duncan humbly.

Glasgow pursed his lips and considered. As a matter of fact, he didn't have anyone else to call on at such short notice, and it hadn't occurred to him that someone would have to take the service at the West Kirk.

'Do I have your undertaking that you will conduct the service in the usual way?'

'Of course,' said Duncan, smiling.

'Then you have my permission,' said Glasgow, reluctantly. He stood up. 'Now I bid you a good morning,' he said, 'and trust that we are left with no permanent ill-feelings over this matter.' He came round the desk, and held out his fat little hand, pulling it away as soon as Duncan touched him then walked briskly from the room.

Duncan followed him with his eyes, smiling, loving his executioner, then after the Reverend Glasgow had gone downstairs and the door had closed behind him, Duncan's glance went up to Jos. McFarland, who was looking down at him from his dark, thin frame, his gentle, almost apologetic expression restored.

Duncan stood up, and with a feeling of overwhelming joy and thankfulness, went over to the glass-covered portrait and kissed Jos. on the lips.

The phone went in the Montroses' hall just as Jean came in, and she picked it up.

'Oh, hello, Larry,' she said, surprised. 'Hold on, I'll go and see if she's in.'

Lisbie was in the morning room watching television, and wearing only a towel wrapped round her.

'For heaven's sake, Lisbie, you shouldn't be walking around the house like that,' she said in as scolding a voice as she could muster against her pretty daughter. 'That's Larry French on the phone, and he wants to speak to you.'

Lisbie let out a shriek of delight that Larry must have heard, and ran to the phone, her towel slipping off unheeded as she went.

'My goodness,' said Jean, coming behind her and really cross this time. She bent down and picked up the crumpled towel and hurriedly wrapped it around Lisbie. She found a big safety pin in the drawer of the hall table, and pinned the towel securely round the back. 'It's just as well for you that your father isn't home,' she said in an annoyed whisper. Lisbie looked around, beaming, and gave her mother a big wink.

'Larry's asked me out tonight,' she told her mother a few moments later, after hanging up the phone. Lisbie was hopping up and down with delight, putting the safety pin's continued effectiveness in serious jeopardy. 'He's going to take me to the Tower Hotel for dinner. Isn't that wonderful?'

'Yes, dear.' In spite of herself, Jean smiled at Lisbie's bright-eyed enthusiasm. 'Now you get yourself upstairs and get dressed before your father comes home. You know he doesn't like to see you or Fiona roaming around the house like that.'

Lisbie laughed, gave her mother a kiss and ran upstairs.

The Montroses were just sitting down to dinner when the doorbell rang, and Lisbie, decked out in a pretty white summery cotton dress with a gay yellow and blue pattern, went to the door, nearly tripping over her high heels, which caused Fiona to choke with amusement.

It was an unfortunate coincidence that Sheila Sutherland had stopped at the same traffic lights, waiting to cross the bridge, when Larry's car drove up. She saw it in her rear-view mirror, and was about to sound her horn to attract his attention, when she saw that Lisbie was sitting very close to Larry, and they were laughing together. Then, to Sheila's utter disbelief, she saw Larry lean over and give Lisbie a quick, affectionate kiss before the lights changed and he drove on, turning right across the old bridge.

Sheila was left at the lights, and only the insistent honking from the cars behind her made her get into gear and drive on. Then she found she had bitten her lip so hard it was bleeding into her mouth.

Chapter Twenty-eight

The next day, at lunch time, Jean went up to the hospital. There were two things she needed to do; one was to visit her patient Jackie Marshall, and the other was to talk to her friend Peter MacIntosh.

Jackie was lying on her bed, flat on her stomach, and making a noise halfway between a cough and a groan. A muscular young therapist was pounding on her upper back. Jean came up to the bed.

'Hullo, Dr Montrose,' said the therapist, and Jackie tried to look round but the therapist wouldn't let her. 'We'll be done in half an hour,' said the young man, smiling but firm, 'if you don't mind coming back then.'

Jean went off, thinking how different things were when she had been a resident. However, the delay gave her an opportunity to go and see Peter, who was one of her favourite consultants. He had trained in Aberdeen, as she had, and they had known each other for years. She found him alone having coffee in the doctors' lounge, and she accepted his offer of a cup and sat down gratefully in one of the tomato-coloured moulded plastic chairs. Jean still hadn't fully recovered from her 'flu, and felt tired all the time, although no one would have guessed.

'I just saw Jackie Marshall,' she said. 'How is she doing?'

'Fine,' replied Peter. 'She should be going home in a couple of days.'

'Good. I had Bob on the phone yesterday. He sounded so harassed with the two children, he'll be glad to have her back.'

'It's a funny thing,' said Peter, smiling. 'There's nothing like a little surgery to make husbands appreciate their wives. If you want, I could arrange a wee hysterectomy or something like that for you.'

'I don't need anything of the sort,' retorted Jean. 'Steven already appreciates me as much as I can stand.'

'So what can I do for you, Jean?' Peter took a sip of coffee, made a face, and dropped the styrofoam cup in the waste basket.

'This may sound a bit strange, Peter, but I'd like to hear your thoughts about Derek Sutherland.' Peter looked astonished, so Jean went on. 'You remember when you were operating on Jackie? That was the day Derek's son was killed.'

'I certainly do.' Peter shook his head. 'You know, Jean, I have a lot of sympathy for him. Losing his son was a dreadful thing to happen, but professionally he makes me very nervous, and on that day he was worse than usual, as you saw. Natural enough, I suppose, considering.'

'I certainly got that impression in the theatre. Peter, did you happen to notice his reaction when Jackie's temperature started to go up?'

'Yes I did. The strange thing was that when her blood pressure fell earlier in the case, he barely noticed, but luckily Morag was there to take care of the problem. That was a far worse situation than Jackie's temp going up half a degree, but that was when he panicked.'

'Yes,' said Jean in a thoughtful voice. 'Yes, that was much less important, wasn't it?'

They talked for a little while longer about Derek. Peter was always very professional about discussing his colleagues, but as Jean was not only a doctor but a good and trusted friend, he was able to tell her exactly what he knew about the various medical scrapes Derek had got into.

'He's not an alcoholic, and I'm pretty sure he doesn't take drugs,' said Peter, always scrupulously fair. 'It's just that he's careless, doesn't think ahead, doesn't see problems coming until he's deep into them, and then he doesn't always know how to get himself out.' I'm not sure where he trained, but apparently he was much the same in his previous job.'

They continued to talk until one of the surgeons came into the lounge, then Jean got up and went back to see her patient.

Jackie was sitting up and sounding cheerful. 'I don't want to go home,' she said. 'Bob had both kids crying on the phone to me this morning. I told him I was going to Fiji to recuperate, and he should put them both up for adoption.'

'I told him yesterday that you weren't to do any lifting for at least six weeks because of your operation,' said Jean. 'Not even the baby.'

'That's all right,' said Jackie. She paused to cough, and put both hands across the lower part of her belly, where her incision was. 'Bob's sister's coming from Huntly to spend a few weeks. She's wonderful; I wish I'd married her instead of Bob.'

They both laughed, but Jackie's stitches hurt, so

she didn't laugh for long. On the way out Jean made a detour and stopped by the administrator's office. Roderick Michie, the Director, was in, and happy to see Jean. The Michies lived a few doors down from the Montroses, but they were all too busy to see each other more than occasionally.

Jean came to the point quickly; she wanted information on Derek Sutherland. After some hesitation, Roderick gave it to her. 'I will swear on oath that I have never discussed this matter with you,' he said. 'And I trust you to do the same, all right?' Jean smiled back at him, although what she had heard made her feel sad and shaky. 'Thanks a lot, Roderick,' she said. 'Why don't you drop by for a sherry sometime on your way home? It's silly that you live so close and we never get to see either of you.'

Chapter Twenty-nine

Soon after the Reverend Glasgow left, Duncan started to make his preparations. There was an inevitability to everything he did now, as if he were on a metaphysical railway track that led only in one direction. Every breath he took, every step, every word was a piece in the jigsaw that was finally putting some shape into his existence. Words and phrases from Rudyard Kipling's *Kim* kept coming back to him, although he hadn't read the book for years. Duncan knew that, like the aged lama in the story, he was now approaching the River of the Arrow, the shining river of ultimate truth.

That Sunday he gave a sermon which he prepared with particular care, as it was to be his last. The church was crowded, and part of his mind knew that many of the people had come to see him merely out of curiosity. And there was a hostility in the air which he sensed but for some reason it affected him not at all. Duncan knew that now he possessed an immunity, a protective mantle that deflected the small shafts of curiosity, the heavier arrows of suspicion, and even the hot and brutal bolts of hatred that only a few days ago would have devastated him. And these bolts were flying out at him now, aimed by certain of the people who were crowding into his permanently polluted and dishonoured church.

It wasn't that Duncan didn't feel these soundless assaults, or even that they didn't affect him. It was simply that he was now living in a different place, inhabiting a different dimension, and such concerns no longer had a place in his life.

It had been Duncan's custom, and the result of his divinity school training, to take a biblical text for his sermon, and build his message upon that. The rules of the church concerning sermon topics were fairly strict, and a rustle went through the church when, after he climbed up the spiral stairs to the pulpit, Duncan announced that his text would be the one word 'love'. A few ribald sniggers were heard from the back of the congregation, and Derek Sutherland, whose gaze transfixed Duncan with an almost palpable beam of hatred, clenched his fists until the nails bit into his palms. Two pews behind Derek, who was not accompanied by Sheila, Jean Montrose listened to the sermon with growing dismay, and watched Duncan's rapt expression and flying arms and hands as he spoke. This was not the sober, thoughtful Duncan Sinclair she had known, and Jean wondered sympathetically if the strain of the last weeks had been too much for him.

Duncan's sermon was long, and not entirely coherent; he talked about the gossamer net of love that united the members of earlier communities, and pointed out the slow and poisonous rise of hatred, suspicion, and greed which had first evicted love from the nest and then destroyed it. But there was a febrile earnestness, a simple and direct honesty about Duncan that transcended his mixed metaphors.

Jean, afraid for him, could see that he was also in

the grip of an ethereal restlessness which gave pause to even the most sinister-intentioned of his parishioners. But only Duncan knew what his restlessness was all about; he felt the most desperate haste to finish, to leave, and to go home and live forever in his Father's house.

The choir sang, and to many of the congregation, Bobby's absence stood out painfully, like a missing front tooth in a pretty girl's smile.

The final organ voluntary was Bach at his fiercest and most complex. Ian Farquar played like a man possessed; no such sounds had ever before issued from the splendid old Willis organ. Maybe Ian had caught the spirit of Duncan's sermon, but if he had, he then modified it; a sonorous diapason followed the exultant sound of trumpets, and eerie bourdon rumblings of imminent death and destruction were slowly displaced by the triumphant, victorious sound of the full organ at maximum volume. The glory and power of the music gave the congregation shivers, and made the entire church shake to its foundations.

Instead of leaving during the voluntary in the usual way, the congregation stood in the aisles or sat, mesmerized, listening to Ian's extraordinary performance. Only Jean, knowing what she knew, felt a growing fear at the overwhelming sounds. When it was finally over, she got up and followed the others down the aisle towards the sunlit door of the church, feeling weak and shaky at the knees, and grateful for the firm support of Steven's arm.

As Jean and Steven, followed by Fiona and Lisbie, moved with the crowd towards the doors, there was a sudden flurry of activity outside. A woman screamed, then another, and a man shouted, then the press of bodies caught Jean and her family and in a moment they were ejected into the bright sunshine.

Someone was lying prone on the ground, his head close to the door, and Jean immediately recognized Duncan from his robes. Two men were struggling with a third, smaller man, but in the scuffle she couldn't see who it was.

Steven, peering over the heads in front of him, said hurriedly to Jean, 'Take the girls with you. I'll see you back at the car,' and pushed his way through the crowd towards the mêlée. A burly man whom Steven recognized as Joe McIver was holding Derek Sutherland with an armlock around his neck, and Mr Archibald the old sexton was hanging on, trying to twist an arm behind Derek's back. Derek, red in the face, furious, his eyes protruding, was shouting obscenities at the fallen man and making ineffectual attempts to kick him. Douglas Niven came up hurriedly from behind. He was dressed in his Sunday suit, but everybody recognized him. Derek glowered but stopped struggling, and Joe relaxed his throttling grip.

Duncan moaned. Jean, having ignored Steven's instructions to go to the car, kneeled down beside him and helped him to sit up. Duncan didn't look severely injured, but his face was bruised and his clothes and hair were all awry and full of dust. A bright trickle of blood oozed out of the corner of his mouth and down his chin. With Jean on one side and Lisbie on the other, Duncan struggled to his feet.

Without warning, Derek broke free and went for Duncan again with fists and feet, but Doug reacted fast, and with a swift and practised movement, brought Derek to his knees with a paralysing half-nelson. Immobilized, Derek panted from the pain, his only weapon a look of sheer hate with which he continued to assault Duncan.

Someone had dialled 999, and an approaching siren could already be heard in the distance. The shocked parishioners dispersed quickly, several of them giving Derek sympathetic looks as they went by. Jean, assisted by Lisbie and Fiona, helped Duncan to limp back into the now-silent church.

'I hope they won't hurt Dr Sutherland,' he gasped, collapsing on to the nearest pew and looking back through the open door at Derek. Even now, in the midst of all the action, Jean could see something other-worldly and beatific about Duncan Sinclair, and his ruffled grey hair standing up like a halo around his bruised head did nothing to dispel that impression.

Ian Farquar came back reluctantly into the church, dragged in by Beth, who was anxious to make sure that Duncan was all right. Ian's usually morose expression was unchanged, but Jean thought she could detect signs of a grim satisfaction as he glanced at Duncan.

'You're not hurt, are you, Reverend?' asked Beth, fluttering around him. 'That was just terrible, a terrible thing to happen, and to think he did it right here outside the church . . .' Beth's voice faded, and she glanced involuntarily up the aisle towards the altar, remembering too late that worse things had happened within these desecrated walls.

'No, I'm fine, Beth, thank you.' Duncan's confused expression had changed, and he was now smiling broadly as if in some way this had been a pleasurable, illuminating experience. He got up from the pew, and rubbed his thigh where Derek had kicked him.

'I must be getting along,' he said, gathering his robes around him. A muscle at the corner of his left eye was trembling uncontrollably, but that was the only sign of stress that Jean could detect. His voice was strong and confident as he said, 'I have to go . . . I have an appointment that I absolutely can't miss.'

He turned to Jean. 'Jean, thank you for your help, and you, Fiona, and of course Lisbie, for yours.' He held Lisbie's limp, unresisting hand in his, and smiled at both girls. That opened up the split on his lip, and a fresh trickle of red zig-zagged through the dried blood on his face.

Looking at Duncan, and dabbing at his lip with a piece of tissue, Jean got the strong and frightening impression that he was beyond recall, and that nothing, absolutely nothing could ever hurt or even reach him again.

By the time the patrol car arrived on the scene, Derek had subsided into something like a catatonic trance. Mute, unresisting, his gaze was completely blank. After handcuffing Derek's hands behind his back, the officers pushed him into the passenger compartment of their car while Douglas placed a protective hand on the top of Derek's head so he wouldn't bump it on the doorframe.

Douglas followed in his own car as the patrol vehicle, with lights flashing and siren howling, sped back to headquarters. It was really very sad, Doug thought as he sped past a lorry. Derek must have been convinced that Duncan was responsible for killing his son, and had taken the law into his own hands, with the result that now he was in the hands of the law. Douglas enjoyed the simple play on words, but not for long, because he had to go fast through an intersection to keep up with the patrol car. As the lights were against him at the time, that resulted in a certain amount of confusion, but he only caught a glimpse of the debacle in his rear-view mirror.

And in any case, Douglas now knew who had murdered Bobby Sutherland, and was trying to decide the best time to arrest the killer. The day before, on Saturday morning, a phone call had been received at police headquarters. It had been for Doug, but he was out of the office, so Jamieson took it. A Mr Bill Inglis was on the line, and he sounded very upset. He was the manager of the Sports Shoppe in Dundee, and remembered reading about the boy's murder in the newspaper. His assistant, Stella Burgess, happened to mention that she'd recently sold a pack of two mylar survival sleeping bags to a person she didn't know. On his own initiative, Jamieson drove over to Dundee with a stack of about twenty photos, and she immediately picked out the individual. Stella, a sunburned, determined-looking young woman with strong brown arms said there was no doubt whatever in her mind. The hair, the face, everything, if Jamieson had a hundred photos, she said, she'd still have known him. The photo she picked out was that of the Reverend Duncan Sinclair.

Chapter Thirty

The next day, Monday, Derek Sutherland was scheduled for a case with Peter MacIntosh. As Peter prepared to go into theatre, Sister Kelso whispered to him what had happened outside the church the day before. Derek had been arrested there, she told him, but Reverend Sinclair had refused to prefer assault charges so Derek had been allowed to go home. As he listened to Jan Kelso's tale, Peter's misgivings increased to the point where he asked her to switch the schedule around so that he would get another anaesthetist.

'I'm sorry,' said Jan after checking the list. 'But everybody's already assigned. I can't change them now.'

Peter was astonished at Derek's attack on the minister. 'Why ever did he do that?' he asked.

'There's been a lot of talk about the Reverend,' said Jan. 'About his relationships with . . .'

She was interrupted by the appearance of Derek, and went off. Derek changed into his operating garb, then went over to the scrub sink next to the one Peter was using, but said nothing, and didn't even reply to Peter's cheerful greeting. Peter, basically a good, sympathetic man, felt very uncomfortable and didn't know what else to say. It would hardly be appropriate to congratulate Derek on getting off so easily.

Sister Kelso had taken the precaution of putting Morag in the next theatre, where several small, simple operations had been scheduled, so that if necessary she could come through and help Derek.

Peter was operating on a young woman with endometriosis; adhesions inside her pelvis were causing her a great deal of discomfort, and she had not responded to simpler treatment.

Peter kept an unobtrusive watch on Derek, but he seemed quite calm and collected. He assembled his equipment, drew up the medicines, labelled the syringes and checked the respirator in the usual way. Derek talked quietly to the patient before giving the intravenous injection of pentothal, and he sounded perfectly normal. Better than normal, in fact. Usually he didn't bother.

Everything seemed to be going well when Peter, while doing a difficult piece of dissection deep in the pelvis, accidentally tore a large vein.

While Peter struggled to get the bleeding under control, Derek dealt with the emergency extraordinarily well; he sent a student nurse racing to get blood, put an extra-large intravenous line into the patient's arm, pumped fluids into her veins to maintain her blood pressure, and while Peter found the bleeding vessel and repaired it, Derek kept everything else under control. Morag's face appeared at the window behind Derek, and Peter, looking up for a second, shook his head to indicate that all was well. When the case was over, Derek went with the patient to the recovery room, and Peter followed.

'Thank you, Derek,' he said quietly after the patient

had been transferred from the stretcher. 'You did a wonderful job back there.'

Derek merely nodded; he was busy taking the patient's blood pressure manually as a check on the monitor.

About an hour later, Peter came back. Derek was still with the patient, and everything had stabilized nicely. While Derek was making a notation on the patient's chart, Peter walked over to him.

'Derek,' he said, 'I have a really difficult hysterectomy to do tomorrow. I'd be very grateful if you'd put her to sleep for me.'

Derek stopped writing, but didn't look up for a long time. 'I'll be delighted,' he replied. There was something strange in Derek's voice. Peter, who had a good understanding of human emotions, gave him a quick, friendly pat on the shoulder before going on his way.

Duncan had got up early that morning, early enough to see the dawn spreading pink across the sky. He made himself a cup of coffee, then went back and sat on the edge of his bed to think out exactly what he was going to do, and in what order. A mood of extraordinary elation gripped him; now that his belief in God had returned, everything had changed, and the power was again within him. Duncan fell to his knees by his bed, clasped his hands together and with a stark and committed intensity thanked his Lord for all the manifold blessings he had received from him throughout his life. Now that he knew His will, Duncan would do it unhesitatingly, and do it happily, with all the new strength that had been granted to his heart and soul. He had no regrets; if at that moment someone had asked him what the word 'regret' meant, he would have laughed aloud and replied that he simply didn't know.

First there were a couple of letters to write, so he went to his desk in the study. Half an hour later, he put them in envelopes which he addressed, sealed, and stamped, one to the Reverend Edmund Glasgow, the other to his organist, Ian Farquar. He looked particularly thoughtful as he sealed the last one, and held it in his hands for a moment before dropping it on top of the other.

For a long time Duncan stood in front of the portrait of Jos. MacFarland and stared into his sepia-brown eyes. It was important that Jos. should understand what was happening and why, so Duncan told him briefly, without any frills or histrionics. Jos. himself had suffered through many a trial and tribulation without complaint, and Duncan felt that nobody would understand better than he.

Then Duncan went up to the bathroom, ran a tepid bath, shed his pyjamas, and for the next hour, washed and shampooed and scrubbed his body with soap and a bristle brush from under the sink in the kitchen, and was not satisfied until his skin was actually scoured raw and bleeding in several places.

Then, feeling hyperalert and anxious to proceed, Duncan went back to the study. Still naked, he spoke a few encouraging and companionable words to Jos., before saying goodbye to him. There was no need for an emotional farewell, because they would be getting together again soon. Duncan's mind was now in a generally benign and approving condition, and he smiled vaguely at his reflection, faintly seen in the glass of Jos.'s portrait, but it puzzled him for a second because it was not the reflection of anyone he had ever known.

Then Duncan set all these things aside and put his entire mind to his preparations. He felt full of the universality of love, and was happier now than at any other time in his life. As he worked, gathering and checking his equipment, it seemed quite natural that he should be enveloped in the white light that enhanced and transformed all his movements.

That morning, after personally taking old Andrew McIver to the hospital for his tests, Jean spent quite a lot of time on the phone, and made a particular effort to note the times and duration of the calls, as they were not on behalf of the practice, and would be paid for out of her own pocket at the end of the month.

The surgery was busy, so it was between patients that she made her calls; several were to the Royal Infirmary in Aberdeen, where Jean still had a number of friends, mostly from her days as a medical student and resident. Some of the people she called were busy doing rounds or in theatre, so she left messages here and there for them to call her back.

Eleanor came in to Jean's office just as she put the phone down. As was happening more and more often recently, Eleanor forgot to knock before coming in.

'They're piling up out there,' said Eleanor, jerking a thumb back at the waiting room and looking pointedly at the phone. 'Dr Inkster has seen eight patients already.'

'Fine, I'm ready. Who's next?' asked Jean. 'And by the way, Eleanor, I notice that you've got out of the habit of knocking before you come marching in here.'

'Mrs Marshall is next,' replied Eleanor, ignoring Jean's comment. 'She says she's having quite a bit of pain in her incision. But she's the complaining type anyway, so I'm not surprised.'

'Send her in,' said Jean. She was not feeling well, had had chills during the night before, and wondered if her bout of 'flu was coming back. She shook her head, annoyed at herself. With every single 'flu patient she saw, she told them not to go back to work too soon, because the 'flu could recur if it wasn't treated properly. And of course that was exactly what she had done.

Jackie Marshall came in slowly, her usually cheerful face now drawn with pain.

'My goodness,' said Jean, concerned. 'You looked a lot better when I saw you in the hospital. What happened?' She helped Jackie to get on to the examination table and undid her blouse and skirt. The incision was red and puffy-looking, and Jean realized she had an abscess.

'Whew,' said Jackie, with a great sigh of surprise after Jean drained it, 'the pain's gone.' She stretched luxuriously while Jean put on a dressing.

As Jackie was leaving, the phone rang; it was one of her calls being returned from the Aberdeen Royal Infirmary. When she put the phone down a few minutes later, Jean sat very still. It may have been partly her 'flu coming back, but she developed a severe bout of shivering. She was beginning to feel really ill again, and the news she had just heard made it twice as bad.

'I don't think he'll give us any trouble,' said Douglas, as they left the office. 'We'll caution him as soon as we get inside the door, but we won't charge him until we get back here.'

Going down the back stairs ahead of Douglas, Jamieson asked why not. 'Won't that just make him angry?' he argued. 'Why don't we take him down to the station and caution him once we've got him inside?'

'It's like this, Jamieson,' said Douglas patiently. 'Suppose that on the way down in the car, he confesses, then after he's been arrested and charged, he gets scared or his lawyer tells him not to say anything more. If he was properly cautioned, what he said in the car could be used in evidence, but not if he wasn't. Do you understand?'

Jamieson struggled with that for a while before giving up. 'Yes, sir,' he said, but as usual, his blank look gave him away.

'When is that woman from the Sports Shoppe coming?' asked Doug, thinking about what he would say to the media people who would be flocking around as soon as the news of Duncan Sinclair's arrest got out.

'I told her about three. We have a six-man lineup organized for that time so she can identify him in person.'

Jamieson held the outside door open for Douglas, and they walked over to Doug's car.

'I talked to the Church people in Edinburgh again this morning,' he told Jamieson as they got in. 'Apparently they knew about the trouble Reverend Sinclair had in his last church, but they decided to give him another chance here.'

'Good timing,' grinned Jamieson. 'Old Reverend Whatsisname drops dead here, but luckily they've got a nice pervert ready waiting in the wings to take over his job.'

Douglas looked over at his subordinate with astonishment. He had never known Jamieson to be so cynical before.

Douglas parked at the kerb outside the manse entrance. There were no other cars on the block, and the whole scene was very peaceful. There was little traffic, and the great ash trees and dark cypresses of the cemetery gave the impression of a country church, far from the city.

The small iron gate at the end of the path creaked when it was opened. 'Could use a drop of oil,' muttered Jamieson, but Doug was already striding ahead towards the silent house, prey to a sudden feeling of unease.

Reaching the front step, Doug pressed the old-fashioned round bell-push, and they heard the ring echoing inside. After a few moments, Douglas pounded on the door panel with the flat of his hand. Nothing happened, nothing stirred. Jamieson looked challengingly at the door, took a couple of steps back and was about to charge when Douglas turned the tarnished brass door-knob and pushed the door open.

Inside, Douglas stood hesitating for a moment, then ran up the stairs with Jamieson thundering along behind him. At the open door of the study Doug stopped in his tracks and Jamieson pulled up next to him.

They stared openmouthed for several seconds at the extraordinary sight.

Douglas pulled a large Swiss army knife out of his pocket. 'If you can hold him,' he said in a tight voice to Jamieson, 'I'll cut him down.'

Chapter Thirty-one

Jean had the papers all out in front of her and was trying to make sense of Helen's rewritten budget application but neither her mind nor her spirit was with the printed pages. Ever since Bobby's death, she had been guiltily trying to find a reason why he had been so pale and withdrawn. She was quite certain now that there was no physical cause; surely if it was emotional, he would have told *somebody*. But who? Not his mother, for sure, and as for Derek . . . Jeremy! Jean sat up. Of course. Jeremy was Bobby's best friend, and he would have told him for sure. She looked at the clock. Jeremy would be at school. Jean jumped up, got into her car and sped the few blocks to the Central School and parked outside the gates. The playground was full of noise and children, but after searching around for a few moments she spotted Jeremy and went over to him.

Jeremy, surprised, answered her question, and she went back to her car, feeling ill.

Within moments of getting back to the surgery, she got a phone call from Douglas.

'You don't have to come, of course, Jean,' he said carefully, remembering the trouble he had got himself into under similar circumstances once before. 'But if you had time I'd really appreciate it . . . No, Dr Anderson's in Dundee today, and there isn't anybody . . . Right, okay, Jean, thank you. Jamieson's outside and I'll tell him to watch out for you. We'll see you in a few minutes, then.'

Doug's voice betrayed his worry; already he saw that he would be on the carpet with his superiors for not having arrested Duncan the day before, and in his mind he was preparing his defence.

After the first shock, and knowing what she knew, Jean was saddened but not entirely surprised to hear about Duncan's suicide. Of course, her cautious voice said, that's assuming that it *was* suicide.

Jean decided to walk. It wasn't too far, and maybe the fresh air would make her feel better. She had been in the manse once before, and remembered its dark wallpaper, long narrow staircase, and an indefinable compound smell which included furniture wax, ammonia, and the musty odour that comes from behind the walls of certain old houses.

Jamieson was outside, as Douglas had said. Some time ago, Jean noticed that his antagonism was more obvious the further they were apart. The deep scowl that appeared when Jean opened the gate was replaced by a controlled immobility of his features as she came up to him.

'The Inspector's upstairs, doctor,' he said.

'Thank you,' Jean replied. Jamieson must be softening up, she thought. Normally he would have merely glared, nodded and pointed upstairs. There was traffic on the stairs; one of the forensic team, the photographer, a pretty young woman with long straight blonde hair was going back to the van for more film; she smiled and stood sideways to let Jean past. The finger-print men were at the top of the stairs, listening to Douglas, who was shaking his head.

'Just do the minimum,' he was saying. 'This was a suicide, no doubt about it.' He looked down the stairs. 'Jean. Thank you for coming. This should just take a second . . .'

When she reached the top of the stairs, Jean leaned against the wall, feeling faint and shaky. Concerned at her pallor, Douglas took her elbow protectively and asked if she wanted to sit down.

'I'm all right,' she answered. 'It's just . . . I think my 'flu is coming back.'

One of the fingerprint men ran to the bathroom and brought back a glass of water for Jean. She didn't really want any, but it was a nice gesture, so she drank a couple of mouthfuls before insisting that she was perfectly all right and ready to go ahead and examine the body.

They had put Duncan on his back in the centre of the floor, directly under the cut end of a white nylon rope, next to a plain wooden chair lying on its side. He had presumably kicked it away, his last considered action. The other end of the rope was tied to the stout central ceiling light fixture.

Douglas caught her glance. 'If he'd tried that in a house built since the war, he'd have just landed on the floor with a thump, looking silly,' he said.

Duncan was almost naked, with abrasions all over his body. Around his waist, tied like a loincloth with a large piece of adhesive tape, was a long, silvery plastic bag.

'Look at this,' said Doug, holding out a piece of paper.

Jean took it. In the middle of the sheet were three

short lines of script, written in Duncan's bold handwriting.

> Naked I came, and naked I go.
> I have found God.
> Death is the price of peace.

Jean silently handed it back and knelt down beside Duncan. The body was already cold and waxy-looking, and beginning to get stiff. His thick grey hair was still wet and sticking to his head. Automatically, Jean waved a large bluebottle away from the wide-open, bulging eyes; their pale blue pupils contrasted vividly with the red sclerae surrounding them. The tight mark of the rope showed as a purplish-white weal around his neck, and his tongue, swollen and blue, protruded from his mouth.

'Several hours,' said Jean, getting up. 'I'd guess about four or five. It's cold in this room, so his body temperature will have gone down fairly fast.' Doug helped her to her feet and she swayed there for a moment, feeling the fever coming back fast into her body.

'Thanks, Jean,' said Douglas, really concerned about the way Jean looked. 'Now let me come downstairs with you. I'll drive you home.'

Under almost any other circumstances, feeling as sick as she did, she would have accepted gratefully, but not today. She still had work to do at the surgery. 'Thanks, Doug, but if you'd take me back to the surgery, that would be just fine.'

In the car, Douglas fastened his seat belt. 'Well, in a way, that's the best possible ending, don't you think? We'd come to arrest him for Bobby Sutherland's murder, and at this point there's not much question that he did it.'

He told Jean about the mylar sleeping bags, mentioning that they were sold in packs of two, and that the shop assistant who'd sold them had recognized Duncan's photo with complete certainty.

Jean started to cough, a deep, hacking cough.

'Are you sure you don't want to go home?' he asked. 'It would be no trouble to drive you.'

'No, thanks,' said Jean, and asked him a question about the bags. Douglas didn't know the answer, and ran back to ask Jamieson. When he came back, looking very subdued, Jean explained to him why she couldn't go home quite yet, but mentioned diffidently that she would be really grateful if he would wait for her outside the surgery.

Douglas, his head reeling, agreed.

There was hardly anyone in the surgery, and Jean started to wish that she had simply gone home as Doug had suggested.

Eleanor eyed Jean from her desk as she walked in. 'You don't look so hot yourself, Dr Montrose,' she said. 'Maybe you should go home. There's nobody here except Mr Farquar, and he's just here for medicine for his wife.'

'It's so cold in here,' said Jean. She was shivering hard.

'Cold?' Eleanor was incredulous. 'This is one of the warmest days of the year, so far.'

Ian Farquar appeared at the door of the waiting room, looking his usual dour and sombre self.

'I thought that was your voice,' he said.

'Come on in,' said Jean, going towards her office. She held the door open for Ian, then closed it after them.

'How's Beth doing?' she asked, sitting down heavily at her desk. Her voice must have sounded odd, because Ian glanced at her sharply. 'Are you all right?' he asked.

'I think I must have got the 'flu again,' she said, and tried to smile. 'But nobody ever has any sympathy for a sick doctor.'

'Aye,' said Ian. 'Beth's doing much better now.' His small, concerned eyes didn't leave Jean's face.

Almost for the first time in her life, Jean suddenly felt seriously worried about her own health. She was really sick this time, she knew it, much worse than her earlier bout. She knew that she should just give Ian the prescription and go home as quickly as Douglas could take her, but she simply couldn't do it. She put her hands flat on the desk in front of her. Her palms were sweating, and she could feel the sweat on her forehead. She knew that at that moment she must have looked dreadful.

'I've just come from the manse,' she said. 'Your minister, Duncan, just hanged himself.'

A look of pure astonishment passed over Ian's normally impassive face, then was replaced by a dark flush. His eyes narrowed. 'Best thing that could have happened,' he said, his small black eyes full of venom. 'That foul bastard, buggerer and killer.'

Jean sat back, disconcerted by the force of Ian's hatred.

'Inspector Niven just told me that he was about to arrest Duncan for Bobby Sutherland's murder,' she said calmly. 'So you're certainly not alone in your opinions.'

'Well, I'd better be getting along.' Ian stood up. 'If you'll kindly give me the prescription for Beth, please.'

'Still,' said Jean as if she hadn't heard him, 'Duncan can't have been entirely bad, Ian, because he did try to save your skin.'

Ian stood frozen for a moment, staring at Jean, then he sat down again, very slowly.

'How so?' he asked. 'Why would he want to save my skin?'

'The first thing that made me realize that it was a very complicated case was the day after Bobby's death, up at the hospital, in the operating theatre.'

Jean coughed, and the spasm shook her for a full minute. Ian watched her without making the slightest movement.

'Derek Sutherland was beside himself with grief,' she went on as soon as she was able to speak. At her words, Jean thought she saw, for the first time, a change of expression on Ian's face, a moment of evil pleasure, but it was only for an instant, and she might have been mistaken.

'Two astonishing things happened that morning,' went on Jean, hoping that her voice would last for a few more minutes. 'One was that a major complication happened in the case he was anaesthetizing, and he barely noticed. Luckily there was somebody there to help him.'

Ian was now showing traces of impatience.

'I'm sorry, Ian,' said Jean apologetically, seeing him shuffling his feet, 'I'm going as fast as I can. The second thing was that a little while later the patient's temperature started to go up.'

Suddenly Ian was paying full attention.

'It was nothing much, not even a whole degree rise, but Derek went almost crazy with it. Something, some bell had rung in his mind to cause such a reaction.'

Ian sat back. 'Why are you telling me this? I just came for . . .'

Jean, flushed and agitated from her fever, went on, her words stumbling over each other. 'I hate to talk about my colleagues, but you know that Dr Sutherland doesn't have the best of reputations among the other doctors, and I found out why. A couple of years ago, while he was working in Aberdeen, he put an injured boy to sleep so that his fractured wrist could be set. The boy, whose name was Victor, developed a condition called hyperpyrexia, a very high fever which sometimes occurs during anaesthesia. Unfortunately Dr Sutherland didn't recognize it in time, and the boy's temperature went up off the scale and he was dead within two hours. Victor's parents, you and Beth, had gone off for a few days' holiday at the time . . .'

Ian's eyes were glassy, and his breathing became rapid, but he didn't say anything.

'At the inquest, the verdict was "Death by misadventure", as I found out yesterday,' continued Jean. 'But you didn't let it go at that. You're not the type.'

As if she just remembered something, Jean interrupted herself. 'When Beth was sick, and I came to your house, there was a photo of you and Beth and Victor standing outside a tent. As a camper, you'd know about those wonderful heat-retaining mylar bags; in fact I suppose you had one handy.' Jean paused, and put her head between her hands, trying to summon up enough strength to go on.

'It must have taken a while before you decided what to do. Killing Derek Sutherland would simply not have been an adequate revenge, because it wasn't painful enough. Then one day you got angry with Bobby and told him that his father was a child-murderer . . . That was unwise, because if he'd told his parents, the whole story would have come out and you wouldn't have had a chance to kill Bobby.'

Jean paused, and wondered if taking some aspirin would make her feel better. Her feet felt cold, although she could feel the sweat on her forehead. She struggled to regain the thread of what she'd been saying.

'Right. By killing Bobby, you could make Derek suffer for ever . . . Of course, Derek had never seen or met you, and that helped. Killing Bobby by making his temperature go up until he died of heat stroke was pure symbolism, pure revenge. And when you *imagined* that Duncan was having a sexual relationship with Bobby, any reluctance you might have had about killing an innocent boy was gone.'

'I didn't imagine anything. That boy wasn't innocent, I can tell you that,' said Ian, pounding a fist into the palm of his other hand. 'And that buggering sod Sinclair . . . They were both subhuman, the pair of them.' Ian's whole body shook, so strong was his disgust.

'Ian, a few days ago I went down to the church with my two daughters. The door between the vestry and the hall is a fine, thick oak door with felt around the edge to stop draughts. Ian, I could barely hear my girls when they were *shouting* on the other side.'

Ian stared at her, then slowly put his hands up to his ears.

'The only person who suspected you was Duncan, wasn't it?' Jean went on. 'He must have seen you with Bobby in the church, or at least had a strong suspicion. Isn't that right, Ian?'

Ian stood up, his short body curved and taut. He put his face menacingly close to Jean's. 'That's a load of rubbish, all of it,' he said, in a voice so soft that

Jean hardly heard it. 'And neither you nor anybody else can prove it.'

'Duncan's last deed was to save you,' said Jean. 'He bought a mylar sleeping bag to wrap around his body before he hanged himself, implying that he'd used a similar one to kill Bobby.'

'I'm sure that's what he did do,' replied Ian.

Jean sighed, and her head was swimming. 'He bought the mylar bag two days after Bobby died,' she replied. She stared at Ian, unable to focus properly.

'Was Beth in on this?' she asked suddenly. 'After all, Victor was her son too.'

Ian's voice was loud and suddenly fearful. 'Beth had nothing to do with it. She didn't know . . .' His face twisted. 'Let me tell you something. If you bring her into this, I'll . . .'

'Now, Ian, don't be ridiculous,' interrupted Jean. 'I can't bring her or anybody else into this. It's a police matter, and has nothing to do with me.' She tried to stand up, but her head swam and she had to sit down.

'Ian,' she finally said, 'Inspector Niven knows all this and he's waiting outside . . . I . . .'

Ian looked at Jean's white face, jumped up and went out of the room to get help. When Helen and Eleanor came running in, they lifted Jean up and put her on the exam table and Helen quickly looked her over.

'Call an ambulance,' she said to Eleanor a few moments later. Her voice was unsteady. 'Now.'

Chapter Thirty-two

'Well, Jean, you really gave us a scare.' Contrary to all regulations, Douglas was sitting on the edge of Jean's bed in her room on the medical floor.

Jean didn't remember getting to the hospital, and even now had only a vague recollection of two days of delirium and fever, interspersed with fleeting visions of the anxious faces of Steven, Fiona, and Lisbie. The evening before, the fever had finally broken, and for the first time she was able to have a night's sleep and was now feeling quite a bit better.

'My, look at all those flowers,' she said, looking around. The room was full of bouquets, colourful lilies, asters, pots of hyacinths and cyclamen, even a large and elegantly displayed vase of exotic orchids. 'How long have I been here?'

'A couple of days,' replied Doug.

Everything was starting to come back into Jean's mind. 'What happened with . . .'

'Ian Farquar? You were right, he did it. We had no trouble with him. All he was concerned about was Beth; he didn't want her involved in any way.'

A thought came into Jean's head, and she tried to

sit up, but she didn't have the strength. 'The bag,' she said, still breathless. 'What about the bag?'

'The bag Bobby was in?'

'Yes. How did Ian just happen to have one in his pocket that evening?'

'He'd been carrying it around for months, or so he said,' replied Douglas. 'He knew exactly what he was going to do, but he couldn't get up his courage until he was sure that Duncan was having a sexual relationship with Bobby. As soon as he felt enough disgust at Bobby he was able to go ahead, and at the same time put the blame on Duncan.'

'But he *never heard* that conversation between Duncan and Bobby. He imagined it.' Jean told Douglas about her test of the vestry door, and Douglas's mouth opened slowly. 'So there was nothing going on between them at all? Oh, my God . . .'

'He had to believe something like that, otherwise he couldn't have done it. And he was in a hurry, for two reasons.'

Doug held his head in his hands, said nothing, and waited.

'Bobby had threatened to leave the choir, and Ian knew it,' said Jean, her voice was weakening. 'Doug, would you get me a glass of water?'

Doug hurried over to the sink. 'It's rather warm,' he said, filling the glass. 'Would you like me to get some ice?'

'No thanks. Oh, that's lovely . . . The other thing, Doug, was that Bobby's voice could have broken at any time, and that would have been the end of his singing. So Ian was under a lot of pressure to get it over and done with soon, because the choir was his only means of access to Bobby.'

Jean sat up suddenly. 'Doug, where's Steven? Where are the girls?'

'They're both out in the waiting room. They've been here all the time, sleeping on the sofas. I tried to get them to take turns and go home, but they just refused, both of them.'

A nurse poked her head into the room. 'One more minute, Inspector,' she said.

'By the way,' said Doug, getting up, 'Duncan wrote two letters before he died, but he didn't post them. They were both stamped . . .' Doug shook his head. 'One was to a minister by the name of Glasgow, a sort of apology. Why he wanted to write to him I don't know, because Glasgow . . . well, he'd helped us in our inquiries.'

Fishing in his breast pocket, Doug took out a folded Xerox copy and opened it out. 'Here,' he said, 'listen to this. It's the letter to Ian Farquar.' Doug took a deep breath. '"Dear Ian,"' he read, '"as I make this joyous sacrifice, I would like you to remember these words of Cardinal Newman. 'O Lord, support us all the day long, until the shadows lengthen and the evening comes, and the busy world is hushed, and the fever of life is over, and our work is done.' Yours in the glory of God, Duncan Sinclair."'

Jean said nothing, but looked questioningly at Doug.

'He underlined the word "fever" three times,' said Doug, showing Jean the paper.

There was a long silence.

'Do you think he knew?' asked Jean.

'It certainly looks like it,' replied Doug.